"We're all going to be married by the year 2000."

Meg began to feel uneasy at her friend's words. But Lena wasn't finished. "Since Oklahoma hasn't done the trick for Kathy or me, we're giving New York a shot."

"You can't be serious about this," Meg said. "You're only here on vacation."

"Extended vacation," Lena amended. "We're staying as long as it takes to keep our vow. Of course, we won't find men by sitting around. We'll have to work at it. You, too, Meg. The three of us took that vow, remember?"

Meg remembered all too well. They'd been three carefree college girls, a bit wild in their time, and on graduation night they'd made the pact: By the year 2000 we'll all be married, settled down.

"How about it, Meg? Are you with us?" Kathy's voice was a little softer than Lena's, but just as determined.

"No. I'm perfectly happy with my life just the way it is. I'm not embarking on any silly hunt for a man."

"That's exactly what it is. A manhunt. Hey, I like the sound of that. Don't you, Kathy?"

"A manhunt," Kathy said solemnly. "Works for me."

Meg didn't have a good feeling about this—not a good feeling at all.

Dear Reader,

If you're like me, there have been times in your life when you've put romance on the back burner. After all, not every man out there is Prince Charming. At twenty-one I was a happy, independent single woman, and I made a vow to stay that way—no prospective husbands need apply. Of course, vows don't always end up the way we intend them. Only a few months later I was making a different sort of promise—a wedding vow to love and cherish one man for the rest of my life. It's a vow I've never once regretted.

I found it intriguing, then, to write about a heroine who's taken a vow she *does* regret throughout the entire story: a vow to be married by the year 2000. It was a lot of fun for me to ask questions about Meg Danley and this inconvenient promise of hers. Had she really given up on love? What lengths would she go to *not* to find the man of her dreams?

I hope you enjoy reading about Meg as much as I enjoyed writing about her.

Sincerely,

Ellen James

THE MAINE MAN
Ellen James

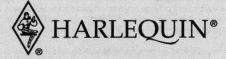

◆ HARLEQUIN®

TORONTO • NEW YORK • LONDON
AMSTERDAM • PARIS • SYDNEY • HAMBURG
STOCKHOLM • ATHENS • TOKYO • MILAN • MADRID
PRAGUE • WARSAW • BUDAPEST • AUCKLAND

ISBN 0-373-70822-X

THE MAINE MAN

This edition published by arrangement with Harlequin Books S.A.

® and TM are trademarks of the publisher. Trademarks indicated with ® are registered in the United States Patent and Trademark Office, the Canadian Trade Marks Office and in other countries.

Printed in U.S.A.

THE MAINE MAN

CHAPTER ONE

THE MAN WAS TROUBLE.

Meg Danley arrived at this conclusion based on two facts. First, he had trespassed into her garden without so much as a by-your-leave. Second, he was far too attractive, with dark unruly hair, resolute features and a strong build evident in jeans and cambric shirt. In Meg's experience, men who were too good-looking were *always* trouble. Arrogant, overbearing heartbreakers.

This man, however, seemed unaware of her critical perusal. Absorbed in his own thoughts, he knelt among the bearded iris. He held a spade, and he looked as if he was about to use it.

"Excuse me," Meg said, "but you must be in the wrong bed." She felt rather foolish as soon as the words were out. The man glanced up at her. He didn't seem particularly surprised at the interruption. He didn't seem particularly concerned, either. His gaze traveled over her.

"Wrong *bed?*"

"You know what I mean," Meg said sternly. "You're in my flower bed. Well, it's not technically *my* flower bed. It belongs to Mrs. Elliott, but I'm tending it for her.'' Meg stepped forward on the roof-top. Her apartment was only on the seventh floor of this charming old New York high-rise, which meant she didn't have gardening privileges in her own right. You had to reside in one of the exclusive penthouse suites in order to claim a portion of the rooftop gar-den. Sixty-three-year-old Helen Elliott was one such resident. However, as Helen was now laid up with a broken ankle, Meg had taken over gardening duties for her.

The man's gaze traveled over Meg once again. ''You must be the Meg who's given up dating. I didn't expect you to be so damn pretty.''

Meg flushed, the blood tingling in her cheeks. ''How on earth—''

The man grinned unapologetically. ''My mother talks about you all the time.''

''Oh.'' Meg paused. ''You're Helen's son… you're Jack Elliott?''

''That's me.'' He straightened. He was even taller and better built than she'd first realized. His eyes glimmered with amusement as he shook her hand. He was trouble, all right. Good-looking…self-assured to the point of cockiness…*trouble*.

''What else has your mother told you about me?'' she asked dryly.

He put on a serious expression. ''Let's see. She says you like caramel corn and old movies, you love your job so much you practically live at the hotel you manage…and you've given up dating. It's the no-dating rule that sticks in the mind most—particularly since you're so damn pretty.''

She could feel her face tingling again, but she managed to remain deadpan. ''I certainly hope you haven't lost any sleep over it—my not dating, and all.''

He gave her yet another slow and appreciative appraisal. Then he shrugged his shoulders reluctantly. ''Matter of fact,'' he said, ''I *haven't* been sleeping all that well lately, but that's another story entirely.''

Meg nodded. ''Right. You've been working too hard with that construction firm of yours, and you won't listen when the doctor tells you that you're headed for an ulcer. But you know what I think the real problem is? Your girlfriend. Kendra, isn't that her name? From what I hear, she's a real handful. Your mom talks about you all the time, too.''

He rewarded her with a sour glance. ''Ex-girlfriend, you mean. I suppose you know all about how she dumped me, right after telling me I was too old.''

Meg couldn't help being interested. ''Actually, your mother didn't get that far. No kidding—Kendra said you were too old?''

Another sour glance. ''Said I was over the hill.''

Over the hill…not likely. What Meg saw was a man utterly in his prime.

''Maybe Kendra's too young,'' Meg suggested. ''Maybe that's the problem right there.''

''Kendra's thirty,'' he grumbled. ''She's thirty.

I'm thirty-nine. Never thought nine years qualified as a generation gap…until now.''

''You know what they say about age—it's just a matter of perspective.'' Meg was beginning to enjoy the pleasant surroundings: the sky tinged pink from the rising sun, the flower and vegetable beds stretching across the roof, showing the vibrant greenery of spring. But then her gaze came back to Jack Elliott, and she made the mistake of looking into his eyes a bit too long. Blue eyes, a deep, intense blue…

''Anyway,'' Meg said hastily, ''how's your mom doing this morning?''

''Complaining, as usual, but not about her health. She thinks I should be married already and settled down. Wonders when she's going to have a grandchild. The usual.''

That sounded like Helen Elliott. A week ago she'd fallen and broken her ankle, and she'd been miserable ever since. The way Meg understood it, Jack Elliott, though he lived in Maine, had immediately arranged for his mother to have around-the-clock nursing care. The only problem was that Helen despised the idea of being nursed.

''Helen says she tried to convince you not to come to New York,'' Meg said. ''All this fuss and bother over such a little thing, she calls it. I gather she doesn't like you to see her in anything but perfect health.''

''That, and she doesn't want me to see how she's

driving the nurses up the wall. One of them already quit.''

Meg took her own spade and knelt down to start digging in the soil. ''Well, Jack, hope you have a good visit in spite of all the chaos,'' she said, giving him a perfect opportunity to make an exit. She'd looked forward to some solitude before work, and this early in the morning there was usually no one else around. She hadn't expected to run into anyone—particularly not someone like Jack Elliott, a man so handsome he was in danger of stealing a girl's breath away.

Jack didn't leave. Instead, he sat down on the edge of a brick planter and studied her all over again.

''You really take this gardening stuff seriously, don't you?'' he asked, the amusement back in his voice.

Very well, maybe she *had* overdone the gardening supplies. She'd brought along a basket that held her work gloves, her bedding fork, her seedling pots and a small bag of peat moss. For good measure, she also wore a gardener's apron, its myriad pockets filled with seed packets, clippers, pruning shears, a weed puller and her lucky trowel.

''I used to garden a lot back home,'' she said defensively. ''It's something I've missed since moving to New York, and now it's generous of your mother to let me have a go at it. She could have brought in a professional gardener instead.''

''Seems you're the one helping her out,'' Jack

said, and now he sounded a bit gruff. "She's told me about all the errands you've been running for her."

"I like your mother," Meg said.

"You just wish she didn't talk so much about you."

"Something like that." Meg had a suspicion he was going to bring up her no-dating rule again, so she quickly changed the conversation. "If you want to garden," she said, "don't let me stop you."

"We can share," he suggested. "I only have a small amount of patience for this kind of thing— stands to reason I only need a small patch of dirt." He made gardening sound like an unavoidable annoyance.

"Why do it at all," Meg asked, "if you don't enjoy it?"

He frowned a little. "Turns out I'm supposed to take up relaxing activities like gardening."

"Of course," she said. "Doctor's advice. The ulcer and all…bet you wish your mother didn't talk so much about *you*."

"Something like that."

She gestured with her spade. "You know, I was thinking of putting some dianthus right about there. You might want to give your input, seeing as you've taken up gardening."

"I'm already thinking about giving it up," he said. "Plants don't seem to inspire me."

"Gardening does soothe the soul," she reminded him.

"I'll let you do it for now. What's life without an ulcer?"

"Don't ask me," she said.

"Happy gardening, Meg." He went off across the rooftop, walking with a forceful, confident stride—certainly not the gait of a man willing to relax. Maybe you didn't get to own one of the most prominent construction firms in Maine by relaxing. He disappeared through the door that led down to the penthouse suites, and Meg finally had her solitude. She surveyed the tulip beds, the rosebushes, the borders of yellow broom, Scotch flower and periwinkle.

She had to admit one thing. Welcoming as this rooftop garden was, it seemed a lot less lively without Jack Elliott around...all-too-gorgeous Jack Elliott.

"New york, Meg, is just swimming in men."

"Yes, Meg. This city is absolutely swimming in guys. And we're here to take the plunge."

Meg settled deeper into her comfortable wing chair, feet tucked underneath her. She studied her two best friends in the entire world, and then she gave a groan of mock despair. "Gee," she said, "here I thought you'd come all the way from Oklahoma just to visit me and catch up on old times. But now you're talking men."

"Really, Meg, think about it," said best friend

number one, Lena Patterson. Lena was as chic and distinctive as ever—the severity of her black mini-skirt and shell top relieved by a necklace of bright fuchsia beads. She wore her red hair in yet another new style—a dramatic bob. Stretched out on the sofa, she gestured toward the window as if to include the entire city. "According to the guidebook, there are approximately seven million, three hundred thousand people in New York. Say about half of those are men. And say at least half of those are single. If we assume half of *those* are eligible, and half of those good-looking...even if only half again are success-ful...let's see, that's still about two hundred and fifty thousand men. A quarter of a million rich, eligible hunks!"

"You always were good at math," Meg remarked.

"If the phone rings," said best friend number two, Kathy Tyler, "and if it happens to be Gary begging me to come home—please tell him I'm not here. Please tell him I'm off having a *wonderful* time with some of those rich, eligible hunks." Kathy sat curled in an armchair beside the phone, and she stared at it as if willing it to ring. Despite her words, Meg saw the sadness in her eyes.

"Oh, honey," Meg said. "Is it bad?"

"Bad enough," Kathy replied tightly. She bent her head, and her long blond hair swung in front of her face. This evening she wore one of the vintage-style dresses she favored—fitted waist, flowing skirt in a soft shade of cameo rose—and it only seemed to add to her air of melancholy. "I've finally figured out that Gary doesn't love me," she said in a low voice. "Maybe he never really did."

"Gary," said Lena, examining the fuchsia polish on her toenails, "is one of those guys who's just never gonna propose."

"I proposed to *him*," Kathy muttered in a tone of disgust. "And what good did it do me? I mean, we've only been dating ten *years*. I'm sure he needs at least another decade or two to even get *used* to the idea of marriage. He is such a coward when it comes to commitment!"

"Honestly, Meg," said Lena. "If Gary calls, don't you dare let Kathy talk to him. He'll manage to convince her their relationship is going somewhere, after all. If we don't watch it, she'll end up on the first flight out of here."

"I have more fortitude than that," Kathy objected. "This time he's not going to convince me of anything."

"Sure," said Lena. "Meg, how many times have we heard this before?"

Meg didn't answer. She just smiled and took a sip of her wine. This felt so much like the old days, when the three of them had sprawled about their college dorm room, talking and arguing and generally being friends. She'd missed all that more than she'd realized.

Meg's tabby cat, Daisy, jumped into her lap and settled down for a good purr. A few years ago, Meg had found Daisy as a stray kitten in front of the hotel where she worked. Now, a warm cat in her lap, a glass of fine wine in her hand, her two best friends visiting from out of town… Meg couldn't think of anything that would make her happier.

"No more waiting around for Gary," Kathy said in a determined voice. She lifted her head, pushing her hair away from her face with an impatient gesture. "Both Lena and I agree. We've been drifting far too long when it comes to romance—and that goes for you, too, Meg. It's time to have something definite happen. Something permanent."

"Besides," said Lena, "don't you remember the vow we made?"

"What vow?" Meg asked.

"You remember," Kathy told her. "It was almost exactly ten years ago. Graduation night. We promised we'd all be married by the year 2000."

"Oh, that," Meg said.

"Meg," Lena said urgently. "The year 1999 is ticking by even as we speak. Two thousand is right around the corner. And not one of us—I repeat, not one of us—is married yet."

"Goodness," said Meg, "to think we're actually in our early thirties and not a husband among us. Time is certainly running out. We'd better nab some guys before it's way too late."

"You always do that," Kathy protested. "Whenever the subject of romance comes up, you get snide. Are you afraid to admit that maybe you're lonely? I mean, heck, *I'm* not afraid to admit I've wasted way too much time on Gary. And *Lena's* not afraid to admit she goes through boyfriends like so many tissues.''

''I don't believe I phrased it quite that way,'' Lena remarked.

''If I recall,'' said Kathy, ''you fully admitted your inability to commit. You said that as soon as you settle on one man, you start thinking about all the others you're missing out on. It's like you're at a restaurant, and your plate's already full, but you can't take your eyes off the dessert cart as it rolls by—''

''Okay,'' Lena cut in. ''Enough already. We get the picture. The point is, none of us is getting any younger.''

''What is this obsession with age?'' Meg complained. ''Only this morning I met a man who thinks he's over the hill because he's all of thirty-nine.''

''A man?'' Lena asked, immediately alert. ''What man?''

Meg could tell she'd made a mistake bringing it up. ''Just a man,'' she said.

''Meg,'' said Lena, ''there's something about your voice that says this isn't 'just a man.' So, fess up. Who is he? What's he like? What's he do?''

''I'll be sure to get you his dossier,'' Meg promised. ''But for now, can we just drop it?''

''If you don't want to talk about him,'' said Kathy, ''he must be somebody special.''

Meg gave another groan. ''I'd forgotten how relentless the two of you can be. Listen, this is a man I barely met. I'm not really interested in getting to know him better.''

''In that case,'' said Lena, ''how about passing him around?''

''For crying out loud,'' Meg objected, ''he's not a plate of hors d'oeuvres. Forget about it, already. Besides, he's too good-looking.''

Lena shook her head. ''What a terrible crime. Let's throw him in jail this instant.''

''I've had it with good-looking men,'' Meg said. ''You know about the last one I dated.''

''Right, right,'' said Lena. ''The blond, bronzed guy who looked like he'd just climbed down from Mount Olympus. Isn't that how you described him?''

''Something to that effect,'' Meg admitted. ''But that's my whole point—he was too damn good-looking. Thought he owned the world, me included.''

''It's amazing, isn't it, Kathy? Meg manages to go out with these incredibly stunning men, but somehow she ends up finding fault with every single one of them. I mean, every time a guy seems promising in the least, she backs off. She starts spending more and more time at work. She acts like managing that hotel is a sacred trust, and no man can possibly be allowed to interfere.''

''For your information,'' Meg said, ''all the men I've gone out with are hopeless. So these days I'm not dating, period.'' Cradling the cat in her arms, she stood and went to the window. Despite the shadows of dusk, she could see the trees flourishing in Central Park. Meg could never take in this view without marveling at her good fortune. An apartment on the Upper West Side, a career she loved. So what if she did have the occasional twinge of loneliness?

"I'm happy," she said with conviction. "I have everything I want. A man doesn't have to be part of the equation."

"Don't you ever wonder," asked Lena, "why every relationship you have ends up going nowhere?"

"Speak for yourself," Meg said as she set Daisy on the sill.

"We're talking about you," Lena said. "You know what your problem is, Meg? Deep down you're scared to death you'll end up like your parents."

Meg rapped her knuckles against the window frame. "Knock on wood," she said lightly, but Lena's words had hit too close to the truth. Just the thought of her parents' marriage still oppressed Meg. Her mother's quiet yet bitter frustrations, her father's stubborn refusal to acknowledge that anything was wrong. Growing up, Meg had looked for any escape from the tension. She'd tagged along after her two older brothers whenever possible. And she'd ended up spending more time at Kathy's or Lena's house than her own home. The divorce, in Meg's junior year of high school, had come almost as a relief.

Now Kathy joined Meg at the window, linking arms with her. "Look at it this way. I've invested too much in one man, Lena's invested in too many guys, and you find fault before you've hardly invested at all. The three of us are equally pathetic.''

"This is supposed to cheer her up?" Lena asked. She slid off the sofa and came to link arms on Meg's other side. "The point is, we can change. We don't have to stay the same. A fresh start—that's what we need.''

Lena had always been a big believer in fresh starts. That was one of the things Meg liked most about her—her ebullience, her perpetual faith in new beginnings. On the other hand, one of the things she'd always liked most about Kathy was her steadiness, her desire that all things should endure. For Meg, the only problem with moving to New York had been leaving her friends behind. The three of them had grown up together in the small, picturesque town of Guthrie—"just a spit away from Oklahoma City," as Lena liked to say. They'd gone to college together, too, at the University of Oklahoma. It was only after college that Meg's intense focus on a career had taken her away from the friends she'd always counted on. Phone calls, letters and infrequent visits simply hadn't done the job. Undeniably, she'd missed Kathy and Lena.

But, once again, her two best friends destroyed her nostalgic mood.

"Kathy and I have decided we're going to fulfill that vow," Lena said. "We're going to be married by the year 2000. And since Oklahoma hasn't done the trick for us, we're giving New York a shot.''

''We're staying,'' Kathy agreed, ''until it's a done deal.''

Meg was starting to feel uneasy. ''You can't be serious about this. You're only here on vacation.''

''Extended vacation,'' Lena amended. ''We've arranged everything so we can stay as long as it takes.''

Much as Meg cared for her friends, her uneasiness only grew. ''But, Lena—what about your job? I thought you'd finally found something you liked. Working for that jewelry broker...''

''Delightful man,'' Lena said flippantly, with just the slightest edge to her voice. ''But here's lesson number one, Meg—never have an affair with your boss. I should have known better. The only good thing is that I made a very respectable salary. I still have enough money to keep me going for a while.''

''Same here,'' said Kathy. ''I've saved up enough. I sure as heck haven't been spending my money on any wedding trousseau. And one of the advantages of working for my aunt is that she's generous about time off. Says she'll manage the travel agency without me for as long as it takes. *She'd* like to see me find someone besides Gary.''

''Well,'' Meg said inadequately.

''We promise not to take over your life,'' Kathy assured her. ''In fact, we've been thinking we should stay somewhere else. We don't want to impose—''

"Nonsense," said Meg. "I want you to stay here. That's why I invited you in the first place. I thought we'd have a long, leisurely visit. The only problem is, the part about finding men doesn't sound leisurely."

"We won't find them by sitting around, that's for sure," Lena said. "We'll have to work at it. You too, Meg. The three of us took that vow, remember?" she repeated.

They'd been three carefree college girls, a bit wild in their time, and on graduation night they'd made the pact: *By the year 2000 we'll all be married, settled down.* It seemed the promise was coming back to haunt her now.

"I thought I'd be the first one married," Kathy said. "I thought it was only a matter of time before Gary came around. Well, it hasn't happened, and I'm finally going to take charge of my life. I'm going to keep that vow."

"I'm going to keep it, too," Lena said grimly. "I'm sick and tired of too many different men in my life. I want something that'll last. How about it, Meg? Are you with us?"

"Don't make it sound like we're the Three Musketeers," Meg protested. "I'm perfectly happy with my life just the way it is. I'm not embarking on any…any silly hunt for a man."

"That's what it is," Lena said, sounding pleased. "A man-hunt. Hey, I like the sound of that. Don't you, Kathy?"

"A man-hunt," Kathy echoed solemnly. "Works for me."

Meg didn't have a good feeling about this—not a good feeling at all.

CHAPTER TWO

JACK ELLIOTT WENT for a run in Central Park, wondering the whole time what the hell he was doing there. Sure, he appreciated the acres of meadow, the elms spreading their branches above, the cool green respite from the fumes and noise of the city. But Jack, by his own admission, wasn't a city person. He felt sorry for a place that needed such a planned oasis. Where he came from, there was nothing planned, nothing tame or organized about the woods and the rocky coastline. Nature engulfed a person in Maine, and Jack couldn't see living anywhere else. He was only a reluctant visitor in New York.

Set in your ways, Jack. First sign of age. It was almost as if Kendra's voice had echoed in his head. He ran a little faster, telling himself that he'd knocked around plenty in his life. He'd traveled all through his twenties, spent time everywhere from Vancouver to the Florida Keys to Panama. Not to mention a year-long stint in Australia.

That was back when you were young, Jack. Now you just wish you were home again. Definitely a sign of age.

He couldn't seem to outdistance the damn voice.

Kendra's voice. Maybe she hadn't said those exact words, but close enough. She'd told him that she needed someone different in her life, someone who could keep up with her. She'd made it sound as if all along they'd been in a race together, and he'd been lagging farther and farther behind. Okay, so he didn't like to go barhopping absolutely every night. So he got bored at parties where everybody seemed eternally twenty-five. Was that so bad?

Face it, Jack. You're getting old.

He upped the pace again, feeling the breath burn in his lungs, until some young guy in a Harvard T-shirt went sailing past him, not even breaking a sweat. Jack tried pushing it even harder, but the distance between him and the young guy only seemed to grow. He eased into a more sedate jog, and when he returned to his mother's apartment a short time later, he wasn't in the best of moods. It didn't help to find her arguing with one of the nurses.

"I can do it myself," came Helen Elliott's adamant voice from the bedroom.

"Mrs. Elliott, the doctor said—"

"I know exactly what he said. I was there, remember? I heard the diagnosis…I don't need to hear it again. Now, will you kindly let me do it myself?"

Jack went into the room. "You can take a break, Mrs. Jansen."

The nurse shot him a grateful look and went out of the room as if she couldn't wait to get away.

Helen Elliott sat upright in bed, attacking her silvery hair with a brush. She was on the small side, but she'd always conveyed a certain presence—due, no doubt, to her energy and sense of purpose. When he was growing up, it had seemed to Jack that his mother was perpetually in motion, pursuing any number of plans and projects. But now her right leg was propped up in an unwieldy cast. Instead of her customary business suit, she wore a terry-cloth robe that seemed to engulf her. It made her appear suddenly frail. As if she was sensing Jack's pity, her expression grew belligerent.

"Go away, Jack," she commanded. "I'm not ready for you."

She'd been saying that ever since he'd arrived in New York, day before yesterday. He got the message. She didn't want him to see her until she was bouncing around on both feet—fit and healthy. Unfortunately, it looked like it would be a while before that happened. Broken bones didn't mend overnight, especially when you were sixty-three.

Helen's dog, Chester, came padding over to greet Jack. Chester was more mutt than golden retriever, a bit too shaggy for proper form. He wagged his tail as Jack patted his head. When Jack sat down on one of his mother's many antiques—a low Victorian fainting couch—Chester attempted to join him.

"Down, Chester," said Helen. "You are *not* a lapdog."

His mother's stern tone didn't fool Jack for a second. "Why not just admit you spoil the dog rotten when nobody's looking," Jack said. "And admit you're going to be out of commission for a while. Take advantage of it. Enjoy the fact that people are waiting on you hand and foot."

"Would you enjoy it?" she countered.

He thought it over. "No," he said at last. "But maybe that's beside the point."

"Sure, because you weren't the one stupid enough to take a tumble and hurt yourself. You weren't the one stupid enough to land yourself in this fix."

"Anybody could fall down and get hurt," Jack said. "It's not a character flaw."

"There was no need for it to happen. If I'd been more careful, it wouldn't have happened at all."

For as long as Jack could remember, his mother had regarded any sign of physical frailty as a moral weakness—an inexcusable breach of conduct. Always she'd prided herself on not giving in to such weakness. It seemed she still refused to give in. No wonder she was driving the nurses crazy.

Helen twitched her fingers on the quilt as if about to fling it off. "I should be at work," she muttered. "I could manage it. Crutches are not a big deal— I'm sure I'd get used to them. But my boss won't hear of it. Insists I stay away from the office until I'm out of this damn cast."

"Consider it a vacation," Jack said.

"Right," Helen replied sarcastically. "Why don't I just sail off to Bermuda while I'm at it?"

Jack figured the conversation wasn't worth pursuing. Helen worked as a copywriter for one of New York's big advertising firms. She'd been with the place five years, but she was still enthralled by it. She acted as though her job was the most wonderful gift she'd ever received, and she still couldn't believe her luck at getting it. Jack felt another stirring of sympathy. Much as he wanted her to relax, he knew how rough the forced inactivity had to be.

"At least give the nurses a little slack," he said. "They're just trying to do their job."

"I can't tolerate a single one of them." Helen moved her hands restlessly. "I'll tell you, the only person I *can* tolerate right now is Meg. She doesn't try to manage me, the way everyone else does."

Meg Danley…the hazel-eyed brunette who'd given up on dating. The very pretty brunette.

His mother was regarding him astutely. "You did say you met her yesterday morning. I should think she's just your type, Jack."

Maybe, if he were in the market, she'd be his type. But after Kendra, he definitely wasn't interested.

When he didn't say anything, Helen looked affronted. "I know you think I'm turning into one of those mothers who tries to arrange her son's personal life. But I was merely making an observation. Truth is, I have enough with my *own* romantic problems." As soon as she'd said the words, she seemed sorry.

His mother—romantic problems? Best not to go there.

Helen looked exasperated. "If you must know—"

"Don't need to know anything, Mom."

"I don't suppose you do," Helen said, "but I don't want you getting the wrong impression. There's a gentleman who lives in the apartment across the hall. Three years he's lived there. We say hello. We wish each other Merry Christmas and Happy Hanukkah and talk about the weather. That's all. It's not as if I'm gallivanting about."

His mother could gallivant all she wanted, as long as Jack didn't know about it. He gave Chester another pat, and Chester wagged his tail.

"Oh, heck," said Helen Elliott, and now she sounded miserable. "You must think I'm nothing but an old fool. At my age...getting a crush on the neighbor man. And even worse, not having the guts to do anything about it."

Jack was beginning to feel stifled in this room. Too much furniture, he decided. Stenciled bureaus, banister-back chairs, fragile tavern tables, ornate candle stands, all crowded together. His mother's penchant for antiques had gotten a little out of control in here. She looked like a prisoner amid the clutter, the posts of the old-fashioned bed frame rising up like the bars of a jail cell. She gazed toward the window, and when she spoke next, her voice was so low that Jack scarcely caught the words.

"Perhaps it's too late," she murmured unhappily. "The man wouldn't possibly be interested in me now—an old lady in a cast, laid up so ridiculously.... Forget any romantic illusions!"

It wasn't like Helen Elliott to talk about romantic illusions. It also wasn't like her to sound insecure or uncertain. In the years since she and Jack's father had divorced, she'd simply gone full tilt after what she wanted in life. Right now, though, she wasn't going much of anywhere.

Jack stared at Chester. Chester stared back earnestly. And Jack wondered, yet again, what the hell he was doing in New York. He'd come here with the idea of straightening out his mother's life. He'd get her to mind the nurses and then he'd be able to go about his own life. That had been the idea, anyway. He hadn't counted on his mother having romantic problems. He also hadn't counted on her seeming so lost...so forlorn.

Maybe straightening things out wasn't going to be so easy, after all. Maybe nothing was easy these days.

AS ALWAYS, Meg savored the view from her office. Her desk was positioned so she could look out into the hotel lobby, where crystal chandeliers from Belgium, walls paneled in Italian silk and wainscoting of English maple served as a backdrop to all the hustle and bustle of guests arriving and departing. This afternoon Meg could see Albert the concierge advising some out-of-towners on theater tickets, and Darlene at the front desk efficiently checking in the latest arrivals. Meg was almost disappointed to see that things were busy but under control. If the situation got hectic, she'd have an excuse to leave her budget reports and do some real work.

Reluctantly, her gaze came back to the computer printouts littering her desk. This was her least favorite part of the job: reviewing the financial statements provided by the controller and then sending them off to the parent company that owned the Alexander. Not too long ago, the hotel had been taken over by a conglomerate that demanded more and more of a profit margin, refusing to accept that running a luxury hotel required certain expenditures for…well, luxury. Meg scanned a column of figures, knowing that the owners wouldn't be happy with it. They'd object to fine linens, arguing that ordinary sheets would do. They'd wonder why Meg replaced broken dishes with real china…again, they'd say that ordinary plates were sufficient. But the Alexander had never been ordinary in any shape or form. Ever since its heyday in the early 1900s, it had been famous for providing only the highest quality. Should a century's worth of tradition change just because some obnoxious penny-pinchers had taken charge?

Meg grumbled under her breath, and Daisy the tabby gave her an unblinking perusal. Meg spent so much time at work that she often brought the cat along with her. Now Daisy presided in her favorite spot, a plump brocade pillow situated beside Meg's desk. Daisy, as the official hotel cat, accepted luxury as a matter of course.

"Smart animal," Meg said. Daisy curled up on

her pillow and gave a contented purr. Meg wished she could feel so relaxed. But work, obviously, was not conducive to relaxation. Neither was her apartment—not with her two best friends so determined to find a man apiece.

Meg wished that she'd been able to go up to the rooftop this morning. Puttering around with gardening claws and pruning shears was a remarkably pleasant experience, very calming. Of course, yesterday morning she'd met Jack Elliott on the rooftop, and that hadn't been exactly relaxing. As for this morning…she'd been reluctant to run into him again. That was why she hadn't gone up to the roof.

"Idiot," she grumbled. Daisy looked at her. "Not you," she told the cat. It was silly. Why would she let someone like Jack Elliott alter her routine? Was she afraid that he'd be even more attractive the second time around?

She forced herself to examine the next row of figures on her budget printout. But then a brisk knock came at the open door of her office. She glanced up and saw Patrice, the hotel's executive chef, standing on the threshold. Patrice, as usual, had arranged her features in a carefully disdainful expression. She was a tall woman in her mid-thirties, and knew how to use her imposing figure to best advantage. She never slouched, never tried to minimize her height. Today, as always, her cook's whites were immaculate. Meg didn't understand how such a talented chef could keep herself so spotless.

"What's cooking, Patrice?" Meg asked.

Patrice drew her eyebrows together. "Must you use that stale joke every time you see me?"

"Sorry...can't help myself. Have a seat. Tell me about the latest crisis."

The woman remained standing. "You should realize by now that I don't allow crises."

How could Meg forget? Patrice prided herself on always having everything under control.

"Very well, then," Meg said. "Not a crisis. But obviously you have something you want to tell me." One safe bet: Patrice hadn't stopped by to chitchat.

Patrice folded her arms. "It's about the staff reductions."

"We've been over this," Meg said.

"I can't run a kitchen with so little help," Patrice went on stubbornly. "The catering department cut by half. No steward. Not even a pastry assistant. It's pathetic."

"You know I didn't have any choice," Meg said as patiently as possible. "The reductions came down from Corporate."

Patrice, if possible, drew herself up even further. "Here's a message you can deliver straight to Corporate. As of this moment, they can reduce their expenses by *my* salary. Because...I quit." Patrice swiveled and went sailing regally out the door.

"Patrice—dammit—" Meg clamped her mouth shut as soon as she saw the concierge casting an interested glance toward her office. She'd let Patrice cool down for a few minutes, and then she'd try to talk some sense into the woman. This was the worst imaginable time for the Alexander to lose its renowned chef—although *Corporate* would no doubt see it as a chance to hire someone with less of a reputation at less of a salary.

The next few hours were mayhem. Patrice, having taken her stand, refused to back down and made a dramatic exit from the hotel. That left Meg to pacify the frantic undercook, who swore he wasn't up to the task of handling the evening's menus, let alone tomorrow's. Meg called a temporary service and got a promise of two more kitchen workers. Then she took the menus in hand, simplified by cutting out all the specials, and finally had the undercook acknowledging that he just might be able to pull off the bouillabaisse. By the time Meg had made certain that room service was still functioning properly and had gone back to her office for a respite, she felt exhausted. She scowled at those budget sheets still scattered across her desk, tempted to tear them in pieces.

"Bad day, I take it."

Startled, Meg glanced up and saw that someone else stood in the doorway now: none other than Jack Elliott. Virile, far-too-handsome Jack Elliott. And he wasn't alone—he had Helen's dog, Chester, on a leash. The dog immediately made a lunge toward the cat's pillow. Daisy didn't move an inch, merely giving Chester a bored, superior look. Jack told the dog to sit. Chester sat, whining a little.

"Impressive," Meg said.

"He knows who's in charge."

Meg tried to think of something halfway intelligent to say, but all she could do was gaze at Jack. She tried to pinpoint exactly why he was so gorgeous. Physique? Those broad shoulders, those jean-clad legs...definitely contributing factors. Dark, luxuriant hair...eyes a deep, dangerous blue...more contributing factors.

Maybe pinpointing Jack Elliott's appeal wasn't such a good idea. Meg realized she was practically gaping at the man.

"Well," she said, shuffling her budget reports. "Fancy seeing you here, of all places. You're not thinking of booking a room, are you?" Meg almost winced as she listened to herself. If she was looking for an intelligent remark, she hadn't found one yet.

"Not a bad idea," Jack said. "Bunking in my mother's apartment is a little confining. Plus, we drive each other crazy."

"Are you going to stay in New York long?" Meg asked.

Humor glimmered in his eyes. "Something tells me you're trying to get rid of me."

She flushed. The truth was, the thought of Jack Elliott in New York City made her feel unsettled. She wouldn't mind at all when he went back to Maine.

"I'm here on a mission," he said. "My mother sent me. Seems you didn't stop by to see her yesterday. Seems she has something important to tell you, and she wants to make sure you stop by today."

Meg felt guilty. Her reluctance to see Jack Elliott again meant that she'd neglected Helen. "Of course I'll go see your mother," she said, "just as soon as I finish work."

He glanced at the clock on the wall. "Way past five," he said. "Quitting time."

"This is the workaholic talking?" she asked. "If your mother's to be believed, *you* never leave your office at five."

"Yeah, but supposedly I'm on vacation," he said. "How about it? Chester and I will walk you home."

She had all kinds of reasons to say no. First and foremost, the kitchen crisis had only been temporarily resolved. Catastrophe could strike again at any moment. But Chester was wagging his tail, and Jack Elliott somehow managed to look more handsome than ever.

"Oh, what the heck," she muttered. "I suppose I can take a short time-out. I'll go see your mother, and then I'll come back here later." She knew her cat would be fine—everyone from the concierge to the housekeeping manager enjoyed coddling Daisy. For once Meg actually wanted to get away from the hotel.

And so, before she knew it, she was out the door with one very enthusiastic dog—and one very good-looking man.

CHAPTER THREE

"So," JACK SAID a few moments later as they went down the street, "guess you really *are* having a bad day."

It was only then that Meg realized how quickly she'd been walking along. She sighed. "That obvious? It's just...the Alexander means something special to me. I started working there eight years ago. One thing led to another, and now...now I run the place, but it's not really *mine*. I have this conglomerate counting every penny I spend and—never mind. You get the idea."

Jack cinched up Chester's leash, trying to keep the dog from tangling with passersby. "Hate working for other people myself," he said. "That's why I started my own business."

"Your mother brags about your success all the time," Meg said.

He got a disgruntled look, and they walked in silence for a few moments. Meg, in spite of the day she'd had, began to savor her surroundings—the skyscrapers, the crowded sidewalks, the neon signs already beginning to brighten the evening air. Even the noise of traffic—the blare of horns, the fitful stop and start of engines—held a certain music for her. New York was so wonderfully, messily full of life.

"You never know," Meg said to Jack. "You might discover that New York is the only place in the world to live."

He didn't seem overly enthused by the idea. "Thought you were an Oklahoma girl," he said.

"Your mother told you that, of course."

"Of course."

"Don't get me wrong," Meg said. "Oklahoma's fine. It's just that I moved to New York right after college graduation, and I fell in love with the city on sight."

"My mother mentioned that, too."

"Just how much *does* she talk about me?" Meg asked with a sense of foreboding.

"You represent the ideal to her—young career woman on the way to the top. Her own career is awfully important to her, but she feels she got much too late a start. Only after she and my dad broke up..."

Meg glanced at him. "Your mother never talks about your father."

He gave a slight grimace. "It wasn't the friendliest of divorces. My dad's a philosophy professor at a very private, very exclusive college. He was happy with my mom being the faculty wife and not very happy when she went back to school to finish her degree. She'd turned fifty-five and decided better late than never. My dad didn't see it the same way. Three

years later she was on her way to New York...
without him.''

"Sounds like a variation on my parents,'' Meg
said. "My mom wanted a career in the fashion in-
dustry, but she didn't know how to go about it—she
didn't know how to assert herself. Dad wasn't looking for a career woman. So she let her dream build
and build...and her disappointments built, too, until
finally it was all or nothing. After the divorce, she
became a buyer for an Oklahoma City department
store. My dad's still trying to figure out what went
wrong.''

"The lesson being,'' said Jack, "that you can be
either married or happy, but you can't be both.''

Meg had never thought of it quite that way.
"Amen to that,'' she said. She didn't know how
she'd ended up trading parental war stories with
Jack. She kept her mouth shut for a while, walking
along with man and dog.

Unfortunately, she couldn't seem to keep silent for
long. "Did you want to marry her?'' she asked before she could stop herself.

"Marry who?''

"You know. Kendra. The ex-girlfriend who thinks
you're too...old.'' She treated that last word as delicately as possible, but it was already too late. Jack
gave her his discontented look.

"For some reason, we started talking about marriage, in an oblique sort of way,'' he said grudgingly.
"Not that either one of us really had that in mind,

but I guess Kendra interpreted our little talk as me wanting to settle down. And then she informed me that only 'old' guys want to settle down.''

"Ouch," said Meg.

"That's what you're trying to avoid, isn't it? Settling down."

"Did your mother tell you that, too?" she asked caustically.

"Something to that effect."

Meg had long since wished she hadn't been so chatty with Helen Elliott. "Your mom needs to get back to work as soon as possible, so she has something better to talk about. But now, as far as Kendra—"

"Thought we'd moved on."

"Not quite yet," said Meg. "I'll bet Kendra was scared even of the idea of settling down, and she just used your age as an excuse."

Jack frowned. "Hell, don't you think I know that? Kendra thinks eating anything but takeout is settling down. It's just...I am getting old. My life's more than half over, and what do I have to show for it?"

"As long as you're not bitter," Meg said.

They walked along at a quick pace, Chester doing everything he could to make them go even faster.

"Chester has the right idea," Meg said. "Push forward. Don't look back. We should be in a hurry— I can't spend much time away from the hotel."

"What with your no-dating policy, no hot date tonight," he said.

"That's right," she said. "And why does everyone assume that women have to be going on dates all the time?"

"Touchy subject," Jack observed.

"It's just that I have these two friends staying with me right now, and their whole purpose is scouting for men. In fact, I find dating tedious in the extreme. All that frantic effort to pair up—and what for?"

"Good question," Jack agreed.

Silence fell between them again. After a few more blocks, they reached the apartment building and rode the elevator to the penthouse floor. Jack opened the door of his mother's apartment, and almost immediately Meg heard Helen Elliott's voice calling from inside.

"Did you bring her, Jack? Did Meg come?"

Jack gave Meg a faint smile. "I believe your presence is required. I'll give the two of you some time alone." He ushered her into the apartment, but then went back out again, closing the door behind him. Meg was sorry to see him go, and then chided herself for it. She was here to see Helen, after all—not Helen's son.

Meg walked into Helen's bedroom, Chester padding along beside her. Helen sat propped up by several pillows, while newspapers, books and magazines were spread around her on the bed. Chester jumped onto the bed, too, and made himself happily at home.

"How are you, Helen?" Meg asked. "Still going stir-crazy?"

"Don't you know it. Thought I'd get caught up on some reading, find out what's going on in the world. Instead it feels like the world is passing me by."

Meg made her way through the delightful clutter of antiques and sat down next to the bed. "I'd go stir-crazy, too," she said. "I'm the same as you. I like being out there in the middle of things."

Helen gave her an approving glance. "You're the only one who doesn't tell me I'll be better in no time, so I might as well enjoy myself. Thank you, Meg."

Meg studied the older woman. She'd struck up an acquaintance with Helen right after moving to this apartment building a year ago. The two of them had often encountered each other while rushing off to work or rushing home again. Helen had obviously liked to rush. How difficult it must be for her now...unwillingly sidelined.

"Helen," Meg said, "Jack says you have something important to tell me."

Helen shook her head. "Oh, I really am foolish. I had Jack drag you all the way here, and now I wonder how I can tell you something so ridiculous."

"It can't be that ridiculous."

"You'd be surprised. I just thought, if only I could have a woman's advice... Blast it, I'm just not used to this kind of thing!"

"Start at the beginning," Meg said firmly. "And tell me what on earth you're talking about."

Helen took a deep breath. "Very well, Meg. You

might as well know the worst of it. You see, I'm in love...I'm in love, and I simply don't know what to do about it.''

IT WAS ALMOST a full hour later that Meg stepped out of Helen Elliott's apartment and glanced at the door across the hall. By now she knew that a gentleman of sixty-two lived behind that door. His name was Russ Cooper, he owned a chain of stationery stores in New York and New Jersey—and Helen Elliott was smitten with him. She was very much smitten, despite the fact that she'd scarcely exchanged a dozen words with him.

Meg was no expert in affairs of the heart, and she couldn't help wishing that Helen had chosen someone else in whom to confide.

Meg had listened to her problem and made encouraging murmurs, but in the end she hadn't had any good advice to offer. That bothered her. Couldn't she think of something—anything—that would help Helen Elliott?

She was still mulling over the situation as the elevator doors slid open, and out stepped Jack Elliott. Not only Jack, but Meg's best friends, as well—Lena and Kathy. The three of them were conversing as if they'd known each other forever.

"Meggie," Lena exclaimed. "Look who we ran into down in the lobby—a friend of yours. We got to talking, one thing led to another, and now Jack's agreed to go out with us tonight, too. It's all arranged. Isn't that fantastic?''

Meg couldn't think of a single thing to say. She glared at Jack. He gazed back at her, his expression unreadable.

''You see, Meggie,'' Kathy said earnestly, ''Lena already had two guys lined up for tonight—you know how fast she works—and anyway she was trying to line up somebody for you. I managed to talk her out of it, seeing as how you don't want to keep our vow. But then we ran into Jack, and we did get to talking…and he did say he'd be glad to be your date tonight. Isn't that convenient?''

''Dreadfully convenient,'' said Meg. She gave Jack a hard look. ''But I'm afraid I can't. I have to go back to work.''

''Nonsense,'' said Lena. ''You give that hotel far too much of your time.''

''Please come with us, Meggie,'' Kathy pleaded. ''This is the first time in ten years I've gone out with anyone but Gary. I'd feel a lot better if you were there.''

''You see?'' Lena said triumphantly. ''You have to come for Kathy's sake. We've always said that we would support each other in times of need.''

Jack studied Meg with that quiet amusement of his. ''I'm game if you are…Meggie. A night on the town can't be that bad, can it?''

Meg could think of all sorts of reasons to refuse, but somehow not a single one came out of her mouth.

And somehow Jack Elliott managed to go on looking gorgeous—in spite of that infuriating grin he wore.

"SO...TELL ME about this vow," Jack said.

He and Meg were sitting at a small table in a murky SoHo nightclub. It was after one in the morning. They'd already been to a comedy club on Broadway, a jazz club in the West Village and a cabaret in the East Village. Meg still couldn't believe she'd let herself be talked into this. What was it about Jack Elliott that she couldn't say no to him? She should have spent the evening working at the hotel. Instead, here she was on what seemed a never-ending date with Jack...when for all intents and purposes she'd given up dating.

"The vow was something silly that happened ten years ago," Meg told him. "I'm sure you wouldn't be interested."

"Try me," he said.

Meg wondered why he had to have such a deep, seductive voice. She sipped her daiquiri and glanced around, trying to find a distraction. A retro fifties band was playing rock music. Lena was out on the dance floor, apparently having a grand time with her date, a stockbroker she'd met while browsing at a bookstore yesterday. She really *did* work fast. Kathy was dancing with the stockbroker's friend, but even in this dim light she appeared uncomfortable. Her first date since Gary—no wonder she couldn't seem to relax.

"I should go rescue Kathy," Meg said.

"Your friends can take care of themselves," Jack said. "You're just looking for an excuse to get away from me. So…what kind of vow did you make ten years ago?"

Meg silently cursed her friends for blabbing so much to Jack. "For goodness' sake," she said, "it was graduation night and we'd had too much to drink, and we all promised…we all promised we'd be married by the year 2000. It was absurd then and it's even more absurd now."

"You don't believe in keeping promises?" Jack asked solemnly.

"I'm sure you find it no end of amusing," she muttered. "Lena and Kathy are determined to keep the vow. I'm not. End of story."

Jack didn't say anything, which only rankled Meg. "I can't figure out why you came tonight," she said. "Barhopping doesn't really seem to be your thing."

He frowned at his Jamaica rum. "Kendra thought it should be my thing."

"I'm beginning to understand," said Meg. "You're still trying to prove something to Kendra."

"Hell, no," he said grouchily.

Meg had no doubt she'd touched a nerve. "So you're not the barhopping type. There are worse things in life. I have a confession to make…I'm not the barhopping type, either."

"Thought you loved New York," he reminded her.

"New York is a whole lot more than nightclubs and bars. If you stay in this city any time at all, you won't want to leave."

"Right now Maine is looking pretty good."

"I've never been to Maine," Meg confessed.

"You're missing out on something." He paused. "Funny thing, after high school I spent a lot of time trying to get away from home. Bummed around, took construction jobs anywhere I could find them. Guess I was rebelling against my dad most of all. Because he taught college, I refused even to go to college. He'd lived in that one small New England town for years, so I was going to live anywhere but. Couldn't help myself, though. Maine kept calling me back, no matter how much I tried not to listen."

Meg was intrigued by this glimpse into Jack's life. "So you finally went back."

"Yeah, guess I stopped rebelling and just started getting on with my life. I figured out maybe I did need a college degree. I went to the University of Maine...and when I decided to go into business for myself, I ended up back in my hometown, after all."

Meg realized that she was staring at Jack. She had a habit of doing that, looking at him as if she couldn't get enough. It was highly annoying. She glanced around, hoping for more distractions, but then Jack took her hand and drew her to her feet. Without a word, he led her onto the small dance floor. The band was now playing an impossibly romantic ballad. Before Meg knew it, she was swaying in Jack Elliott's arms.

"Oh, no," she murmured, but somehow her protest got lost in the music. Jack held her close. She felt tantalized, all too tempted to rest her cheek against his shoulder. Jack, for not liking to barhop, was a very good dancer. He maneuvered her slowly in the confined space, and Meg could almost believe the two of them were alone.

She told herself it was dangerous, dancing with Jack. The romantic music, the dark atmosphere, the late hour all combined to intoxicate her senses. If she had any sense at all, she'd sit down right now. She wouldn't let this go on…

But she didn't want the moment to end. She wanted to remain in Jack's arms, feeling his warmth. Slowly she lifted her head and gazed into his eyes. She couldn't read his expression, but that didn't stop her. A reckless impulse was carrying her along, making her heart pound. She twined her fingers in Jack Elliott's hair, brought his face nearer to hers. And then, quite of her own volition, she kissed him.

CHAPTER FOUR

EARLY THE NEXT MORNING, Meg woke slowly, luxuriously. She stretched her arms above her head, then wiggled her toes. A feeling of lazy, unfamiliar contentment pervaded her. Eyes still closed, she relished the silkiness of fine sheets against her bare skin...

Heart thudding, she opened her eyes and sat straight up in bed. It was a large bed, king-size, just right. Everything about this hotel room was just right—the embossed wallpaper, the rosewood furniture, the draperies patterned richly in gold and burgundy.

The door of the bathroom was open, and she could hear the sound of the shower running. "Oh Lord," she whispered. "What have I done?" She saw clothes strewn everywhere: skirt, blouse, pants, shirt...her bra dangling from the bedside table. She could hear the shower being turned off, and she told herself that she had to get out of this place. But somehow she couldn't move. She waited, frozen. And a few seconds later Jack Elliott appeared from the bathroom, a towel fastened casually around his waist. Meg stared at his broad shoulders, his muscular chest.

"Good morning," he said.

Meg grabbed her bra and tried to struggle into it while holding the sheet up as a protective screen.

"Like some help?" Jack murmured.

"I can manage." Somehow Meg got the bra fastened, and then she plucked her blouse from the floor. "If you don't mind, Jack," she said, "I'm running late. Have to get to work and all that. Wouldn't want anyone at the Alexander to find out I'd spent the night at a rival hotel." She knew her attempt at being flippant had failed miserably, but now she was desperate to get out of here. She searched around on the mattress for her underwear but couldn't find anything. Her face began to flame.

Jack came to sit on a corner of the bed. "So," he said. "Let me guess what comes next. You figure last night was a big mistake, and you want to forget all about it."

"Something like that." She found herself staring at him again. His hair was wet from the shower, still uncombed. He looked virile and handsome, and she had an almost overwhelming urge to reach over to him and kiss him. But that very same urge had already gotten her into enough trouble! She'd been dancing with him at that bar, and she'd gone ahead and given in to the urge. She'd kissed him....

After that, somehow she'd ended up saying goodnight to her friends. And then, somehow, she'd ended up taking a cab with Jack to this very posh midtown hotel.

"I don't have any excuses for what happened," she said grimly. "Sure, I could say that I had too much to drink—all that barhopping. I could say that it had been a long time for me...too long...and a woman has her needs. I could say a lot of things...but I don't have any excuses."

"Something tells me," Jack said, "that you don't do this kind of thing very often." He sounded matter-of-fact, but Meg felt her face burn all the more.

"I'm not exactly...inexperienced," she muttered. "But I usually don't hop into bed after the first *date*."

He regarded her seriously. "We seemed to need something from each other last night. It's not something you should feel bad about."

How could he sound so calm and rational? But he'd been that way all along. He'd even had the foresight to take care of birth control. Meg had been the one who'd lost control, who'd allowed herself to be swept away by a tumult of sensation. She could feel the turmoil inside her even now, the longing to go into his arms, the desire to lose herself all over again. How could this be happening? No other man had affected her this way. Before, she'd always been able to stand back, keep a distance from her emotions— her desires. But with Jack Elliott, standing back obviously hadn't been an option.

She searched the bed again and at last found her briefs. Fumbling awkwardly, she put them on while still using the sheet as protection against Jack. She couldn't think of anything more humiliating than putting on her underwear while he sat there, observing her impassively.

"Dammit," she said. "Didn't you get carried away at *all*?"

His eyes darkened as he watched her. "I thought I proved that to you."

"I don't mean just…sex. Oh, hell, I don't know what I mean." At last she gave up the protection of the sheet. She slid out of bed, pulled on her skirt, grabbed her shoes and purse and made a beeline for the door. Only once did she glance back.

"It *was* a mistake," she told Jack. "The worst kind of mistake."

And then she left.

"YOU CAN'T AVOID Jack Elliott forever, Meg," said Kathy.

"And why would you want to avoid him, anyway?" asked Lena. "He's gorgeous."

Meg sighed. "I explained, didn't I? I barely know the man, yet I slept with him. Of course I have to avoid him!"

The three women had congregated in the living room of Meg's apartment. Lena as usual had taken over the sofa, and Kathy sat curled in her favorite armchair. Meg sat in another armchair, cradling Daisy in her lap. It was Sunday afternoon—two days since Meg had been so reckless, so unthinking. Two days since she'd gone to bed with Jack Elliott. Even now she felt her face heating at the memory. How could she have done it? What had possessed her? The questions remained unanswered.

"You haven't been sleeping very well the last couple of nights, have you?" Kathy observed. "I've heard you up, prowling around."

It was a small apartment, and Meg couldn't seem to hide much of anything from her friends. It was true that she'd been inordinately restless. At work she could keep her mind occupied with the myriad problems of running the hotel, but at night self-recriminations assaulted her full force.

"I shouldn't have done it," she said bleakly. "One minute I was kissing the man, and the next I was imagining—well, never mind. I wish I'd left *everything* to my imagination. I wish I'd left well enough alone!"

"No one," said Lena, "is disagreeing that you did something extremely foolish."

Meg frowned. "Gee, don't try too hard to console me."

Lena stretched out on the sofa. She looked as sophisticated as ever in a sarong-style skirt and sleeveless T-shirt, her toenail polish a bright vermilion. "I'm just being realistic," she said. "I know you, Meg. You take sex far too seriously. Remember Bruce Layton?"

"How could she forget Bruce Layton?" asked Kathy. "It was her first time."

Meg groaned. There was a distinct disadvantage

to having friends who knew absolutely everything about her. "Do we have to dredge up the embarrassing details of my past?"

"Dredging is good," pronounced Lena, "when it has instructive value. So, remember Bruce Layton?"

"Of course I remember Bruce Layton," Meg grumbled.

"Your first true love," Kathy said a bit dreamily. Perhaps she was influenced by her overly romantic attire—lacy blouse and gored skirt in a soft fawn color.

"Kathy," said Lena, "stick to the point—when it came to Bruce, Meg confused sex with love."

"Please," said Meg. "Can't we discuss something else?" But she remembered all too well. She'd been nineteen, in her sophomore year of college, when she'd met senior Bruce Layton. They'd shared an anthropology class together, and later they'd shared a whole lot more. Meg had been utterly convinced that she'd found the love of her life. Bruce hadn't harbored the same conviction, and he'd started dating a dance major. Meg had declared her heart broken, sobbing her despair to her two college roommates, Lena and Kathy. They'd commiserated and comforted, but even back then Lena had astutely pointed out the most likely possibility: wasn't it logical to assume that Meg had simply confused love with the desires of a healthy young body?

"All right," Meg admitted grudgingly now.

"Maybe I was naive in those days. But I've changed. I've learned how to handle men."

"What you learned after Bruce," said Lena, "was to keep guys at a distance. Face it, you haven't exactly had a whole lot of relationships since then. You find fault with men, you back off, you tell yourself you've made a lucky escape because no way are you gonna end up like your parents. To sum matters up, you haven't had nearly enough sex in your life."

Meg gave another groan. "Enough is enough. Let's talk about something else."

"No, let's talk about sex," said Kathy. "It's very interesting."

Lena was already going on inexorably. "You haven't had a lot of sex, Meg, and that means you still take it too seriously. You still confuse it with love. So when a dreamboat like Jack Elliott comes along…a guy you can't possibly resist…you make love to him, and next thing you know you're all starry-eyed. Look at her, Kathy. Isn't she starry-eyed?"

Somehow Meg had known this exasperating conversation would return to Jack. "I'm not in love with the man," she insisted. "I may have exhibited a serious lack of judgment, but I am *not* in love with Jack Elliott."

"First sign," said Lena. "Protesting too much."

"Wait a minute," said Kathy. "What's the problem here? So Meg went to bed with a gorgeous man.

So maybe she's already falling in love with him. Isn't that the idea?''

Lena's expression was long-suffering. "Kathy, the idea is to do this thing right. You have to sample a lot of men before you find the one and only—''

"You certainly know about sampling," Kathy interjected, "but I don't see how it's helped *you* any.''

"At least I haven't devoted my entire life to Sit-on-the-Fence Gary.''

"Girls," said Meg. "No bickering.''

"Okay," agreed Kathy amenably. "So, tell us, Meg. How was it?''

"How was what?" she muttered.

"How was sex with Dreamboat Jack?" asked Lena.

Meg shook her head in disbelief. "I'm not going to talk about this. I'm just not.''

Lena and Kathy didn't say anything, merely watched her patiently.

"For crying out loud," Meg sputtered at last. "It was...wonderful.''

"Could you be a little more specific?" asked Lena.

Before this, Meg had confided all manner of information to her friends. But when it came to those few impassioned hours she'd spent with Jack Elliott...no, she simply couldn't be more specific. The experience had been too private, too intimate—too overwhelming. She couldn't put it into words. Somehow that made her feel lonely, as if she'd left her friends behind. As if, in fact, she'd left all familiar landmarks behind.

Kathy was carefully observing Meg's expression. "Wow," she said. "That good, huh?" She sighed wistfully. "Boy, I really do miss Gary. Can't help it."

Lena and Meg exchanged glances, then burst out laughing at the same time. Meg was grateful for the release of tension.

Kathy looked miffed. "I don't see what's so funny."

"You," said Lena. "We're talking about sex, and you just naturally bring up Gary. If you're going to do that, you have to dish. What's it *really* like, making love to the same guy after ten years?"

Kathy folded her arms. "Gary and I have—*had*— a perfectly satisfactory sex life. It's just that…"

"Just what?" prodded Lena.

"I wish you hadn't brought up all this talk about sampling other men! You know Gary was the first man I ever slept with…the only man I ever slept with. And sometimes…"

"Sometimes," said Lena, "you've wondered what it would be like with someone else."

Now Kathy looked unhappy. "I know I wouldn't have those thoughts if Gary would just—just commit, dammit. He'd be the only person I'd ever need."

"Don't count on it," Lena said. "Remember that old saying—variety is the spice of life."

"But you're the woman who's going to be married

by the year 2000," said Meg. "Hate to remind you of this, but marriage kind of means sticking to one guy. No variety, so to speak."

Lena sat up and began strapping her feet into black sandals that were improbably high-heeled. "If a woman experiences enough men, she'll know for real when she's found the one she *can* stick to. Both of you have to make up for lost time. Here's the plan—"

"The master plan," Meg said dryly.

"Right," said Lena, not sounding perturbed in the least. "The master plan is that we meet as many of those eligible, rich, successful New Yorkers as we can. Only later do we narrow down the field."

"In plenty of time for the year 2000," said Meg.

"It's going to work," Lena assured her. "Just you wait and see." She stood and slipped into a designer jacket that perfectly matched her vermilion nail polish. "Off to the hunt," she announced cheerfully. "This time I even have my red coat."

Kathy stood and put on her own jacket—fringed brown suede, an evocation of Oklahoma's Old West days.

"Happy hunting," said Meg. "The two of you look suitably armed—the New York male doesn't stand a chance."

"You won't come with us?" asked Kathy. "Best thing in the world to get your mind off Dreamboat Jack."

"Do we have to call him that?"

"Here's my advice," said Lena. "Go to bed with him again. Enjoy. Then see what else is out there. Compare. It's the only way to figure out if you really do love the guy."

"I do not want to enjoy," Meg protested. "I do not want to compare. And I am under illusion of being in love with Jack Elliott!"

"Whatever you say…" With a debonair wave of her hand, Lena escorted Kathy out the door. Meg finally had the apartment to herself.

She didn't know why she felt so bereft. A little solitude for once should be appealing. Stroking Daisy's fur, she glanced around, telling herself this was her sanctuary. She saw the prints she'd had so much fun arranging on the walls—several watercolors, as well as reproductions from a nineteenth-century fashion catalog. She saw the bright ceramic bowls she'd scattered across the mantel, the hand-painted cupboard she'd discovered at a flea market, the lacquered fire screen that had been another find. Every detail was something she'd chosen with care, creating her own special world. Why, then, did she feel unaccountably stifled? Was it because she'd decided to hole up here rather than run the risk of facing Jack?

The phone rang, and she picked up the receiver, glad for any outside contact. "Meg Danley."

"Meg, it's Helen Elliott. Can you forgive an old woman for intruding on your life?"

Meg felt the guilt that was becoming all too common where Helen was concerned. Avoiding Jack meant avoiding his mother, as well.

"You're not intruding—you know that."

"Don't suppose you could drop by," said Helen.

Drop by…and no doubt run into Jack. Meg's heartbeat accelerated just at the thought.

"I'm being silly," said Helen. "I'm sure you have a hundred better things to do."

Meg hesitated a second longer, but she'd heard the loneliness in the older woman's voice.

"Of course I don't have anything better to do," she said. "I'll be right there." She hung up the receiver. She tried to be reasonable. She couldn't avoid Jack forever, could she?

If only she could.

SEVERAL MOMENTS LATER, Meg knocked on the door of Helen's apartment. She held her breath as she heard the locks being undone on the other side. The door swung open, but it was not Jack Elliott who greeted her. It was one of the nurses who looked after Helen. Meg let her breath out, battling a strange mixture of relief and disappointment.

She went into the living room and found an enthusiastic welcome. Chester wagged his tail. Helen smiled from the sofa, where she sat with her cast propped up.

"I've missed you, Meg. Of course, they keep you terribly busy at the hotel, and that's just as it should be."

Meg sat down in a chair next to the sofa, feeling guilty all over again. No matter how busy she'd been before, she'd always found time to visit Helen. Meg debated telling Helen the truth: *By the way, I slept with your son the other night, and that's why I've made myself scarce.*

On second thought, sometimes the truth was better left unsaid. Meg fought the urge to ask where Jack was. She felt certain if he were here in the apartment, she'd sense his presence. But asking would be a mistake, surely. Somehow Meg had to play it cool.

"Tell me about work," Helen said. "Tell me all about it."

Meg settled back and recounted her latest adventures at the Alexander. She talked about the fact that she'd finally hired a new chef—adequate but no comparison with Patrice. She discussed her ongoing efforts to snag a well-known jazz quintet to play at the hotel bar, and confessed her ambitions to have the hotel host one of New York's more prestigious charity events.

"All very worthwhile, my dear," said Helen, "but you know that Corporate is going to come down on you for any added expenses."

Meg nodded ruefully. "They'll be in a snit when they hear about some of my plans, but I'm going to barrel forward. I know what's right for the Alexander, even if they don't."

"Give 'em hell," said Helen.

It occurred to Meg that Helen understood her dedication to the hotel more than anyone else. The older woman knew it was more than a job to Meg—it was what gave meaning and shape to her days, just as Helen's job had once done for *her*.

"I know it's going to seem like forever," Meg consoled her, "but you will be back at work."

"I'm sixty-three," Helen said. "My boss is pushing me to take early retirement. He's acting like my little accident is a sign I should be put out to pasture."

Meg was indignant. "Don't listen to him. Fight back. You have years of good work ahead."

Helen gave a slight grimace. "Sometimes that's what I'm afraid of, Meg. Afraid I have years and years of work."

Meg stared at the other woman in surprise. "But I thought you loved your job."

"I did…I still do, actually. But, I don't know, perhaps it's not enough. Being laid up *does* make you look at life from all angles. I need to make time for other things in my life—something besides puttering around and looking for antiques by myself. I'd like to travel, and go to some of those concerts I keep meaning to attend. Problem is, who will I share all that with?''

''You can do a lot of things on your own,'' Meg replied promptly. ''A woman doesn't need a man in order to be happy or fulfilled—or busy.''

Helen smiled almost pityingly. ''Five years ago, I would have said the same thing. I was so grateful to be out of my marriage. But I'm older now, and I hope a little wiser. Just because my ex and I didn't get along is no reason to toss aside all men.''

''I suppose,'' said Meg, ''you're thinking about the gentleman across the hall again.''

Helen's face seemed to light up. ''I know I already told you about him, but I've learned more. Claudia is a very reliable source, thank goodness.''

Meg knew that Helen was referring to Claudia Romero, the building super.

''Turns out he's divorced, just like me,'' Helen told her. ''He has two grown sons and five grand-children. And he goes to the opera. Do you know, Meg, I've always wanted to learn more about the opera. He likes Chinese food. Claudia knows, because he's always ordering takeout from a place on Broadway. Did you know, Meg, that I adore Chinese food?''

Meg hadn't known. But even as she watched, the light seemed to fade from Helen's eyes.

''Of course,'' Helen murmured unhappily, ''it's ri-diculous to pretend I actually know the man. Everything I learn about him comes from someone else. I've barely said more than hello to him.''

Meg thought it over. ''Helen, maybe it's time you did say more than hello.''

''That's impossible right now. No one looks appealing on crutches, and I spend too much time in a wheelchair these days. I won't be running into him anytime soon—not in my situation.''

''I'm not so sure about that.'' Meg couldn't help grinning. ''You know what you need, Helen? You need a master plan.''

Helen's expression was extremely doubtful, so Meg explained.

''A master plan—that's what my friend Lena would call it, anyway. Instead of sitting around bemoaning the circumstances, we need to take fate into our own hands.''

Helen looked even more skeptical.

''Listen, I have an idea,'' Meg began. ''A way to kick things off.'' She leaned forward in her chair and outlined the details.

Now Helen began to look scared. ''Oh, Meg, I don't think I could do what you're asking. It's a good idea—ingenious, in fact—but I'd feel so awkward.''

''What are you risking?'' Meg asked. ''If you don't take some sort of action, you'll always wonder.''

''If I could only wait until I'm on my feet again...''

"I have a feeling you'll always find an excuse," Meg chided gently. "You spent three years saying hello to Mr. Cooper in the hall, but never took it further. Once your ankle heals, you'll just find another reason to stand back. I say the time for action is *now*."

Helen made a restless gesture. She still seemed scared—but she also seemed excited. "Oh, what the hell, Meg! Let's just do it. Before I change my mind—let's do it."

CHAPTER FIVE

IN LESS THAN AN HOUR, Meg had everything ready.
She'd managed to get the nurse out of the apartment,
dispatching her on several errands. And Helen had
assured her that Jack was gone for the afternoon.
Then Meg had tidied up the place and done a little
work on Helen. The older woman looked quite fetch-
ing in a ruffle-collared robe, her silvery hair curling
attractively about her face.

"Perfect," Meg said.

"I'm not so sure I can go through with this,"
Helen said anxiously.

"You'll do great," Meg reassured her. "I have a
good feeling about this, I really do." Meg found herself very caught up in the scheme she'd devised; she
liked focusing on someone else's romantic problems.
"Okay," she said. "I'm leaving now. Plan A is
about to go into action."

"Meg..."

"Yes, Helen?"

"Just—thanks. I feel as nervous as a teen-
ager...but thank you."

"Helen," said Meg. "I *do* have a good feeling
about this."

She let herself out of the apartment and stepped across the hall. According to Helen's sources, Russ Cooper was invariably home this time of day. Meg tapped on his door.

Sure enough, he answered her knock. He was a balding man who looked younger than his sixty-two years.

"Yes?" he said rather distractedly.

"Mr. Cooper, I'm Meg Danley from 7C. I wondered if I could ask you a favor."

He hesitated for a second or two, but then he nodded. "Certainly, Ms. Danley. Please come in."

Meg stepped across the threshold. The first thing she noticed was a bicycle propped up in the middle of Mr. Cooper's living room. It was a classic bike— big red fenders, generous handlebars.

"Nice," Meg said.

"Had it ever since I was a boy," Russ Cooper told her. "Don't ask me why I've held on to it all these years, because usually I don't save anything. But here it is…I finally dragged it out of storage. Thought maybe one of my grandkids might like giving it a whirl."

Meg studied Mr. Cooper without being too obvious about it. He seemed to be in mint condition— just like the bicycle. He wasn't one of those men who made the mistake of trying to hide his bald spot. What hair he had left was neatly trimmed, obviously under the care of an expert barber. His clothes had the expert's touch, too: cashmere tie, herringbone vest and trousers, suede shoes.

"Don't suppose you know your way around a spoke wrench," he said. "I have a wheel that's wobbling, and darned if I can fix it."

"Let me have a go at it," Meg offered. With Mr. Cooper's help she turned the bicycle upside down, used the wrench, and soon had the wheel spinning smoothly.

"I'm impressed, Ms. Danley," he said.

"I grew up with two older brothers. Anything they did, I learned too. No way was I going to be left out."

"Ms. Danley, seems you're the one who's done me a favor."

She straightened. By now she'd had a chance to glance around Mr. Cooper's apartment. Unlike Helen's place, it was uncluttered in the extreme. The furnishings had been pared down to a few essential— and expensive—items: a Scandinavian-style sofa, chairs of bleached oak, a glass-topped table with two or three books situated precisely upon it. Russ Cooper seemed like the type of person who had such refined tastes that not very many objects could meet his standards. He probably wouldn't know what to think of Helen's apartment, where no antique was considered too lowly to occupy a space. Meg began to experience a niggling little doubt. What if Helen and Russ Cooper weren't exactly compatible...?

She pushed the thought aside. "Mr. Cooper, you

can still do me a favor. I'm a friend of Helen Elliott's—"

"Ah, yes," he said, his tone formal. "Mrs. Elliott. I was sorry to hear about her taking a fall. How is she doing?"

"Very well, considering the circumstances. But here's where the favor comes in. She's going to be alone for the next few hours, and I was hoping you might check in on her. Just to make sure she's okay, and all."

Russ Cooper looked uncertain. "I'm not very good with people when they're sick."

"Helen isn't actually sick," Meg said. "She just has a bit of trouble getting around at the moment. I have a key here. Ordinarily I'd do it, but I have to go out. If you could let yourself into her apartment, say, in fifteen minutes or so, and ask how she's doing… I'd very much appreciate it."

He hesitated, then gave a reluctant nod. "Anything I can do to be of assistance," he said, not sounding altogether convinced. Other doubts were beginning to surface in Meg's mind. Mr. Cooper didn't seem what you'd call the nurturing type. Meg also suspected he was set in his ways. Nonetheless, she wasn't going to back out now. She handed him the key.

"Thank you so much, Mr. Cooper. Goodbye for now." She exited his apartment, closing the door behind her. The rest was up to Helen. You never knew about this type of thing. Opposites *did* attract. With any luck, Mr. Cooper and Helen would get to talking, the time would fly, and Meg's plan would be well on its way.

Having managed to reassure herself, Meg stepped toward the elevator. Before she could press the down button, however, the doors slid open and out stepped Jack Elliott.

All she could do was stare at him. Dark-haired, blue-eyed, dangerously handsome Jack Elliott. She tried to unravel the emotions he made her feel, but it was hopeless. She was entangled by the most elemental of sensations. A warmth coiling through her…an awareness skimming every nerve ending… She might as well be back in that hotel room with him, wrapped in his arms.

· Her face burned as a potent mixture of desire and regret swept over her. "You're not supposed to be here," she said at last. "Your mother said you'd be gone for a while."

He regarded her gravely. "Trying to get rid of me?" he asked.

More than anything, Meg wanted to take the elevator down to the seventh floor and barricade herself in her apartment. Seeing Jack again was even worse than she'd feared it would be—her composure was rattled, her self-command vanished. Getting away from him seemed the only solution. On the other hand, she couldn't very well let him go into his mother's apartment, not with Plan A about to go into effect.

"Jack," she said, "you and I need to…talk. What do you say we go somewhere, and we…talk."

He continued to observe her with that solemn expression. He didn't budge, as if he knew full well that something was up. Finally Meg grabbed hold of his arm and drew him into the elevator. She punched the down button and didn't say a word until they'd reached the lobby. Then she grabbed his arm again and propelled him out of the elevator. She did her best to ignore the glimmer of amusement in his eyes.

"Don't ask any questions," she muttered. "Just come with me."

Soon she had him walking down the street with her, but she had no idea what to do with him next. She couldn't let him go back to his mother's apartment for at least a couple of hours. The only way she could make sure he *didn't* go back was to stay right beside him.

"Jack," she said almost desperately, "ever been to the Empire State Building?"

"No…but something tells me I'm about to."

She flagged a cab, glad to have a goal in mind. Only a short while later the two of them were in another elevator, this time traveling to the eighty-sixth floor of the Empire State Building. They shared the cramped space with several tourists, which meant that Meg found herself pressed close to Jack. She became all too conscious of the lean, powerful lines of his body. Slowly she lifted her gaze to his, and saw that he was regarding her with a faintly quizzical expression. He gave no sign that her proximity affected *him*.

They reached the observation deck, and now all of New York was spread before them, buildings jumbled together like dominoes. Windows glinted in the sun, and the sky was a springtime blue. Despite the jumble of tourists, Meg and Jack found a small space to themselves.

"Have you ever seen anything like it?" she murmured. "No city in the world can compare to this." When she glanced at Jack, however, she saw that he wasn't admiring the view. Instead he continued to study her.

"You did say you wanted to talk," he remarked.

"Yes, well…" Her voice trailed off as she tried to think of a neutral topic.

"We have to discuss it sooner or later, Meg. What happened between us the other night."

Once again she felt her face heating up. Around Jack, all her temperature controls seemed to go awry.

"There's nothing to discuss," she said. "We already decided it was a mistake."

"No…*we* didn't decide anything of the kind. You came to that conclusion on your own."

She hugged her arms against her body. "And you don't think it was a mistake?"

He frowned a little. "It wasn't something I planned on happening. Lord knows I don't need another involvement. But it did happen, Meg. And we have to deal with it."

"I'm dealing with it," she said tightly. "I'm admitting it was wrong, and I'm putting it behind me."

"I want to make love to you again, Meg. And I'm pretty sure you feel the same way."

She was suddenly having trouble catching her breath. Blame it on the altitude. Or blame Jack Elliott.

"Dammit, Jack—"

"We might as well be honest with each other."

No chance now of losing herself in the view. "Very well," she said in a low voice. "Maybe I do want to make love with you. But that's no reason to give in. I shouldn't have given in to my impulses the first time."

"I already told you…maybe we needed something from each other."

"What exactly *did* we need, Jack? Did you need to prove that you're still young? And did I need to prove that I was still desirable, even though I hadn't gone to bed with a man in ages?" She couldn't believe what she'd just said. Being honest definitely had its drawbacks. Quickly she turned away from him. "We shouldn't be talking about this. We don't have any privacy."

"No one is paying attention to us." He drew closer to her, put his arm around her. "We just look like we're out having a good time on a Sunday afternoon."

"Not that good a time," she said. His arm felt so natural across her shoulders, but it also interfered with her thought processes. "Darn it," she muttered, "I can't remember what I was saying. What I wanted to say..."

"You were talking about the men in your life."

"It's too late to be diplomatic," she told him. "I was talking about the *lack* of men in my life."

"I already knew that part. How you'd given up dating."

Meg told herself she was getting altogether too cozy, snuggled against Jack this way. But somehow she couldn't seem to move.

"No," she admitted. "I'm talking about even before I gave up dating. Even then, I suppose I didn't let anyone get too close. Physically...sometimes. Emotionally...maybe not ever."

"Is that what you're worried about?" he asked. "The fact I might get too close?"

She felt compelled to look at him again. "What about you, Jack?" she asked quietly. "Aren't you worried about the same thing—that somehow *I'll* get too close?"

He didn't answer, but his eyes darkened as he gazed at her. And now, at last, she drew away from him.

"You know what happened, Jack? We made things go too fast. One minute we were little more than strangers—the next we were in bed together. It didn't stop us from being strangers. It certainly didn't stop us from being people who live in different states…and who don't have a whole lot in common."

He rubbed his neck. "Okay. Let's start over."

She stared at him. "What are you talking about?"

"Exactly what I said. We'll start over. Pretend we never ended up in that hotel room together. Go back to the beginning. Get to know each other a little."

She almost laughed. "That's impossible. We can't just erase what we did."

"Maybe not. But we can start on a fresh page. How about this—come out to dinner with me right now. That's all it'll be…dinner."

Meg wondered how he could make one simple, ordinary meal sound so alluring. She glanced at her watch. "Bit early for dinner, isn't it? It's not even five yet."

"So it'll be an early dinner. Can't ask for anything more innocent than that."

Innocent…nothing could be innocent where Jack was concerned. She could swear she still saw a hint of humor in his eyes. Was he making a joke of this, or did he really want to start over?

"Dinner," she repeated. "That's it?"

"That's it." He grinned. "Trust me, Meg."

The real problem was…did she trust herself? But she found herself giving in.

"Dinner," she agreed, "and then good-night."

MEG CHOSE the restaurant—one of her favorites, a place that served Spanish food. The decor was nothing fancy, just plain tabletops and booths with slat-wood benches. However, a lovely mural had been painted on one wall, depicting a sun-drenched Mediterranean villa, and the food was delicious. Both Jack and Meg ordered the paella, a savory mixture of mussels, shrimp, fresh green peas, pimientos, and saffron-flavored rice. Because they had, indeed, arrived early, they had the place almost to themselves. Meg was surprised to realize how hungry she was. She hadn't thought she could relax enough around Jack to enjoy a meal, yet they shared the food companionably.

Meg broke off a piece of crusty bread. "Tell me, Jack," she said, "how is it you've reached the ripe old age of thirty-nine without accumulating at least one ex-wife along the way? And don't tell me about Kendra—we all know how *she* felt about settling down. There had to have been other women, though." How could there *not* have been other women? A man like Jack Elliott would never lack for admiring females.

He looked reflective. "So far there've been two stages to my life, Meg. In my twenties I traveled around so much, no relationship had a chance of sticking. In my thirties I've focused so much on building my company, no relationship's had much of a chance, either. Now I guess the third stage is around the corner."

"Hmm, which one is that?" she asked with interest.

A dour expression took over his face. "The stage of not knowing what the hell comes next in my life."

"Maybe you just have to decide what happens next."

He gazed at her for a long moment without saying anything. But from the way his eyes darkened, she could tell what he was thinking...yes, she could tell.

"Dammit," she swore under her breath. "You said we were going to start over, Jack."

"I am starting over. I'm sitting across the table from a beautiful woman, trying to get to know her better."

"You're making love to me just by looking at me," she murmured, her voice unsteady.

"I'll stop," he said, but he didn't. At last she wrenched her gaze away.

"This isn't going to work," she said. "We're not getting to know each other better. We're just... reliving our mistake."

He sat back. "Okay, let's try again. Tell me everything about yourself, Meggie."

The way he spoke her nickname sent an odd little shiver through her. "Everything...that's a tall order."

"Just start at the beginning," he said. "Let's see...what's your first memory?"

"This is ridiculous—"

"Humor me."

Now she was the one who sat back. Her first memory...an image tantalized her, just out of reach. She closed her eyes, trying to capture it. And then, almost absently, she began to speak. "I guess I was three—maybe four. I was sitting in the swing set out back, and my brother Ryan was pushing me. I kept telling him to push me higher and higher. I couldn't understand why my mother came running out the back door and told Ryan to stop before I got hurt. I knew I could never get hurt, not as long as I was with one of my brothers."

Slowly she opened her eyes and saw that Jack was regarding her thoughtfully. At once she felt self-conscious.

"I don't know if that was my *first* memory," she said. "It's just what came to mind."

"Obviously you were close to your brothers," he remarked.

"Yeah, sure, when I wasn't trying to beat them up, or get better grades than they did, or generally outdo them."

"Why are you embarrassed to admit your brothers were special to you?"

"I'm not embarrassed," she grumbled. "It's just that…"

"Maybe it's hard to admit you've actually had a couple of guys in your life who didn't let you down."

She stared at him in exasperation. "What makes you think you know so much?" She paused. "Oh, all right, it's the truth. Out of all the men I've known, my brothers have been the ones I could count on.

Even when they teased me mercilessly, I knew they wouldn't let me down on the important things.''

''What about your dad?'' Jack asked.

This getting-to-know-you business was uncomfortable. ''We've talked enough about me,'' she said.

''We're just getting started.''

She wanted to protest, but facts about her life kept tumbling out. ''My dad's never been what you'd call an emotive guy. For example, we had a big scare once, when my brother Shaun got really sick and the doctors couldn't figure out what was wrong with him. Turned out to be some kind of allergic reaction, but we all thought it was going to be a lot worse. Anyway, later I saw a copy of a letter my dad sent to some relatives, explaining the crisis. And he was so…unemotional. So dry and clinical about the whole thing. As if he were talking about a stranger, not his firstborn son.'' She shook her head. ''I'm sure he'd been scared to death, but he didn't know how to admit it. To this day, he's never said that he loves any of us. When he writes letters to me, he signs them 'Father.' Not 'Love, Father,' or even 'Sincerely, Father.' Just 'Father.''' She took a breath and stopped herself. ''Now I've definitely said enough.''

''Guess I've reopened old wounds.'' Jack's tone was gruff.

Meg gave a shrug. ''All families have their share of wounds, I suppose. Mine are no worse than anyone else's. I've learned you can't change people. My father is never going to open up—he's never going to let his guard down, that's for certain. The positive side of that is that my brothers aren't likely to change, either. They're still the two guys I can call in the middle of the night, if I need to.''

Jack's expression remained reflective, but he didn't ask her any more questions about herself. She was glad to concentrate on dessert, a creamy parfait topped with candied walnuts. Then she and Jack lingered over coffee and an orange liqueur. They stayed so long that the restaurant filled up around them, and evening shadows darkened outside. They spoke of inconsequential things now—no more family secrets revealed—but Meg felt the same unsettling intimacy between them.

Jack paid the bill, leaving a generous tip. Meg smiled a little, and Jack gave her an inquiring look. She felt compelled to explain.

''It's just that when Kathy and Lena and I were in college, we had a list of standards we judged men by. A rather silly list, but one of the items was whether or not a man knew how to tip properly.''

''Do I pass?'' he asked wryly.

''With flying colors. Kathy was a waitress once, so she positively cannot abide poor tippers.''

''What other standards are you judging me by?'' he asked as they left the restaurant.

''I told you—it was just a silly list. Hardly something we'd take seriously anymore.''

''That's not what I gathered from your friends the

other night,'' he said. ''Seemed like they had a list a mile long.''

''Well, *I* don't have a list anymore, so rest easy— I'm not judging you at all.''

''Too bad,'' he said. ''I like a challenge.''

Mentally, she ran over the items of that absurd, long-ago list: handsome, intelligent, ambitious, sense of humor, confident, outgoing but definitely not the partying fraternity type....

''Tell me, Jack,'' she found herself asking, ''did you ever belong to a fraternity when you were in college?''

''Didn't have the time for that kind of thing,'' he replied. ''I was an older student. Wanted to get my degree and then get on with the rest of my life. Why?''

''Nothing important,'' she said. No sense telling Jack Elliott that so far he fit every qualification on her college-girl list.

They strolled down the street, neither one of them seeming to be in much of a hurry. Meg savored the bustle of a Sunday evening in New York: people moving with a sense of purpose, on their way to movies and plays, other people stopping at the deli after a long, leisurely afternoon at the park.

''I love this city,'' she said.

''That's the idea I keep getting.''

''And I keep getting the idea you don't feel the same way. You'd probably like to get back to Maine.''

He gave her a sardonic glance. "Message received. You want to make sure I realize how incompatible the two of us are. Hell, we don't even live in the same town."

So maybe that had been her point. Maybe it was a good idea for them to remind each other that they lived different lives...incompatible lives.

It was something of a walk to Meg's apartment building. She didn't suggest a cab, though, and neither did Jack. They simply went along, the silence between them surprisingly companionable again. At last, however, no matter how much they hadn't hurried, they did reach the building. Meg stopped outside.

"Well, I guess this is good-night," she said.

"That's what we agreed on. Dinner, and then good-night."

"So...good night, Jack."

"Good night, Meg."

She wished he would go inside first, because she didn't seem able to wrap things up.

"Good night," she repeated, for good measure.

"Good night," he said. And then he took her in his arms and kissed her.

A kiss—not a good idea. Look at what had happened last time they'd kissed. But Meg couldn't seem to make herself leave Jack's arms. His touch, the caress of his lips...these were things she already knew too well. She knew the warmth gliding through her, and how quickly it could flame into something more. She knew the reckless way Jack made her feel, as if nothing in the world mattered but his touch.

Somehow, from somewhere, she found the strength to resist his embrace. She drew away, even as she trembled deep inside.

"No, Jack," she whispered. "We're still moving too fast—way too fast. And... I can't. I just can't."

She turned and went quickly into the building, trying to ignore the loneliness spreading through her. The loneliness, and the longing.

CHAPTER SIX

THE MAN AT THE BANK was annoying the hell out of Jack. Bradley, read the nameplate on the man's desk. Bradley was methodical to the point of tedium, and yet he couldn't seem to get a complete sentence out of his mouth.

"Yes, well, Mr. Elliott..." Bradley stared at the numbers on his computer screen. He punched numbers into his calculator and stared at those, too. Then he stared long and hard at the numbers on his screen, as if to make sure they hadn't misbehaved while he wasn't looking. "Yes, well..."

Jack shifted in a chair on the other side of the desk. He just wanted to get on with it. At last Bradley took a sheet of paper and laboriously wrote a figure on it. He inched the paper across the desk toward Jack. Bradley acted as if there were something underhanded, something devious, about this whole transaction. To Jack, it was pretty damn straightforward— he was only trying to pay off his mother's debts.

Jack glanced at the figure on the sheet of paper. It was a sizable amount, more than he'd expected...a lot more. Without hesitating, though, he opened his checkbook, wrote out a check and handed it over. Bradley picked up the check and stared at it.

"Yes, well… "

Jack had had enough. He left the bank and found himself once more on the streets of New York. He walked without paying much attention to where he was going, his thoughts occupied by the newest development in his life: it seemed his mother was on the brink of financial disaster.

Not that his mother had been the one to tell him. No—that would have been too easy. Jack had received the first hint this morning from the super of Helen's apartment building. Claudia Romero had come to Jack in confidence. She liked Helen, thought she was an excellent tenant. There was just one small matter that Claudia hated to bring up but felt she had to, for Helen's benefit. Namely, Helen was two months overdue on her lease payments.

Jack had taken care of that "small matter." Then he'd started some poking around in his mother's finances and discovered she was overdue on loan payments to the bank, as well. He hated to think what he might find next.

Traffic had come to its habitual standstill and Jack crossed the street, threading his way between vans and cabs and other cars, all with engines idling. When he reached the other side of the street, he chose a direction at random. He needed to walk and to think.

He considered the past five years since his parents'

divorce. From all appearances, his mother's financial position should have been stable. Despite the acrimony of the divorce, she'd received a generous settlement. Jack's father wasn't cheap. The combination of his salary from the university and a substantial inheritance from Jack's grandparents had enabled him to set up his ex-wife in comfort. And Helen hadn't just been sitting around the past five years, either. Undaunted by the fact that she was reentering the job market in her fifties, she'd simply knocked on doors until one had opened to her. She'd worked hard ever since; the considerable energy she'd once applied to being a faculty wife had gone into her late-blooming career. With proper money management, she should have been fine.

But it seemed that Helen Elliott hadn't been one for fiscal responsibility. And it seemed it was up to Jack to find out why.

"Hell," he muttered. He didn't like poking into his mother's finances. But he also didn't like the thought of her being destitute.

Gradually he became aware of where he was headed—turned out he was half a block from Meg Danley's hotel. He hadn't intended to come this way, but apparently his subconscious had led him here. Meg Danley…another complication to his New York City visit. A big complication.

Yesterday she'd hauled him off to the Empire State Building. Then they'd shared dinner, and then he'd taken her into his arms—and then she'd run away from him. He'd wanted her to stay. He'd wanted to touch her again—feel her bare skin against his fingers. And after that...he hadn't thought any further than that.

He stood where he was, staring down the street at the Alexander Hotel. It had a graceful, if somewhat overwrought Gothic facade. Jack pictured Meg going about her work as hotel manager, running the place, leading a life totally separate from his. She would welcome no intrusion from him, that much was certain.

He turned and headed in the opposite direction, away from the hotel. Away from Meg.

"IT'S NOT THAT I want to quit, Meg," said Albert, peering at her over a pile of towels. "I may simply have no other choice."

Meg took the towels from the concierge and set them down on a table in one of the hotel's supply rooms. "Albert, don't give up on me yet—please."

"I'm not giving up on *you*," he said. "I'm giving up on Corporate. Ever since they took over this place, things haven't been the same. It's not your fault, Meg. You've done everything you can to keep the Alexander up to spec."

"Yeah, right, it's just that everything I can do isn't enough." Meg shook out one of the towels and gave it a critical glance. It was very expensive, the soft and thick variety, expertly laundered, but it was starting to look just a tad off-white. Guests of the Alexander expected their towels to be pristine—and rightfully so. Meg sighed. ''One more item that I need to replace. But Corporate doesn't include luxury towels in the budget. I'm supposed to go with the bargain brand.''

Albert brought another pile of towels over to the table. He'd been working at the Alexander even longer than Meg—fifteen years in all. He'd started out at eighteen as a bellboy, advanced his way to the front desk, then to assistant concierge, and finally to the position of head concierge. He was superb at his job, seeming to know what guests needed before they knew it themselves. He could magically produce tickets to sold-out Broadway musicals, name virtually every restaurant in Manhattan and unsnarl the worst of airline-ticket mix-ups. In short, Meg considered him irreplaceable.

''You don't have to help me do this,'' she told him as she separated acceptable towels from the ones that needed replacing. ''You have better ways to spend your break.''

''With Brenda being out sick again, you need all the help you can get.''

Something in Albert's voice made Meg look at him more closely. ''Brenda's not really sick, is she? No doubt she's out on a job interview.''

Albert's famous discretion came to his aid, and his face remained perfectly impassive. But Meg suspected the worst—Brenda, the hotel's executive housekeeper, was already looking for another job.

Meg sank into a chair. Pushing the towels aside, she propped her elbows on the table. Barely one o'clock on Monday afternoon, and already the day was well on its way downhill.

"I feel like I'm on a sinking ship," Meg said, "and everybody but me is jumping overboard."

Albert pulled up a chair and sat across from her. He had sandy hair and endearing blue eyes. The way he teased her sometimes reminded her of her brothers, and that was one of the reasons they got along so well. But if he left the hotel, Meg would start to feel she didn't have any friends left here.

She rubbed her temples wearily. "I wish those wretched people had never bought the hotel. They seem to have absolutely no...no *soul.*"

"Not to mention they didn't give us any raises this year. I have to think about money, Meg, especially now that I'm getting hitched."

In a very short time, Albert would be marrying a woman who had two young children. No wonder he needed to think about money.

"I understand," Meg said. "I really do. It's just that...if you leave, I'll know this place really *is* falling to pieces."

"So why don't you bail out, too?" he asked. "Look for another hotel to run."

"It's not that simple. The Alexander is too important to me. I can't just abandon it to those people."

A smile twitched at the corners of his mouth.

"You're doing it again. Talking about this place like it's a person."

She shrugged. "That's the way it feels to me. It's been around all these years, and it deserves better. But you know what really gets me the most about all this? The fact that I feel so damn out of control!"

"The problem is, you're a control freak," Albert said seriously. "You need to lighten up."

She drew her eyebrows together. "I'd like to know what on earth qualifies me as a control freak."

"How about taking responsibility for every single thing that happens at this place? Here's some free advice, Meg," Albert offered, unusually earnest. "Let go of this place. Get a life."

"Have you ever noticed," she said, "that people about to be married are impossibly smug? They think they've found the secret to the universe, and all the rest of us are poor ignorant fools."

Albert didn't look perturbed. "Maybe you should try it—pull out all the stops and get engaged."

"Not likely," she muttered. Then she glanced at him. "Don't you have any doubts about it—any doubts at all?"

"You've met Natalie. Think I should have doubts?"

"Natalie's wonderful," she said. "It's just that… marriage. It's an awfully big step."

"It's the control issue again," he remarked in a tone of annoying superiority. "You figure if you get married, you won't be able to keep a handle on everything. Too many volatile variables. So, in your mind, better not to get involved at all. That way, at least you retain the illusion of control.''

''Why is it,'' asked Meg, ''that lately everyone has an opinion on why I'm not married?''

''Maybe it's because you've been wondering about it yourself,'' he suggested helpfully.

''I don't wonder in the least. I'm glad *you're* the one getting married, not me.'' She pulled some more towels in front of her and scowled at them.

''Someday you'll realize what you're missing.'' Albert looked at his watch and pushed back his chair. ''Gotta get back to the desk. Listen, Meg, I'll tell you if I get a bite from another hotel. I won't quit on you all of a sudden the way Patrice did, but I can't promise much more.''

''Thanks, Albert,'' she replied unenthusiastically.

The glance he gave her now was almost sympathetic. ''Don't give too much to this place,'' he said, and then he left her alone in the supply room.

She took her clipboard and began tallying the towels. Yet she couldn't muster any enthusiasm for the job, and she set the clipboard down again with a clatter. Albert's assessment continued to nettle her. *Was* she a control freak? She thought back, remembered herself as a kid. Perhaps even then she'd taken on more responsibility than she should have. She'd believed that if somehow she did the right thing, said the right words, she'd be able to make her family into a happy one. She'd felt guilty when she had started trying to escape the tension in the house, as if she were reneging on an important trust.

The supply room was starting to make her feel claustrophobic. She went back to her office, but that didn't help the closed-in feeling she had. Daisy was stretched out regally on her pillow. Meg picked up the cat and held her as she paced. Out of control...that was exactly how she felt. And it wasn't just because of the situation at the hotel.

It was because of Jack Elliott. All day Meg had tried to keep him out of her thoughts, but he'd intruded nonetheless. She kept replaying that moment last night in front of the apartment building, when he'd kissed her. And when she'd wanted so much more than kissing.

She'd known him such a short while, but he made her think about all kinds of crazy things. Things like making love again, when she scarcely knew him.

Meg told herself to get a grip. Instead she just felt more and more confused. She sat down at her desk, tried to work. But thoughts of Jack Elliott kept intruding. Thoughts that ought to be censored.

"Hey, sis. Why the frown?"

Meg glanced up and saw a man in the doorway of her office. Forget frowning. A slow grin broke over her face.

"Shaun...oh, Shaun, what a great surprise." She stood and ran over to her oldest brother, treating him to a big hug. "It's so good to see you! I didn't know you were coming to New York. You should have told me. How else can I roll out the red carpet?''

"A hotel like this—I bet you really do have a red carpet. Ouch—want to crack my ribs?'' But he returned the hug in equal measure. Meg knew that deep down he loved the fuss she made over him. Shaun had always been the more reserved of her two brothers. He'd never teased her quite so mercilessly as Ryan had, nor had he been able to express Ryan's easy affection. He'd simply been the one most protective of her, all during their years of growing up together.

Now she took a step back and studied him. His reddish-brown hair was tousled, as usual, his jacket a bit rumpled. That, too, was usual. Shaun never looked quite put together, as if he had more lofty matters to consider than a proper wardrobe. It was part of his charm.

"So what brings you here?'' she asked.

"Maybe I just wanted to see my kid sister.''

"Try again,'' she said severely. "For months I've been begging you to visit me, and now I'm supposed to believe you suddenly got the urge, after all.''

"Okay, okay. Medical conference, last-minute decision to attend.''

Shaun was an eye surgeon in Oklahoma City, darn good at what he did, and Meg didn't think that just because he was her adored older brother. She knew his reputation was growing, and she was immensely proud of him.

"Did Barbara come with you?" she asked. Instantly his expression became guarded.

"No," he said, his voice oddly brusque.

Meg felt more than a little uneasy. Shaun and Barbara had been married almost five years, and they had the nearest thing to an ideal relationship that Meg had ever witnessed. So why was it that now she saw a flash of unmistakable misery in her brother's eyes?

She wanted to ask him outright, but she also saw the way his face had tightened. For the moment, she let it go.

"I suppose this conference is putting you up somewhere, but I wish you'd stay here, Shaun. I'd even offer you my apartment, if Kathy and Lena weren't visiting at the same time."

Shaun made the necessary brotherly joke about her "crazy" friends, but his heart didn't seem in it. Meg was relieved when he agreed to stay at the Alexander. The next twenty minutes were spent in a pleasurable flurry, getting him settled in one of the premier rooms on the fifteenth floor. Meg went around the room, making sure everything was in order—cedar hangers ready in the closet, bureau and other furniture dusted immaculately, draperies drawn wide to afford the best possible view of Manhattan.

"It's fine, Meggie," said Shaun, his tone flat.

Meg studied him closely.

"What's wrong?" she asked.

"A little jet lag, that's all."

She shook her head. "No—it's more than that. And something tells me it has to do with you and Barbara. Shaun, you know I'll get the truth out of you sooner or later."

He gave her only an imitation of a smile. Then he sank into a chair. "Hell, Meggie," he said after a moment, "you always were good at prying stuff out of me." He glanced at her, and she saw the misery in his eyes again—unmistakable.

"I don't know," he went on, his voice bleak. "I had to get away, that's all. I had to get away before I made the biggest mistake of my life."

"Mistake?" Meg echoed.

"What else would you call adultery? Because that's what I almost did, Meggie. I almost betrayed my wife. I almost went to bed with another woman. And the urge was so strong, I just had to get the hell out of there."

A COOL BREEZE BLEW over New York Harbor. From the top deck of the ferry, Meg gazed at the Manhattan skyline. As the ferry moved farther out into the water, all those towering buildings receded, growing smaller and more manageable. Meg could almost pretend that she was leaving her problems behind for a short time. As she leaned against the railing of the ferry, she was sandwiched between Kathy and Lena. The three friends were on their way to visit the Statue of Liberty. Even though it was only Tuesday, and at this hour of the afternoon Meg was usually at the hotel, Lena and Kathy had convinced her to play hooky.

"You're thinking about Jack Elliott, aren't you?" Kathy asked, on Meg's right side.

"No, I am not thinking about Jack," Meg said rather testily. "Maybe I was thinking about him *five* minutes ago, but at the moment I am mulling over various catastrophes at the Hotel Alexander." Not to mention her brother's unexpected arrival yesterday and the unhappiness she'd seen in his eyes...the painful words she'd heard him speak.

"Meg's touchy today, isn't she?" Lena stood on Meg's left side. "Jack Elliott's influence, no doubt."

"The hotel," Meg insisted. "It's the hotel that's driving me crazy."

"But you *were* thinking about him only five minutes ago," Kathy said. "You admitted it."

"Okay, so I was thinking about the man. This, however, is not a fact that should make world headlines."

"She's touchy, all right," Kathy agreed.

Meg reminded herself that she was on an outing with her two best friends, and that she ought to be enjoying herself. "So I won't be grumpy anymore," she said. "And we'll stop talking about Jack. Deal?"

"I suppose we ought to talk about Lena instead," said Kathy. "She's been behaving oddly today. Haven't you noticed?"

Actually, Meg had noticed. Lena seemed in a daze. She would smile to herself and stare off into the distance. This wasn't like her. She'd never been moony before.

"Uh-oh," said Meg. "You'd better tell us what's going on, Lena. What have you done now?"

Lena gave another of those silly smiles. "I suppose I can't keep it to myself forever. It's just that…I've found the perfect man! Don't look so surprised, Kathy. You must know who I'm talking about."

"The stockbroker?" Kathy asked.

"No, of course not the stockbroker. For goodness' sake—you have to know who I mean."

Kathy's look of puzzlement only grew. "The guy who owns his own software company?"

"*Absolutely* not him," Lena said.

"You can't be talking about that other man," said Kathy. "The one you only met last night at the party? The lawyer?"

Lena sighed exuberantly. "Yes! That's the one!"

Meg didn't have a good feeling about this. She usually didn't, where Lena was concerned. "The perfect man, eh?" she said. "Less than a week in New York City, and you've found the perfect man. What happened to sampling from those quarter of a million others?"

"Oh, that." Lena gave a dismissive shrug. "I've already had enough experience with men to know when I've found the one and only." She rested her chin in her hand and stared dreamily over the water. In the distance rose the Lady, her blue-green robes shimmering in the sun. With her beacon held high, she was a majestic sight, one that Meg never took for granted. But apparently Lena still had other things on her mind. She proceeded to talk at great length about Nathan the lawyer. It was amazing what she'd already learned about him. She knew that he had one sister and one brother, that he'd grown up in Connecticut, and that he'd had a German shepherd as a child.

"I do so like a German shepherd," enthused Lena. "They're very intelligent dogs, you know."

Meg was really starting to worry about her friend, but Kathy actually appeared to be envious.

"Sometimes," said Kathy, "it seems like everyone around me is falling madly in love. Does it feel that way to you, Meg?"

"More like losing their heads," Meg observed. But she couldn't deny it. Everywhere she turned, people were turning their lives upside down for the sake of love. Helen Elliott pining for the man across the hall...Albert annoyingly certain that marriage was the only way to go...and now Lena, convinced overnight that she'd found her one and only. It was as if springtime in New York had infected everyone with romance. But romance didn't last. Surely Meg's parents had proved that. And now her own brother...

If romance *was* contagious, Meg had to make certain that, Jack Elliott notwithstanding, she didn't catch the bug.

CHAPTER SEVEN

JACK PUT ON the reading glasses he hated and scanned the fax that had just come in. He'd set up an impromptu office in his mother's living room, consisting of his laptop computer and the fax machine. More sheets were rolling out of the machine. He picked those up, looked them over, too. He had to hand it to Ron Ballard. It was a generous offer— a very generous offer indeed.

Ballard Development of Portland, Maine, was Jack's principal competitor in the commercial and industrial construction field. And now Ron Ballard wanted to buy Jack out. Jack looked over the fax sheets one more time, then set them down. The offer didn't really surprise him. He'd known for some time that Ron didn't like the competition. What better way to get rid of a rival than to make an offer too good to refuse?

Except that Jack *could* refuse…if he wanted to continue heading up Elliott Construction. The firm had given him a lot of satisfaction over the years. Starting virtually from scratch, building up the business himself—that had been the good part. And with every success, he had raised the bar a little higher, seeing if he could outdo past accomplishments. Yes, that had been good, too. The question was, could he continue to raise the bar? Or was it time to accept Ballard's offer?

He stood restlessly and tried to stretch his legs. What with all the antiques in the living room, it wasn't an easy proposition. He felt hemmed in by fanback chairs and the hoopback sofa, by corner cupboards and sideboards and hanging cabinets. When a knock came at the front door, he didn't mind the distraction.

He opened the door to find Meg Danley on the other side. The very pretty Meg, with her hazel eyes and with her chocolate brown hair skimming her shoulders. Today she wore jeans and a white cotton shirt with the sleeves rolled halfway up her arms. The simple, unadorned lines suited her, only hinting at the curves underneath. But Jack already knew how beautiful Meg Danley was underneath.

She stared at him rather defiantly, a blush tinging her cheeks. "Dammit, Jack," she said. "Can't you even say hello first? Before you…before you start…"

"Before I start what?" he asked, leaning against the doorjamb.

"You know exactly what. Before you start looking at me as if we're still…" Her voice trailed off. He knew they were both picturing that hotel room and the things they'd done there. The very enjoyable things.

The lovely flush on her cheeks deepened. "Can't you stop?" she said, almost in a whisper.

Reluctantly, he straightened. "Next you'll tell me that you're here to see my mother, not me."

"Yes. I came to visit Helen."

"She's sleeping right now," he said. "Finally taking a nap."

"Oh...guess I'll come back later then. Please tell her I stopped by." As Meg delivered this polite speech, she was already turning to go. He reached out and took her hand.

"So visit me instead."

"You don't need any visiting."

"Sure I do," he said gravely. "Don't forget—I'm a stranger in town."

"You seem to be doing all right for yourself."

"Not as all right as I'd like." He drew her into the foyer, bent his head toward her. His mouth almost brushed hers, but she slipped past him. A shame.

"No way," she said in a low voice. "We're not doing *that* anymore."

"Is this another vow?" he asked.

She gave him a stern look. "What do you mean?"

"You seem to like making vows. So maybe you've made a vow not to have anything to do with me."

"For your information," she said, "I do *not* like making vows. That was a silly promise Kathy and Lena and I made ten years ago. As for now—" She stopped herself and stared at him in exasperation. "Why am I getting involved in this conversation?"

"Because you know I'm a good listener." He reached for her hand again, but she sidestepped him neatly. She went toward the living room.

"Hmm, something smells delicious," she said.

"Mrs. Jansen has taken over the kitchen. I think she'd rather bake all day than try to take care of my mother."

Meg deftly changed direction. "I'll go say hello to Mrs. Jansen." She disappeared into the kitchen, and after that, Jack heard the murmur of feminine voices as Meg spoke with the nurse. He had a suspicion that Meg was going to stay in there for her entire visit, doing anything she could to avoid him. He sat down in the living room again and examined the fax sheets. At this moment they didn't interest him, despite the momentous decision they represented.

Meg surprised him by joining him a short time later. She carried in a plate of cookies, Chester padding after her.

"Mrs. Jansen is very strict," she said. "She won't let the dog have even a bite of cookie. He thinks he'll have better luck with us." She sat down in a Windsor chair and carefully set her plate on a butterfly table. "All these valuable antiques. I'd hate to harm one of them."

"You don't have to worry about that," he told her. "I'll say this for my mother—she uses antiques, doesn't just collect them. She believes if a piece of furniture has lasted two hundred years, it'll keep on lasting.''

After hearing this, Meg seemed to settle back more comfortably. She took a cookie, broke off a piece and gave it to an ecstatic Chester. Then she ate the rest.

''You should try one of these,'' she said. ''Peanut butter and coconut. Absolutely wonderful. Mrs. Jansen could go into the bakery business.''

''She might decide to change her line of work. She and my mother haven't had the best couple of days together.''

''And that's why you're still in New York,'' Meg said. ''Trying to straighten out your mother and the nurses.'' She made it a statement, not a question. He gazed at her.

''That…and other reasons.''

The flush had come back to her cheeks. ''Jack, you're not staying in New York because, well, because of us. After all, there is no us.''

He felt a stirring of regret. ''Something else you don't have to worry about, Meg. I'll go back to Maine when the time comes.''

She relaxed again. ''You really should try one of the cookies,'' she said.

He took one and started eating it. Meg was right— it tasted great. ''Wednesday afternoon,'' he said. ''Kind of early for you to be off work.''

She looked vaguely guilty. ''I'm taking some time

off, that's all." As if eager to change the subject, she studied him. "I like the glasses. They suit you."

He'd forgotten about the reading glasses, and now he took them off. "Hell," he said. "Next thing you know, they'll be telling me I need bifocals."

"Glasses don't make you look old, Jack," she said. "They make you look...sexy." She said this last word grudgingly, as if afraid he might take it the wrong way.

"I never used to need glasses."

"Goodness, this age thing really *is* getting to you, isn't it?" She dusted the cookie crumbs off her fingers and stood up with an air of purpose. "I know what you need, Jack Elliott. Maybe I'll regret doing this, but you're coming with me."

He didn't argue. Right now, with Meg, he was game for just about anything.

JACK HADN'T COUNTED on in-line skates. But after a half hour or so, he was almost used to them. Meg appeared to be an expert. They skated down one of the paths in Central Park, Chester trotting eagerly behind them.

"Want to try the rink?" Meg asked a bit breathlessly.

He took her hand. "I like this."

"Jack..."

"You have to help me keep my balance," he said.

She gave him a skeptical glance. "At least tell me this is helping you to feel young."

"Either that, or an old fool. In my day, it was strictly skateboards. These in-line skates are new technology."

"At least you're moving with the times," she assured him. "And now you own a pair."

Meg believed in going all out. She already owned skates, but she'd taken him to a store and had him outfitted. He'd drawn the line at knee pads and elbow guards, though.

Now he veered off into the grass. Jack, Meg and the dog landed in a somewhat ungainly heap.

"You did that on purpose," Meg accused him. He didn't give her a chance to say anything more. Instead, he drew her into his arms and kissed her. He found her lips as soft and warm as he'd been imagining. She responded to him naturally, provocatively, her hands reaching up to twine through his hair. The kiss went on for quite some time, but then Meg seemed to recover herself. She pulled away a bit.

"Chester isn't doing a very good job," she said, her voice unsteady. "He's supposed to be our chaperon."

"I think he's doing a great job," Jack remarked. The dog was exploring contentedly, nose to the grass, paying no attention whatsoever to his human companions. Jack took advantage of the opportunity to kiss Meg again. Her lips were pliant under his, seeming to invite yet more from him....

This time it was quite a few moments before she

broke contact. She scooted away, perhaps to what she thought was a safe distance.

"Dammit, Jack. This wasn't supposed to happen today."

"Why not?" he asked.

"You *know* why not."

He supposed he could list the reasons. After Kendra, he wasn't looking for a relationship. Meg wasn't looking for a relationship, either. But none of that changed the fact that he wanted her in his arms, wanted her close to him.

As if sensing his thoughts, she moved away a little farther.

"Meg," he said, "what are you afraid of?"

"I'm not afraid," she said. "It's just…I don't trust this. What we're feeling. It's not something we should indulge."

When he was around Meg, he couldn't think of anything but indulging. "You think we're moving too fast again."

"Yeah, something like that." Her voice held a hint of irony.

"So we'll start over again."

She frowned. "You keep acting like we can do that. But we can't—"

"We can keep trying," he said. "Who knows, one of these times we may actually get it right."

"You really think we can start over?" she asked skeptically.

He stretched out on the grass, resting his head on

his arms. "Try me. Ask me anything you want. Get to know me—I'm not such a bad guy."

She gave him a caustic look. "I don't doubt your integrity."

"We're in the middle of starting over, remember?"

"Oh, for goodness' sake," she muttered. "All right—tell me this. What were you like as a kid?"

"That's easy," he said. "I was hell. Drove both my parents nuts, but especially my dad. I figured it was my job to be as unlike him as I could."

"Why?" Meg asked.

It was a question he'd often asked himself, but never had any good answers for. All he had were theories. "Maybe it was my nature to be a handful. Maybe my dad and I had different personalities from the very beginning. Or maybe it was because he assumed his way was the only right one."

Meg scooted back toward him. She wrapped her arms around her knees and studied him. "What *was* your father's way?"

"The life of a scholar. Losing yourself in books. Writing monographs and sharing your knowledge with a small, select group of students who admire you enormously and who never seem to question your judgment. I think that's what my father wanted from me all along. He wanted me to treat him the way his students did. He wanted me to be admiring, respectful—maybe even overawed. Guess I didn't come through." Jack stopped. This was something he'd never quite realized before, that his dad had hoped he'd be like one of those adoring students.

"Tell me more, Jack," Meg murmured.

"Yeah, well, there's not much. Except that maybe I was jealous of my dad's students...of the camaraderie he seemed to have with them. He and I never got along."

"That was when you were younger," she said. "You're an adult now. Haven't things changed?"

"Sure," he said. "These days, my dad and I can actually have a discussion about history or philosophy. I don't mind shooting the breeze about arcane subjects. But he gets ticked when I disagree with him, as if somehow that's proof I still don't admire or respect him."

"But do you, Jack?" she asked quietly. "Do you admire and respect him?"

"I respect his intelligence. I respect his love of knowledge, the way he can still get excited about learning something new. But I don't respect what he needed from me—that unquestioning admiration, that awestruck, thoughtless devotion." Jack paused to think for a moment. "I just realized that it's always been that way with my dad...what *he* needed from me. What *he* wanted. Never what I needed in a father."

"Jack, maybe you should tell him what you need. It's never too late for that."

"Maybe it is," he said. "I look at my dad now and I see someone who's getting old. Someone who doesn't wield nearly as much authority as he once imagined. I can't picture myself accusing him for all the years past.'' Jack shook his head. "I've wanted to rebel against him, but I've sure as hell never wanted to pity him.''

Meg moved yet a little closer. "It's hard, isn't it? Finding out that your parents are a lot more vulnerable than you'd ever bargained for. When I was growing up, even though I knew my mother was unhappy, I always thought she was so in control of everything. And then one day, when I was about thirteen, I found her crying after she'd had an argument with my father. She was sobbing in such despair...such hopelessness. And that was when I knew the truth. She *wasn't* in control—she was just putting up a front. Scared the heck out of me.''

"So ever since, you've made sure the same thing didn't happen in your own life. You've made sure no one took away your control.''

Meg didn't appear pleased by his assessment. "That's the second time this week somebody's called me a control freak.''

"Wouldn't have been exactly my choice of words,'' he commented.

"Yes, but you *do* think I'm a control freak, don't you?''

Meg's hazel eyes seemed to reflect her moods in varying shades of gold and brown, and her lovely face was expressive. In the little time he'd known her, he could already tell when she felt concern or amusement…or desire. But he could also tell how much she wanted to keep her emotions under restraint.

"I think," he said, "that it really bothers you how much your feelings influence your actions. If you're a control freak, you're not a very successful one."

"Not successful," she echoed, sounding miffed.

"Like right now, for instance. I can tell you want to come over here next to me. You've been fighting the impulse, but you're closer than you were a few minutes ago." He reached out, took her hand, pulled her gently toward him. She ended up stretched beside him on the grass. Sunlight filtered down upon them through the tree branches. He trailed a finger across her cheek, felt her tremble.

"Damn you, Jack Elliott…"

He waited, allowing her to decide what the next move would be. He saw the struggle of emotions on her very pretty, very expressive face. He heard her sigh, as if in defeat, just before she leaned closer to kiss him.

It was a slow, leisurely kiss this time, the kind made for spring days in the park. It went on for quite a while. But Meg was the one who ended it, just as she was the one who'd started it. She drew away, then rose quickly to her feet as if to avoid further temptation. She went gliding away from him on her skates, her dark brown hair waving out behind her in the breeze.

"Come on, boy," Jack told Chester, "or she's going to leave us in the dust."

For the next half hour or so, it seemed to Jack that Meg did everything she could to keep things impersonal between them. Friendly, lighthearted…but impersonal. She told Jack he was doing very well with his in-line skates. She chatted about the sights he ought to see while he was in New York—the Metropolitan Museum, Rockefeller Center, Coney Island. Yet through all this, she scarcely glanced at him, and she kept her tone distant. When they left the park and bought pretzels from a street vendor, Meg had one more impersonal topic of conversation—the delicious food of New York.

"Meg," Jack said at last, "you don't have to be my tour guide."

"Why not? Somebody should tell you about the places to go, the things to do."

"You're making it very clear you expect me to do them on my own—without your company," he said.

She kept her gaze set resolutely forward. "I'll be too busy for sight-seeing. The fact that I took off work this afternoon is an aberration. I was just feeling a little…stir-crazy. Giving in to that simply isn't a luxury I have very often."

"In other words, I'd better not get any ideas. This afternoon won't be repeated."

"I *do* have a job," she said.

They went along one street, then another, heading in roundabout fashion back toward Meg's apartment building. Perhaps it was only coincidence they ended up approaching the hotel where, not so very long ago, they'd spent the night together. Meg came to a halt so quickly that Chester almost bumped into her. The expression on her face was one of chagrin.

"Jack, did you purposely lead us here?"

"No," he said. "I thought you were leading the way."

She stared at the entrance to the hotel. Jack stood beside her and took her hand. Her fingers curled in his, but she didn't pull away.

"We were no better than two teenagers," she said in a low voice. "Trying to find a place to be alone, sneaking out to a hotel."

"I don't regret what happened," he said. "You shouldn't, either."

"The worst part of it is…wanting it to happen again." She was careful not to look at him.

"I want it, too, Meg. Is that so terrible?"

"What do you see for us?" she countered, her voice taut. "We keep sneaking off to hotels, stealing a few moments from our real lives? What happens afterward?"

Jack hadn't gotten to that part yet…the afterward part. Meg continued to stare at the hotel for several more moments. And then, without another word, she did pull away from Jack and took off down the street.

When they reached her apartment building, she sat down on the curb and took off her skates. Jack sat beside her. She was still careful not to look at him.

"You know what I was thinking back there?" she said, hugging her arms around her knees. "I was thinking that if it weren't for Chester...and if it weren't for these silly skates...I would have gone right back into that hotel with you, Jack."

"Would it have been such a mistake?"

"I told you—I don't trust whatever's happening between us. How do I know how I really feel? Maybe Lena's right. She says I don't have enough experience with men to judge my reactions properly. She says I ought to get more experience."

Jack didn't especially like the sound of that. But what claim did he have on Meg?

"Don't worry," she said dryly, as if reading his thoughts. "I don't expect to follow Lena's advice. I don't see that as the answer. Frankly, I don't know what the answer is."

"Maybe," said Jack, "you and I can just keep getting to know each other."

Now at last she did look at him, her expression sardonic. "We both know what that means. We trade a few confidences and then we hop into bed again because that's what we've been wanting to do all along."

"Doesn't sound so bad to me."

"You know what, Jack? We have this—this physical thing, but it's clouding judgment for both of us. You keep acting as if we can start over, but you're wrong. We jumped into this too fast, and now—now I don't even know what I think or feel. If we'd gone slower...who knows, maybe something would have worked out."

"I'd say you're breaking up with me." He knew a farewell speech when he heard one.

She stood. "How can we break up, Jack, when we never had a real relationship to begin with? We had sex, that's all...sex too soon." She stared at him a moment longer, as if debating whether to tell him anything else. But then she turned and disappeared inside the building.

Jack sat at the curb, Chester beside him. "Well, boy," he said, "guess you were a pretty good chaperon, after all." He tried to ignore the disappointment inside him. Disappointment and regret. He'd made love to Meg...and already lost her because of it.

CHAPTER EIGHT

MEG WAS A MUSEUM BUFF. Today her brother was trying to convince her he liked museums, too. So far he hadn't done a very good job.

Together they'd visited the Museum of American Folk Art, the Carnegie Hall Museum, the New York City Fire Museum. Shaun had forged through every exhibit with a grim, relentless determination, lost in his own thoughts but refusing to slow down. Finally, when they landed at the Museum of Modern Art, Meg couldn't take it anymore. She sank onto one of the benches.

"Enough," she informed her brother. "I know you're not having a good time. You're just going through the motions. And you're trying as hard as you can not to talk about anything personal. Shaun, you know that sooner or later I *will* get it out of you."

He sat down next to her and propped his elbows on his knees, staring at the wall opposite.

"I feel exactly like that painting over there," he said. "Churned up. Out of focus." He paused, and after a moment he continued in a low voice.

"I suppose Barbara and I have been having problems for a while now. Somehow we've both changed. She's changed. Meggie...do you remember what she was like when I married her? She had a million things going on in her life, and she was always trying something new. It made her exciting. That's the way she used to be, anyway, until last year, when she lost her job.''

Meg was startled. ''Lost her job? You never said anything. Neither did Barbara.''

''That's the way she wanted it. Said it made her too ashamed, being fired like that. I kept telling her it wasn't her fault. Her company got bought out, that's all. But she didn't see it that way. She saw it as a personal failure. She took it hard, all around. Meggie, I tried to give her the support she needed. But then...one month went by. Two months...three. And she was still brooding, still blaming herself. Still holed up in the house—not doing a damn thing.''

Shaun stopped again, then finally went on. ''I tried to help her get her confidence back. Encouraged her to look for a new job. Recommended a counselor. Told her she had to stop feeling sorry for herself. But everything I did only made it worse. She started blaming me, not just herself.''

He sighed heavily. ''Look, I can't lay this entire thing on her. Maybe I've lost the ability to listen the way I should...the ability to sympathize. But how long can she go on like this? She's acting the way Mom used to when we were growing up. Discontented, yet too apathetic to do anything about it.

What if Barbara turns out to be just like Mom? I don't know if I could stand it.''

Meg's heart went out to her brother. She remembered all too well her mother's unhappiness.

Shaun moved restlessly. ''I know what you'd say, Meggie. None of this is an excuse for almost betraying my wife. But the truth is, there is this other woman. Christine. And she isn't unhappy or apathetic. She sure as hell doesn't remind me of Mom. So I almost went through with it. I almost did it, Meggie. What does that tell you about me?''

''It tells me you had the strength to stop.''

''Not by much. If I hadn't flown to New York…''

''But you *are* here,'' Meg said.

''What really scares me is that I don't have a clue what the hell to do next.''

Meg didn't know, either. She had no answers of her own—not where love and heartache were concerned.

''I'M ENGAGED!'' Lena announced triumphantly that evening as she sailed into Meg's living room. She held up her left hand, showing off the sparkle of a large diamond. Meg and Kathy looked at each other, then looked at their friend. As usual, the three of them had agreed to congregate for a glass of wine and girl talk. Lena seemed to have timed her entrance for the most dramatic effect. She was so effective, in fact, that for a moment both Meg and Kathy were speechless.

"Wow," said Meg at last.

"You're kidding, right?" said Kathy.

"How about congratulations?" Lena asked, sounding miffed.

"She's not kidding." Kathy went over to Lena and gave her a hug. "Definitely congratulations. This is so exciting! And what a rock."

Meg went to hug her friend, too. "Oh, honey... congratulations. You took us by surprise, that's all. Say, that *is* a rock."

Lena allowed them to admire the ring thoroughly. But then she seemed to grow a bit defensive. "I know what you're both thinking. You're thinking that I'm just being my usual self. Impetuous, impulsive, reckless."

"You getting engaged isn't usual," said Meg. "This is a first."

"Yeah," Kathy agreed. "You've never gotten engaged before."

"Okay," said Lena. "But you're probably thinking I've only known this guy, what—a couple of days? And he's already given me a ring—"

"It's better than dating someone for ten years," muttered Kathy, "and no ring in sight."

"If love's going to hit," said Meg, "I guess it can hit fast."

Lena seemed mollified. She sank onto the sofa and propped her feet on Meg's coffee table. Tonight she wore slim black capri pants, a bright copper-colored blouse and oversize copper hoop earrings. Somehow the ensemble all went perfectly with her vivid red hair. "I didn't expect to fall in love so quickly," she said, "but there you go. And when a man like Nathan Quinn proposes, you accept. You don't tell him it's only been three days and he should wait awhile. You grab him up when you can."

Kathy grinned. "You make it sound like you're at Macy's, and Nathan's a cashmere sweater you just have to have."

"Oh, he's cashmere, all right," said Lena. She held up her hand again, admiring the sparkle of her ring. "How'd I get so lucky? Rich, handsome *and* generous."

Kathy looked wistful. "You were right about New York. It's made things happen—for you, at least. You're engaged all of a sudden. And Meg has Jack."

Meg thought about yesterday afternoon and the time she and Jack had spent in the park. She had as much as said goodbye to him. She knew it had been the right thing to do, so why did she feel such an emptiness inside?

"I don't have Jack," she said. "In fact, as of yesterday, I stopped seeing him altogether."

"I didn't tell you to break up with the man," chided Lena. "I said get to know a few other guys, that's all."

Meg didn't want to talk about it. She lifted her wine glass. "A toast," she said firmly. "To you and Nathan."

A clinking of wineglasses, more congratulations.

But then Kathy went to sit by the phone and picked up the receiver. This time it was Meg and Lena who glanced at each other.

"Kathy," said Lena, "are you okay?"

"I'm calling Gary, all right? There...now I've said it."

Lena swung her feet off the coffee table, went over to Kathy, took the receiver and hung it up.

"Mistake," she said. "Big mistake."

"I have to call him," Kathy said stubbornly. "Don't you see? Everything's happening to everybody else right now. I have to call Gary and make something happen for *me*."

Lena kept her hand placed on the phone. "Can't let you do it, honey. We'll make something happen for you here, in New York. But Gary and Oklahoma—you've moved on. Don't make the mistake of trying to turn back."

"Dammit, I'm going to call Gary," Kathy insisted. "Maybe he's not drop-dead gorgeous like Jack Elliott, or rich, generous and handsome like Nathan, but he has his good points."

"Maybe we should let her call," said Meg. "She seems determined."

Lena hesitated, then lifted her hand from the phone. "Maybe she has to get it out of her system," she acknowledged. She and Meg watched as Kathy punched in the number. They waited as the phone rang...and rang...and rang. Meg felt the tension mounting. But then, apparently, Gary picked up.

"Hello," Kathy said too cheerfully. "It's me. Yes…oh, yes…I've missed you, too.…" She listened intently for a long moment, and when she spoke next, her voice was brittle. "Things *do* change for some people, Gary. Take Lena, for instance. She's engaged…yes, that's right. Engaged to be *married*. Now, Gary, don't let the M-word make you faint." There was another long pause, then Kathy said brusquely, "Goodbye, Gary. I have to go now." She hung up the phone. "Gary says congratulations," she mumbled, and then she burst into tears.

Instantly, Meg and Lena went into action. They patted Kathy's back, made consoling murmurs and managed to get her seated on the sofa. Lena poured her another glass of wine. Meg produced a box of tissues. And at last they had Kathy in a condition where she was able to speak.

"Gary wants me to come home," she said soggily. "He says he misses me…and he wants me back."

"I suppose that's good enough reason to sob your heart out," Lena said.

"Sure, he wants me back—but he wants everything just the way it was before. He wants to pick up where we left off. Nothing different. Nothing changed."

"Honey, he's not worth the trouble," said Lena.

"Not by a long shot," added Meg.

Kathy took a tissue and blotted her eyes. "I realize what I've been doing. All along, I've been holding out the hope that Gary will change. Deep down, I thought this trip to New York would wake him up. He'd realize that he'd lose me if he didn't commit. Only now, after talking to him, I finally get it. He's not going to change. Not ever.''

Kathy set aside the box of tissues, smoothed back her hair and stood up. "Lena, do you think your fiancé has any friends he can introduce me to?''

"I'm sure he does. I'll call him right now, and we'll make a night of it. Are you in, Meg?''

Meg shook her head. "Count me out. I'm going to visit Mrs. Elliott tonight.''

"In that case," said Lena, "you might as well make up with Mrs. Elliott's son.'' She smiled mischievously. "And *then* I'll introduce you to some of Nathan's lawyer friends.''

"No males for me—thanks all the same," Meg said firmly. "No lawyer friends. And no Jack Elliott.''

A SHORT TIME LATER, Meg stood before Helen's apartment. She hadn't knocked yet. She was worried that Jack would answer the door. She hadn't spoken with him since the two of them had "broken up.'' What would she say? How would she act?

"Idiot,'' she muttered to herself. And then she knocked a bit too forcefully.

One of the nurses answered, no Jack to be seen. Meg told herself that she felt nothing but relief. She went into the living room and gave Chester a pat. Helen sat in her wheelchair, an unopened book in her lap. She looked a bit peaked tonight, almost list-less. That wasn't like her.

"Hello, Meg," she said in a subdued tone.

Meg sat down on the sofa. "I'm sorry it's taken me this long to get back up here. You were asleep when I came yesterday, and—"

"No need for apologies, Meg. I know you've been trying to avoid my son."

Meg felt disconcerted. "Does it show that much?"

"I'm not going to pry. I'm not going to ask what's going on between the two of you. But a person would have to be completely obtuse not to notice that some-thing *is* going on." Helen gave a slight grimace. "I may be confined to this wheelchair, but I can still see what's right in front of my nose."

"Well, hmm, you see, Jack and I…"

"Stop floundering, Meg. I told you I wouldn't pry. Let's talk about my romantic problems instead."

Meg was all too happy for the change of subject. "I've been awfully curious to know how it worked out."

"Our little setup, you mean. Luring the neighbor man into my apartment. I'll tell you how it went, Meg. It all went terribly wrong!"

Meg studied Helen in consternation. "I hope you're exaggerating."

"No. I'm being honest. Russ Cooper came to look in on me, just the way we planned. He was very polite. Only we couldn't seem to think of a single thing to say to each other. Not a single thing, Meg.

I have never known moments of silence to stretch out so agonizingly. At last the poor man put himself out of his own misery. He got up and left.''

"Oh, dear,'' said Meg. "It seemed like such a good idea. A way to get the two of you together.''

"We got together, all right. Looked at each other and completely lost our tongues. I'm sure neither one of us is eager to try it again.''

"I'm sorry,'' Meg said. "It was my idea. My fault—''

"Don't go blaming yourself,'' Helen interrupted. "It was my fault, if it was anyone's. The truth is, I've lost the knack for talking to men. I'm fine in a business situation. But make it social—make it personal—and I'm hopeless.''

"We can work on that,'' Meg said.

"What are we going to do, send me to charm school? I don't think so. No, Meg. Best to leave it alone. I blew it with Russ Cooper. That was my chance, and I blew it.''

Meg might have desisted, but Helen looked so unhappy. "You still have a thing for him, don't you?''

"More than ever,'' Helen confessed. "If you could have seen him… I could tell how hard he was trying to think of something to say. It made him more appealing than ever.''

"Maybe he was thinking the same thing about you,'' Meg said.

"I'm afraid not. I may have lost my knack with

men, but I can tell when someone wants to hightail it out of here and never see me again.''

''If we could just come up with another plan—''

''No more plans, Meg,'' Helen said. ''One fiasco was enough.''

Chester came to put his head on Meg's knee and gazed at her soulfully. She gave him another pat.

''Chester, don't look at me like that. If I can't solve my own romantic crisis, how can I solve anyone else's?''

''So you're having a crisis with my son,'' Helen said.

Jack again. Why could Meg never seem to get away from the topic?

''Not exactly a crisis,'' she hedged. ''We've just come to realize that our lives are widely divergent and—''

''Do you love him, Meg?''

She gave an unsuccessful attempt at laughter. ''I hardly even know him! How can you love someone you don't know?''

''I seem to be enthralled with my neighbor, and I don't know him.''

Meg stood and paced among the antiques. ''Why is everyone so obsessed with love?'' she asked. ''It's not just you. It's my friends Lena and Kathy, as well. They're doing wild, silly, reckless things—all in the name of romance.''

''There's your answer, right there,'' said Helen.

"It's a lot more interesting to be wild and reckless than it is to play it safe."

"So why are *you* going to play it safe?" Meg countered. "If you really like this guy, go ahead. Be wild. Be reckless."

Helen huddled back in the wheelchair. "I've already taken my one shot at that. It didn't work. I'm back to playing it safe."

"You'll give up that easily?" Meg asked.

"Yes," Helen said emphatically. But she continued to look unhappy. Meg couldn't help feeling responsible for the Russ Cooper debacle. It had been her idea in the first place. Now she wanted to fix what had gone wrong.

But how on earth did she go about doing it?

THOMAS P. RILEY of Corporate was an imposing, yet seemingly good-natured man. Although he was probably only in his early forties, his hair was a startling white, just long enough to be gathered into a neat ponytail. His husky build was well complemented by a double-breasted wool suit; the contrast between the ponytail and the designer suit suggested that he did not take life altogether seriously. All during the morning he'd spent with Meg, he'd seemed to maintain a remarkably genial outlook. Now, as he sat across from her in the restaurant of the Hotel Alexander, he sampled the lunch menu: poached scallops in cream sauce, artichokes and prosciutto and grilled mushrooms.

"Sauce is a little flat," he pronounced in regard to the scallops.

Meg took a deep breath. "When Patrice was chef here, the sauce was never flat. Of course, she quit in protest over staff and budget cuts." She waited to see if her words would have any effect whatsoever on Thomas P. Riley. So far, all he did was give her the half smile that seemed to be his perpetual expression. During the past few days, Meg had initiated three somewhat heated telephone conversations with Mr. Riley—heated on her part, at least. He had maintained his good humor throughout. This morning he had surprised her by flying in from Corporate to meet with her in person, but he continued to maintain his good humor. Did nothing faze the man?

"Mr. Riley," she tried yet again, "your budget cuts are seriously harming the Alexander!"

He patted his mouth with his napkin. "I don't believe it's cause for such alarm. Take the sauce, for instance. Very few people have my discernment in these matters. They'll think the sauce is fine."

"But our guests *are* discerning—"

"Perhaps the guests of former times," he said. "Nowadays we're going after clients who are happy just to get a room in a posh Manhattan hotel. Throw a little luxury their way, they won't notice the other luxuries we've cut out."

Meg gritted her teeth. She'd tried to be as polite as possible with Mr. Riley. He was her boss, after all. But this week, every time she'd had a phone conversation with him, she'd been so annoyed that she'd ended up ditching work. Talking to him in person was no better. She felt like tossing down her napkin and ditching *him*.

Instead, she remained seated, doing her best to retain a professional demeanor.

"Mr. Riley," she said. "In the long run, those budget cuts *are* hurting the Alexander. Pretty soon we won't be seen as a 'posh' hotel. Our reputation will slide, we'll lose our most important customers—"

"We'll make up for it in volume," he told her. "We'll knock down room rates enough to keep full occupancy."

Meg took another deep breath. "If it were only the rates you'd be lowering, fine. But you've already started to lower salaries. Not to mention employee morale. Our turnover's becoming way too high—"

"We can always find people willing to take less of a paycheck. Just as we can always find customers willing to accept less. It's only a matter of degree. We still provide an adequate living for our employees. We still provide adequate services for our guests." He gave her that half smile.

"Adequate isn't good enough," Meg said. "Not for me, anyway. Mr. Riley, I don't think I can work at the Alexander under these circumstances." She wasn't speaking impetuously. She'd given the matter a great deal of thought these past few days. Now she went on. "This hotel means a lot to me. Maybe because I've been here a long time, or maybe just because of what it's stood for—something special, something better than 'adequate' or 'average.' But I have to move on if all that's going to change.''

He contemplated her. ''Are you trying to call my bluff, Ms. Danley? Do you believe threatening to quit will make me change my ways?''

She gave a sigh. ''No, I don't think that at all. I think you'll go right out and find someone else to take my place...somebody less experienced, who'll accept less of a paycheck. Somebody who'll care a whole lot less than I do about the Alexander. And you won't mind, will you?''

''When it comes to the Alexander—no, I won't mind,'' Riley said. ''Location alone will keep this hotel functioning adequately, much as you despise that word, Ms. Danley.'' He examined the prosciutto with a critical air, then set aside his plate. ''I've recently purchased another hotel, in London, and this one's a different matter altogether. It needs to be posh, because the competition is way too posh. I need someone to bring it up to scratch, and something tells me you're the person to do it.''

She stared at him. ''You're offering me another job? In *London?*''

''Exactly, Ms. Danley. Or may I call you Meg? You have very high standards, Meg. Very definite ideas about what a hotel should be. In London, I'd give you full rein with those ideas. You want the best chef around? Hire him—or her. You want the best service, the best quality? I'll foot the bill.''

"But why—''

"This one's different. I know what market I'm playing in. Sometimes you need to shell out the bucks, sometimes you don't. The Alexander is already established, but in London, I'm not established yet. If you can create a luxury hotel there and still show reasonable profits, I'll be satisfied. You would be providing a flagship institution for me, so to speak.''

"In other words,'' she said wryly, "you want to impress the Brits.''

"Meg, I appreciate your straightforwardness. I expect you to continue being blunt and straightforward. Tell me exactly what you need in London. I'll be listening, I promise you.''

"Mr. Riley, I haven't accepted the job yet,'' she said.

"Yes, but why wouldn't you?'' he asked, as if he couldn't possibly imagine anyone turning him down.

"Well, for one thing, a luxury hotel in London doesn't change the fact that you've still lowered standards at the Alexander.''

"I can't believe you're that sentimental about this place,'' he said dismissively. "You'll be across the Atlantic, Meg. You won't have time to think about the Alexander. Did I mention that I'd be giving you a sizable salary increase?'' He proceeded to mention a figure that made her sit up just a little straighter.

Thomas P. Riley observed her with a somewhat smug expression.

"I thought that would get your interest," he said. "And don't forget the autonomy part…the place will be yours to run as you see fit."

She wanted to tell him that money and control didn't make any difference to her. She wanted to tell him that New York was the city where she belonged. And yet…London! She couldn't deny the attraction. She'd romanticized England since she was a kid. To actually live and work there… She could tear herself from New York for *that*, surely.

Thomas P. Riley continued to eat his lunch imperturbably, behaving as if her acceptance were inevitable.

"Mr. Riley," she said, "I still don't understand why you're offering the job to me and not someone else. I haven't exactly been a quiescent employee."

"You've been the opposite. Difficult, argumentative, questioning every decision I make. You don't take kindly to authority. You trust your own intuition, your own opinions, and you're willing to fight for them. In other words, you possess all the qualities I will need in London."

She gave him a skeptical look. "I'm really to believe that you'll give me complete authority? Even though you refuse to give me real control at the Alexander?"

"As I've tried to make clear, Meg, London is a new venture for me. New rules apply."

She didn't know if she could believe him. And yet, if he stuck to his end of the bargain...London! And a hotel to create according to her own vision.

"Mr. Riley," she said at last, "your offer's tempting—very tempting. But I'm going to need some time to think about it. I can't give you an answer right away."

He gazed at her in that cool, steady way of his, as if she'd said exactly what he'd expected. "I understand that it's a big decision. Just keep in mind that I want to get started on this project as soon as possible."

Would he truly have the ability to step back and let Meg make all the decisions in London? On the other hand, maybe this was the opportunity of a lifetime, and Meg was a fool not to snatch it up as quickly as she could.

Maybe, just maybe, she was delaying because London was so far away from New York...and Maine.

Maybe, just maybe, she was thinking far too much about Jack Elliott.

CHAPTER NINE

EARLY THAT EVENING, Meg carried her gardening basket up to the rooftop of the apartment building. She found Jack Elliott already there ahead of her, poking a spade among the nasturtium.

Meg stopped, then took a step backward, as if somehow she could escape his notice. He glanced up.

"Hello, Meg," he said.

"Hello, Jack. I didn't expect to see you up here."

He gave a slight grimace. "Thought I'd find out if gardening really is a relaxing activity."

"What's the verdict?"

"Negative. No way is it relaxing—at least, not for me."

She set down her basket and studied him. He did seem a bit wound up, his energy barely restrained.

"Maybe you should go for a jog or something," she suggested.

"Trying to get rid of me, Meg?"

She walked slowly over to him. "I guess it's too late for that," she said. "I knew we'd have to run into each other again, sooner or later."

He gazed at her. She gazed back, an odd stillness

washing over her. It was as if she waited for something, not even knowing what that something might be.

"You're growing a beard," she said.

He rubbed his jaw. "Yeah. For now, anyway."

"I like it." The dark stubble defined his features all the more clearly, and also gave him a hint of danger. Not that he needed it. He was already dangerously attractive. "Changing your life, Jack? Or just growing a beard for the heck of it?"

He gave his spade a frown. "Damned if I know."

She took out her own spade and knelt to dig in the bed she intended to plant with periwinkle and pincushion flowers. "Too bad you can't really immerse yourself in this gardening thing. It would do wonders for that ulcer of yours."

"I don't have an ulcer yet," he reminded her.

"No, but you're so tense I'm afraid the doctor's right—if you don't learn to relax, that ulcer's coming. What has you so pent up?"

"You mean more than the usual?" he muttered.

"Yes—something's different. Can't quite put my finger on it, but I'd guess something new is bothering you."

He put down the spade and sat with his back against one of the brick planters. "Turns out I've been thinking about something a lot lately...the fact that I have a chance to sell my construction business at a very good profit."

She waited, sensing there was more. And, after a moment, he did go on.

"I'm considering it," he said. "I'm actually thinking about selling. But that's not what bothers me. What really bugs me is that I want to sell without knowing what comes next. It's not like I have a big plan for what I'd do with my free time."

"Gee," said Meg. "Maybe you could follow doctor's orders and actually relax for a while."

He gave her a disgruntled look. "What do you picture me doing—taking up golf? Playing a little bingo?"

"I get it," she said. "In your mind, only *old* people have time on their hands."

He shook his head. "It's not that simple. In my twenties, I had the knack for free time. I did a lot of traveling without knowing what would come next— just living day to day."

"Now I get it. What bothers you is that *young* people know how to live in the moment, and you don't."

He treated her to another sour glance. "Next you'll tell me that age is just a matter of attitude."

"Something to that effect. Heavens, you really are tense. Let me try something." She perched on the edge of the planter and reached over to massage his shoulders. "Yep...lots of tension. Your muscles are all knotted up. If you could just sit where this would be a little easier..." She ended up with his back resting against her knees, and she proceeded with her impromptu massage.

"You're good at this," he said.

"Are you relaxing?" she asked.

"Getting there."

Only gradually did Meg realize that this could be described as a sensuous activity—the warm pressure of Jack's body against her legs, the movement of her hands upon his shoulders. It was almost as if she was caressing him....

With a mumbled curse, she slid away from him. Scarcely knowing what she was doing, she went to the roses, cupped her hand around one of the stems— and promptly pricked her finger on a thorn.

"Dammit," she said.

Jack came to her and cradled her hand in his. "Running away from me, and you only end up hurting yourself."

"Very funny." With her free hand, she fumbled in her pocket for a tissue. Jack took it from her and pressed it against the small welling of blood on her finger.

"I wasn't making a joke," he said. "Meg, why do you keep trying to avoid what's happening between us?"

"Nothing's happening." She knew she sounded almost desperate. "And besides—Jack, my life could be changing drastically in the next few months. I've been offered a job in London."

He studied her. "Congratulations," he said in a quiet voice.

"It really is an opportunity," she rattled on. "I'd be managing a hotel, with a lot more authority than I have now. If I go for it, I'll be so far away. And you and I...well, your life is in Maine, and mine would be across the ocean."

"You keep doing that," he said. "Explaining to me why the two of us can't be together. You tell me it's because we had sex too soon. Or because I live in Maine, and you live in New York. Now it's the possibility that you could move to London."

"All *very* good reasons," she said.

"Sure, they sound good, anyway. But they're smoke screens, Meg. The real reason is that you're afraid as hell of getting involved with me."

She looked into his eyes, and they seemed a darker blue than before. "Of course I'm afraid," she said. "You and I don't have anything in common, we barely know each other—"

"Smoke screens again," he said. "What's really behind the fear?"

"Damn you, Jack—"

"Maybe you're afraid I'll make you disappear. That's what happened to your mother, isn't it? She married your dad, lost her dreams and lost herself. You watched it happen, and maybe you've been running scared ever since."

She hated him for seeing inside her. "Why shouldn't I be scared? Take right now, for instance.

You're probably thinking I shouldn't take that London job—not if I want to have any kind of relationship with you. So already it becomes a matter of giving in, giving up.''

''Maybe sometimes the woman follows her dreams and the man jets over to see her, at least now and again. And nobody gives up anything.''

''That wouldn't be a relationship at all, would it?'' she countered. ''That would only be a way for the man to play it safe too. Listen to yourself! You come over to see me…'now and again.' What kind of situation is that?''

''A situation where we would both have our own lives, and neither one of us loses.''

''It never works that way,'' she said stubbornly. ''And in the scenario you're describing, each of us would be giving too little.''

He regarded her gravely. ''Problem is, Meg, you seem to see only one other alternative—giving too much. Where does that leave us?''

''It leaves us going our separate ways,'' she said in a low voice.

''Meg…are you breaking up with me again?''

''Dammit,'' she said. ''You *are* making a joke about all this.''

''Just trying to lighten the mood, that's all.'' He sat again with his back against the planter, drawing her down beside him. He held her hand, the one she'd pricked with the rose. ''Meg,'' he said, ''I'll admit I wasn't looking to get involved again. And I sure as hell don't have anything to bring to a relationship right now—not when I don't know what's coming next in my life. But you and I…we can enjoy this moment, at least, can't we?''

This moment…and no more. Meg didn't say those last words, but they seemed to echo mournfully in her head. She and Jack sat beside each other, hand in hand. The rooftop garden surrounded them with the lush yellow and greens of spring. The vivid sunset offered more color—gold and lavender and burnt orange. Everything was so beautiful that Meg felt an ache inside her. She wanted to capture this moment forever, but how? Already it seemed to be slipping away.

Jack turned to look at her. She felt that odd stillness again. He tilted her chin toward him, placed his lips upon hers. And now she knew what she had been waiting for all along…his touch, his kiss. All the colors of this evening seemed to blend and shimmer with her longing. She leaned toward Jack, leaned into his kiss, and with her own touch required more of him.

Music blared suddenly on the rooftop, shattering the moment. Meg pulled away from Jack in confusion. She peered over the edge of the planter and saw one of the penthouse tenants—Mrs. Larkin—complete with boombox and hoe. Meg struggled to her feet.

''Why, hello, dear,'' said Mrs. Larkin, raising her voice to be heard over the music, a Broadway tune going full blast. "Wonderful time of day to garden, isn't it?" She raised her eyebrows a bit as Jack got to his feet, too, and stood beside Meg.

"Just wonderful," Meg murmured under her breath. The beautiful moment was definitely over.

JACK HATED to do it, but there wasn't any choice. He sat down in a chair beside his mother and spread a sheaf of papers across the coverlet on the bed.

"We have to talk," he said. "We have to discuss how you got yourself in this fix, and how we're going to get you out of it."

Helen Elliott gave him her best stony look. "If you're trying to discuss my finances again—forget it. I've taken care of myself for the past five years, and I will continue to do so."

"You need help," he said. He gestured at the figures he'd jotted on one sheet of paper. "You've made too many unwise investments. Not to mention living in an apartment way too expensive for your budget."

"Stop," she ordered. "Stop right now, Jack. I never gave you permission to go poking your nose into my personal matters." She picked up some of the other papers strewn on the bed—bank statements that had never been balanced. "Where did you get these?" she demanded. "They're my private documents."

"They were on the desk in the living room," he

said, "out in plain view. Almost as if you wanted me to see them."

"I suppose you're looking for some sort of neat psychological explanation," she said icily. "Incompetent woman subconsciously begging son for help. But these statements were on my desk because that's where I always keep my important papers. You had no business rifling through them."

He hadn't enjoyed doing it. But the untidy stack of papers on that desk had been difficult to avoid once he'd learned his mother was in financial trouble and she refused to talk about it. He had to find some way to help her, whether she wanted it or not.

"I needed a clear picture of your situation," he explained. "We can't work on solutions until we know exactly what the problems are."

"'We' will not do anything. I will continue to manage my own affairs."

It had been this way every time he tried to bring up the subject of her precarious finances. She got angry. She refused to listen. And she flat out refused to acknowledge that she'd made one bad financial decision after another in the past five years.

"Look," Jack said. "It's not hopeless. Not yet, anyway. We can still turn things around—"

"It was very high-handed of you to go to the bank the way you did. Not to mention discussing my private matters with the super."

He didn't mention that the super had been the one

to bring up—as delicately as possible—Helen's overdue lease payments.

"Okay," he began again, searching for a different tack. "Why don't you tell me what you see for yourself in the next five years. What financial plans have you made?"

"None of your business, Jack. You're my son, not my financial counselor."

"You don't have a financial counselor," he reminded her. "That's part of the problem. You made those investments yourself, without any knowledge of the market."

"You sound just like your father," she said, her voice suddenly too calm. "He never believed I could handle anything on my own. Oh, when it came to being a hostess for him, throwing parties for the faculty, that type of thing, he didn't mind if I took charge then. It was even fine for me to have my own bank account, as long as he controlled how much money went into it. But anything important was strictly off limits. He told me he didn't want me to worry about investments and all those other big financial decisions. You know my mistake, Jack? I went along with your father. It was the easiest thing to do. Except that now I don't go along anymore. I don't take the easy way out. And if I mess up, it's *my* problem, not anyone else's. I no longer hide behind a husband. And I certainly will not hide behind my son."

Although her manner remained almost unnaturally

calm, Jack saw the hurt and anger in her eyes. She looked at him as if he were an unwelcome stranger intruding on her life. He recognized that expression. Helen Elliott had looked at his father much the same way in the last difficult months before their divorce.

"I'm not against you," Jack said. "I can even understand how your problems happened. Five years ago, you began handling money—real money—for the first time in your life. It's the kind of thing most people get to do in their early twenties or so. That's when they make all their mistakes...buy the things they can't afford, whatever. It's something of a learning process. After a few years, hopefully they straighten things out and the repercussions aren't too bad. But you've been going through the process at a time in your life when the repercussions can be serious. That's why we have to straighten things out now, before they get any more out of hand."

"Now you're patronizing me, Jack," she said in a cool, distant tone. "And you still sound like your father. He patronized me, too. All those years he belittled me so expertly, so subtly. I thought you understood how damaging he could be—the way he seemed so kindly on the surface, and yet denigrated his own wife, his own son. The way he could be arrogant and overbearing, and completely dismiss what you and I were feeling. I really believed you *did* understand. After all, you rebelled against him, didn't you? But now I wonder if you're not turning out just like him."

The conversation had gone too far, and Jack knew it. Somehow they were no longer talking about his mother's finances. Instead, they'd treaded into a far murkier area—the dynamics of the Elliott family. It wasn't ground Jack wanted to explore. He suspected his mother didn't, either, but perhaps he'd pushed her to it. He'd confronted her with the evidence of her mistakes, tried to bulldoze her into recognition of them. It had gone downhill from there.

He gathered up the miscellaneous papers and put them back into the file folder he'd provided for them. There was something ironic about him trying to organize the chaos of his mother's finances. Maybe it meant he had been overbearing, just like his old man. Again, an area Jack didn't want to explore.

But that didn't mean his mother wasn't in trouble. And it didn't mean Jack could stand by and do nothing. Somehow he had to find a way to get through to her.

New York was getting more complicated all the time.

MEG STEPPED into her apartment after a long day's work at the hotel. As she went into the living room, she saw Lena. She saw Kathy. She also saw Gary—Kathy's longtime, commitment-phobic boyfriend.

"Isn't it wonderful!" Kathy exclaimed, her cheeks flushed and her eyes shining. "Gary just suddenly showed up! In New York!"

It seemed to Meg that everyone was showing up

in New York these days—her friends, her brother, and now Gary.

"Welcome to the Big Apple, Gary," she said dryly. Maybe the guy didn't know how to commit, but she'd always found him likable enough. Lanky and fair-haired, he was a high-school teacher and track coach. Back in Oklahoma, he'd always seemed most relaxed when surrounded by his students. Here in New York, however, he seemed cast adrift. He looked uncomfortable, standing in the middle of the room as if he couldn't decide where to sit.

"Hey," he said to Meg, apparently eager to latch on to a new presence. "Congratulations. Hear you're engaged, and all that."

Meg stared at him. "*Lena's* engaged."

"Oh, don't be silly, Meg," Kathy said, sounding altogether too nervous and excited. "Don't forget *you're* engaged, too. I told Gary all about you and Jack."

Meg couldn't believe what she'd just heard. "Kathy—"

Kathy grabbed her arm and propelled her toward the kitchen. "Let's see what the two of us can rustle up for dinner," she said brightly. "Lena, you'll entertain Gary, won't you?"

"Oh, sure. Gary and me, it's old home week. Right, Gary?"

He looked unenthusiastic, his usual response to Lena. But Meg didn't have a chance to make any further observations. Next thing she knew, she was in the kitchen, and Kathy was swinging the door shut.

"Whew." Kathy leaned against the counter. "Close call."

"Okay. Mind telling me what the hell—"

"Shh! He might hear you. Meg…oh, Meg. You've got to help me!"

Meg went to the fridge and got out a raspberry yogurt. Next she opened the silverware drawer and found a spoon. Then she sat down at the table and popped the lid off the yogurt. "Something tells me I'd better not hear this on an empty stomach," she said.

Kathy paced. "I didn't expect him to show up. It was a complete surprise. After that last phone call I had with him, well, *you* heard."

"I seem to remember Gary being out of the picture after that."

"That's what I thought. But then he showed up today, out of the blue. When I saw him, I just felt so…so damn happy. Meg, he came all the way from Oklahoma to see me! Don't you think that's highly significant?"

"Oh, highly," said Meg, eating a spoonful of yogurt. "But maybe now you'll explain the little part about my *engagement*."

Kathy sat down, propped her elbows on the table and leaned intently toward Meg. "Here's the thing. When Gary showed up a couple of hours ago, he was so incredibly sweet. Said my being away had shook him up something bad. Said he'd missed me so much he just had to be with me. If you could have seen the hug he gave me…and he was even nice to Lena. Asked about her engagement, admired the ring—the whole bit. I tell you, Meg, I've never seen him like that. I mean, actually able to *talk* about somebody's engagement. Actually showing a little interest.''

''How touching,'' Meg said.

''It was remarkable,'' Kathy sighed. ''I guess this whole New York thing really did shake him up. Only then, well, then it began to wear off. He started to get cynical again, just like the old Gary. He said he couldn't imagine Lena, of all people, getting married. He made some more snide remarks, and she made remarks back. I had to do something. So I said *you* were engaged, too. I swear it wasn't calculated—it just popped out of my mouth. Out of desperation, you see. But it worked! Gary stopped, and he just looked at me. He said if *you* were getting married, that was really food for thought. Can you imagine, Meg? 'Food for thought.' Those were his exact words.''

''He gets no points for originality,'' Meg remarked. ''And now we have to go back out there and set him straight.''

''Oh, no, Meg,'' Kathy said urgently. ''We can't do that! Don't you see? It made an impact on him, your being engaged. He knows your history—how you've always backed away from any promising relationship. He knows how adamant you've been about your independence. The fact that you've actually succumbed...it does have impact, a lot more than hearing about Lena. Gary thinks she's flighty. But he thinks you're sensible. So if *you've* given in, it has to be food for thought.''

Speaking of food, Meg wasn't so hungry anymore. She pushed away the yogurt. ''How grand that I've made such an impression on Gary. Too bad none of it is true.''

''Couldn't we pretend, Meg?'' Kathy asked in a small voice. ''Just for a little while? This is so incredible, to have Gary actually thinking about people being engaged and getting married and all the rest of it. It might make him believe he could do the same. I know I said I was ready to look for another man...but he's the one I want. Can you possibly understand how I feel, Meg?''

Meg looked at her friend. When it came to being sensible, Kathy was usually the one you could count on. She'd always been cautious, thinking her decisions through, looking at them from every angle. For her to have done something this far out...she had to be feeling desperate.

''You really love Gary, don't you?'' Meg asked.

Kathy rested her head in her hands. ''Yes, I do,'' she admitted a bit wearily. ''Why else would I stay with him for ten years? He has a good heart, Meg, he really does. All he needs is a little encouragement. And today, somehow, I seem to have hit on just the right encouragement. I've even come up with a plan, Meg. I think it's a good one. I think it'll work."

Meg shook her head. "I know I'm going to be sorry I asked this," she muttered, "but what exactly do you have in mind?"

Kathy immediately perked up and proceeded to give Meg an outline. Meg listened with a growing sense of dismay.

The plan was worse than anything she could have imagined.

CHAPTER TEN

"I NEED A FAVOR," Meg said.

Jack didn't think she sounded too happy about it. A short while ago, she'd knocked on the door of his mother's apartment and asked him to come up to the rooftop garden with her. So here they were on the roof, 10:00 p.m., the lights of Manhattan glittering all around them. The air was cool. He couldn't see Meg very well in the darkness, but he sensed her shiver.

"Cold?" he asked.

"No."

He took off his jacket anyway and draped it over her shoulders. They sat on the edge of a brick planter. Meg seemed tense, as if she wanted to jump up and leave.

"I'm available for favors," he said.

She gave a humorless laugh. "You haven't heard this one yet. Oh, for goodness' sake, here goes. The fact is, I need a fiancé for a few days. And not just any fiancé. It has to be you."

He smiled a little. She'd definitely gotten his attention. "I'm listening," he said.

"This is so humiliating, Jack," she said. "Today

Kathy's boyfriend showed up all the way from Oklahoma. Seems Gary really missed her—so much that he got in a mellow mood and was even willing to talk about Lena's engagement. And when he didn't want to talk about *that* anymore, Kathy lost her head. She came up with another engagement to chat about. Namely, mine…and yours.''

''We're already engaged?'' he asked solemnly.

''According to Kathy, we are,'' Meg informed him in a grim tone. ''She spun a very imaginative little tale for Gary. She told him that we met up here on the rooftop and fell in love at first sight. Gary was impressed. Apparently he's always thought of me as someone who'd hold out till the bitter end. He's willing to admit that if *I* finally gave in, an engagement could happen to anyone.''

Jack thought it over. ''Sounds reasonable.''

''Sounds crazy, is more like it,'' Meg said. ''But Kathy has this theory. I'll try to repeat it with a straight face. She says psychologists use desensitization when they want to help you get over your fears. Little by little, they expose you to your fear until you're not scared anymore. You know, if you're terrified of dogs, the psychologist has you look at a picture of a schnauzer until you're comfortable. After that, maybe you listen to the sound of a dog barking. Step by step, you keep moving along. You look at a collie from three blocks away…then two blocks… then one. Eventually you're ready for the big trip to the pet store. You look at a Scottie dog close up.

Maybe you pet him. And maybe you even fall in love with him and take him home with you.''

Jack nodded. "Pure logic—makes sense to me.''

"Wait till you hear the rest of it. Kathy thinks the same thing will work on Gary. She says that all his life he's been afraid of marriage. In the past she's tried railroading him, and that hasn't worked. Now her plan is to expose him little by little to the idea. She says he's already taken the first step—at least he's talking about engagement and marriage. Hell, he's talking about *my* engagement—that's the problem. But anyway, Kathy thinks the next step is for Gary to see you and me in action. We're supposed to be this wildly happy couple while he looks on, and hopefully he'll realize that an engagement is not the end to life as we know it.''

Meg paused, then gave a sigh before she went on. "I tried to argue with Kathy. I told her I didn't like deception. I told her that Gary should see Lena in action with her fiancé. At least that way things would be real. But Kathy disagrees. She says Gary's already started to be a cynic about Lena's engagement, so the 'impact value' has been lost. No, you and I are supposed to provide the entertainment. We're supposed to be the convincing ones.'' She laughed again, rather gloomily. "Can you believe it? We're supposed to pretend to be authentically happy. If that isn't irony for you, I don't know what is.''

"Yeah, it's irony,'' he agreed.

Meg made an impatient gesture. "I know it's ridiculous for me to even be considering this. Getting over a fear of marriage is not like getting over a fear of dogs. And yet, Kathy seems convinced this will work. More than anything, she seems so in love. Can you believe it? Ten years with the guy, and she's still in love. You know what she said to me? She said if there was a chance her plan could work—just the slightest chance—wasn't it worth it? Any chance at all that Gary would finally commit, and they could begin the rest of their lives together. I didn't have an answer to that. I couldn't honestly say the chance wasn't worth it. Besides, Kathy's been my friend since grade school, and I hate to see her unhappy…and somehow I couldn't say no.''

He thought it over some more. ''Meg,'' he said gravely, ''are you proposing to me?''

''Very funny,'' she grumbled. ''Although I suppose you're entitled to your share of jokes. I'm asking you to pretend to be my fiancé, and no doubt you find that incredibly amusing.''

''Actually, I'm taking the request very seriously,'' he said. ''I'm thinking it over. But seems I should know a little more about you before I sign on as your intended.''

''Jack—''

He took her hand, clasped it companionably in his. ''Ever been in love, Meg?''

''Jack, for crying out loud…all right. Yes. Once. At least, I thought I was in love. I was a very naive college student at the time. His name was Bruce, and he threw me over for a dance major. End of love affair. Now, could you just tell me yes or no?''

"You weren't engaged to the guy?"

Her fingers moved in his. "It never got that far with him. It never got that far with anybody."

"I've never been engaged, either," he told her. "Sounds like we're both novices at this."

"The whole thing is ridiculous," Meg said. "Why did I listen to Kathy? Why did I let her persuade me at all?"

"Because you're loyal to your friends," Jack answered, "no matter what kind of wacky thing they ask you to do."

She slipped her hand away from his and stood. "Listen, Jack, I'm sorry I wasted your time. The truth is, I don't like deception. Kathy says we wouldn't be forcing Gary into anything. She says if he does end up proposing, it'll be of his own free will. But I just don't like it."

"What the hell," he said. "I'll do it."

She didn't say anything for a moment. And then, reluctantly, "You will?"

"You sound like you wanted me to say no."

"Oh, damn," she muttered. "You know something? That's exactly what I wanted you to say. A big, unequivocal no. I figured I'd present the idea, you'd turn me down flat, and that would be the end of it. I'd be able to tell Kathy I tried, but it didn't work out. That way I'd have the best of both worlds—I'd still be the good friend, but I wouldn't have to go through with the ridiculous charade.''

He went to stand beside her. All around them were the scents of the garden—rich, moist earth, the lingering perfume of flowers. Or maybe it was just Meg's perfume that got to him. He drew her into his arms and kissed her. She placed her hands against his chest, but she didn't resist beyond that. She returned his kiss with the warmth and the banked passion he was familiar with. Meg felt right in his arms...very right.

When at last she pulled away, she was breathing unsteadily. "No one's watching us right now," she said. "We don't have to pretend."

"I wasn't pretending." He drew her close again. The next kiss took them further. Meg's lips opened under his. Her hands wove through his hair, her body melted soft and warm against him. He thought about making love to her amid the iris and the English ivy. The idea appealed to him. Making love to Meg anywhere appealed to him.

As if sensing the direction of his thoughts, she pulled away from him once more.

"Jack," she murmured distractedly. "Even if we go through with it...our so-called engagement...it's not an excuse for anything."

He felt sorry about that. "So we'll do it for purely altruistic motives," he said.

Meg stared at him through the darkness. "You're already having fun with this, aren't you?"

For an answer, he took her into his arms yet again and kissed her before she could protest. Words didn't seem necessary at the moment. Nothing seemed necessary but Meg, soft and warm and womanly against him.

THE RESTAURANT WAS one of Manhattan's most elegant, with silk-backed chairs, linen napkins, candles flickering in crystal sconces. Meg's gaze traveled around the table where she sat. Lena sparkled in a beaded sheath and leaned close to her fiancé, Nathan the lawyer. Nathan had light brown hair and brown eyes that seemed to have no focus other than Lena. Across from him sat Kathy and Gary. Kathy looked very pretty in a filmy lavender gown that evoked the 1930s, her long wavy blond hair caught up with jeweled combs. Gary still wore the expression of someone who hadn't quite found his footing in New York, but he looked handsome in what appeared to be a brand-new sports jacket.

Meg forced her gaze to slow, but she could not avoid the last occupant of the table…the person sitting right next to her. Jack Elliott. When at last she glanced at him, she felt the oddest constriction in her throat—an undeniable physical reaction to his good looks. The other two men at the table seemed to fade into insignificance. Jack was devastating in his dark suit coat, the shadow of beard along his jaw giving him a hint of rakishness. He looked at Meg, his eyes the deepest blue she had ever seen.…

"My," Kathy said. "You two really *are* wrapped up in each other. I guess that's what being engaged does to people."

Meg winced. Kathy had been laying it on a little too thick all evening, making pointed remarks about the advantages of betrothal. That wasn't part of the plan. The plan was for all three couples to share a meal together, and for Gary to make whatever conclusions he preferred.

Jack put his arm around Meg until she had no choice but to snuggle close. "Meg and I just feel lucky we've found each other," he said.

She winced again. Now she saw a subtle glimmer of humor in his eyes. He was having far too good a time. She had no doubt that was the only reason he'd agreed to this crazy scheme—he found it amusing. Perhaps it was a distraction for him, a way to spend his time until he went back to Maine and his real life.

Meg wondered for the umpteenth time why she'd agreed to this...until she saw the half-hopeful, half-wistful look on Kathy's face. That alone motivated her to play her part well. She allowed Jack to keep his arm around her.

Lena held up her left hand and moved it back and forth in the candlelight. "I can't get over what a rock this is," she said unabashedly. "Nathan pulled out all the stops when it came to an engagement ring." She gave Jack an innocent glance. "What about you,

Jack? What kind of diamond are you going to buy for Meg?''

Meg glared at her friend. Lena was also enjoying this game a little too much. But Jack answered readily, with no apparent qualms.

''Meg and I are still working on an engagement ring. Everything's happened so quickly, we haven't had a chance to get the details down.''

That was an understatement. Meg was grateful when the musicians began to play. She grabbed Jack's hand. ''Come on...darling. You haven't treated me to a waltz yet.''

Jack moved obligingly to the dance floor with her. He managed to waltz superbly and at the same time hold her close.

''Don't fight me,'' he murmured.

''I'm not...''

''You're all tense,'' he said. ''A woman dancing in her fiancé's arms isn't supposed to be tense. She's supposed to be mellow.''

''As if you would know,'' Meg retorted caustically. ''Between the two of us, we have a deplorable lack of experience. Lena almost threw us on the engagement ring.''

''So we need a little practice,'' he said, expertly whirling Meg.

''Thank goodness Gary will be in New York only a few days,'' she said. ''He has to get back to his teaching job. We won't have to do this for long.'' Gary was staying at one of the mid-priced hotels

Meg had recommended. With any luck he wouldn't be at her apartment very often. Surely in her own home she wouldn't have to keep up the front.

"We need to be more convincing," Jack told her. "Have you ever taken an acting class, Meg?"

"No. Of course not."

"When I was in high school," he said, "I hung out at the drama club for a while."

"No kidding." She gave him a considering look. "You have ambitions for the stage, and you haven't told me?"

He grinned, holding her a little closer. "Not likely. I was just trying to get out of social studies. In spite of myself, though, I learned a few things about acting. First, you have to immerse yourself in the role."

"Very interesting, Jack, but—"

"Which means," he went on, "that you and I have to figure out what it feels like to be engaged. We have to immerse ourselves."

She frowned. "You're finding no end of amusement in all this, aren't you?"

"When I accept a job," he said, deadpan, "I always try to do my best work."

"What you do," remarked Meg, "is hide behind that mock-serious attitude of yours. Very convenient. That way you don't have to risk showing any real emotions."

She couldn't be sure because of the hazy lighting, but he seemed disconcerted for a second or two. He recovered quickly, however, waltzing her away from the dance floor to one of the window nooks.

"Wait," said Meg. "We have to get back to the table. We have to play our part."

"That's exactly what we're doing," he informed her. "Engaged people are expected to sneak off by themselves." He twirled her under his arm and she landed gracefully—if breathlessly—on the brocade window seat. Beyond shimmered the lights of the city, and Meg felt as if she were floating among the stars. But she knew it wasn't the surroundings that made her feel this buoyant sensation. She'd felt that way last night, too, on the rooftop with Jack...as if she were floating in the sky, all moorings gone except for her awareness of him.

Now he sat beside her and studied her. "You're beautiful," he said, his voice low and husky, and for once he sounded completely serious. The truth was, she'd invested far too much time preparing for this evening. She'd lifted her hair off her neck in a loose chignon, curls escaping free. And she wore a body-hugging dress of jade shantung that was more daring than her usual attire. It seemed to be having the proper effect on Jack.

She quickly reminded herself that she'd merely dressed for the part. With firm resolve, she gazed out the window, turning away from him as well as she could.

"You're still tense," he said.

"Darn it all, I'm not going to do any so-called

immersing in the role. It wouldn't be a good idea, believe me. I'd only see the bad things about being engaged.''

''Bad things,'' he echoed reflectively. ''Most people act like getting engaged is a positive step.''

''I'm not most people,'' she countered. ''As far as the downside of engagements—all you have to do is analyze Lena's behavior this evening. Instead of being her usual independent self, she's let Nathan make all the decisions for her. Which wine to drink, what food to order. She's…she's *deferring* to the man. It's as if she's forgotten that she has a mind of her own, because she's trying to please him. She's never been like that before, let me tell you.''

''Maybe it's only a temporary effect,'' Jack suggested.

''No matter what it is, it's scary,'' Meg told him. ''If that can happen to my strong-willed, irrepressible friend, what hope is there for lesser mortals?''

''Maybe it's just the wrong combination,'' he said. ''Maybe she wouldn't be that way with another guy.''

Meg shook her head. ''It's not that I'm blaming Nathan. From everything I can see, he's remarkably easygoing. He's not trying to force anything on her. He keeps asking her opinion, and she keeps refusing to tell him, so she can follow his lead instead. Lena's never been like that with a man before…voluntarily abdicating.''

"So you think it happens to all women," Jack said. "They abdicate."

"It happens to far too many of us. Even my sister-in-law—" Meg stopped herself. She'd told Jack that her brother was in town, but she didn't think she had a right to divulge Shaun's marital problems... problems that seemed to have a lot to do with Barbara no longer being as independent and self-sufficient as before.

"Don't forget your mother," Jack reminded her.

"It doesn't always come back to my mother," she protested. He didn't answer, and that only nettled her. "Jack," she said, "I'm an observant person, that's all. I see what's going on around me. I don't travel through life in a romantic fog."

"You're a realist, then."

Why did she get the feeling he was laughing at her again? "Yeah, I'm a realist." she said. "And I'd bet you are, too. I don't see you carting around any romantic notions."

He put his hands on her shoulders, drew her gently back so that she was half leaning against him. Their bodies seemed to fit together enticingly.

"Jack…"

"Just striving for authenticity," he said. "Your friends are looking at us."

Meg glanced over and saw that Lena, Kathy and company did seem to be craning their necks this way.

"You don't suppose they're talking about us," Meg wondered.

"They're probably commenting on what a fine job we're doing."

"*Are* we doing a fine job?" she asked. "I wonder."

"It's working for me," he said.

He didn't try to kiss her, didn't try to deepen the contact between them. Maybe that was why she felt free to lean back against him a bit more. Maybe that was why she turned her head until her lips brushed his cheek. Maybe that was why she trailed her fingers across his jaw. Maybe that was why she made sure that eventually her lips found his.

And maybe, just maybe, she was starting to get too involved in this engagement thing.

"IT'S WORKING, Meg!" Kathy exclaimed. "It's really working!"

It was late that evening, after they'd returned from the restaurant. The three men—Nathan, Gary, Jack— had gone their respective ways. And now the three women—Lena, Kathy, Meg—had congregated in Meg's bedroom.

Kathy kicked off her shoes and fell back against the bed, spreading her arms wide. "It's working," she repeated dreamily. "Gary thinks you and Jack are a wonderful couple."

"His exact words, I'm sure," Meg remarked.

"Close enough. He said being engaged didn't look so bad. And those *were* his exact words. 'It doesn't look so bad.'"

"A ringing endorsement," Meg observed wryly. She belted her robe and ran a brush through her hair. Meanwhile, Lena kicked off her shoes, too, and sprawled on the other half of the mattress.

"You and Jack did an impressive job," she said, back to offering her opinions left and right. "So impressive you almost had *me* fooled." She gave a mischievous smile.

"Good," Meg said. "Just fine. Just dandy. And as far as I'm concerned, it's over."

Kathy straightened, looking alarmed. "What do you mean?"

"Just that. It's over. I set the scenario—now you and Gary can talk about engagements ad nauseam. But Jack's services are no longer required."

"Oh, no," Kathy said. "Gary has to see the two of you in other situations. He has to see that no matter what the circumstances, an engagement isn't stifling! And that it's not limiting in any way, shape or form!"

"Kathy," Meg explained, as patiently as she could, "the very definition of an engagement *is* limiting. It's saying that you're promised to one person, and one person alone. I assume Gary's figured that out by now."

"Of course he has," Lena said snippily. "Why else do you think he's been avoiding it all these years?"

"Lena," Kathy said in a stern voice, "Gary has never had a problem with fidelity. He's never balked at sticking to just one woman...me. It's the other aspects that frighten him. Thinking that suddenly his whole routine, his whole schedule will have to change. That kind of thing.''

"Poor Gary, having to deal with the terror of a new schedule. But I still don't understand why you can't use Nathan and me as an example of the perfect couple.''

"You act like a ninny every time you're around your fiancé, that's why. You practically coo at the man, and he doesn't have the sense to realize how obnoxious you're being.''

This was similar to Meg's assessment, but her friends' tempers were fraying and she wanted to inject a little moderation.

"Time out,'' she said. "Let's stick to the point— the point being that Jack and I have done our parts. Kathy, if you must continue the fiction with Gary...go ahead. Tell him that Jack and I are amazingly compatible in every possible situation. Just don't ask us to prove it.''

"Meg, one more time. That's all I ask. I'm taking Gary on a sight-seeing tour tomorrow. If you and Jack come along, Gary will *really* see how happy the two of you are. And then maybe he'll admit that being engaged is more than just not so bad.''

Meg groaned. She sank onto the stool in front of her vanity. "Kathy, are you listening to yourself? Are you listening at all?''

"She obviously doesn't want Nathan and me

along tomorrow.'' Lena sounded injured. ''She doesn't want a *real* engagement. That would be too obnoxious.''

Kathy ignored Lena. ''Please, Meg. Gary's softening up, I swear it. Just one more time.''

Meg knew she was going to regret it, but she nodded grudgingly. ''All right,'' she said. ''Once more. And that's it.''

CHAPTER ELEVEN

NEXT MORNING at the hotel, Meg watched a sheet scroll out of her fax machine. Then she picked it up and read it. Thomas P. Riley of Corporate was growing impatient. He wanted a decision about London, and he wanted it soon.

Meg set the piece of paper on her desk. She'd already stalled Mr. Riley by phone; she'd already left two faxes unanswered. But she knew she couldn't delay much longer. She had to make a decision, one way or the other.

She'd scribbled pro lists and con lists, but they hadn't helped at all. She'd paced her bedroom at night, searching for the answer. But still she felt confused. This wasn't like her. Why was she having so much difficulty making up her mind?

Daisy curled up on her pillow beside Meg's desk. Meg contemplated the tabby. "You have it easy," she murmured. "No big decisions to make. No conflicts. No uncertainties. No wonder cats think they're superior to humans."

"Mind if I join the conversation?" asked Jack Elliott from the doorway.

Meg started guiltily. "I don't always talk to my

cat,'' she said. She surveyed Jack. He wore khaki pants and a denim shirt, the perfect attire for a New York outing. But then, any clothes would look perfect on his muscular frame.

''You're early,'' Meg said.

''There's something we need to do before we meet your friends.''

''Really? What's that?''

''It's a surprise,'' he said in the solemn way she'd come to distrust.

''I can't leave just yet. I have some loose ends to tie up,'' she told him.

''Go ahead—I'll wait.'' He sat down in a chair and picked up a magazine from the table beside him. In only a few moments he seemed engrossed in an article, as if to show Meg that she could go about business as usual.

She tried to concentrate on her work. She signed a few letters. She returned a few phone calls. She reviewed departmental reports, jotted notes for tomorrow's meeting with convention services. But all the while she worked, she was intensely aware of Jack's presence. He didn't speak, didn't try to intrude. Yet his presence was undeniable. Meg's gaze kept straying to him. He'd slipped his reading glasses out of his pocket and put them on. He didn't seem very accustomed to them; they kept sliding down his nose. Somehow those wire-framed specs made him look more gorgeous than ever.

He glanced up, caught her gaze and immediately put the glasses away.

"They're not a sign of weakness, Jack," she said. There was still a pile in her "to do" basket, but she knew she wouldn't accomplish anything else. She pushed back her chair. "Okay, let's get on with it. What's the surprise?"

"We have to walk a little," he said unhelpfully. A few moments later, they were outside. Jack didn't seem in a particular hurry. He took Meg's hand and strolled with her down the street.

"I'm kind of glad we get to be engaged again," he said. "Maybe we could get used to this."

She gave him a sharp glance. "You can't be having *that* much fun."

"Think about it, Meg. How many times do you have the opportunity to try something on for size, risk free?"

"I don't know about the risk-free part," she muttered.

"We've opened the door, we're looking in. But we don't have to buy the house."

He seemed serious, but she'd already learned that didn't mean a whole lot.

"Pretending isn't a bit like the real thing," she argued.

"It's close enough. I can't help being intrigued, Meg. Can't help wondering if there aren't some positives to this engagement thing."

She had absolutely no doubt he still considered

this situation a huge joke. "Not a one I can think of," she said flippantly.

"You're not trying. Humor me. Imagine something positive."

She rolled her eyes, but she did think about it. "All right," she said at last. "Maybe—for some people—it would be nice to feel that you could put your faith in another person. Enough faith that you'd promise to be with that person always."

His fingers were warm around hers. "I can think of another positive. Finding the one person you can let your guard down with. The one person who won't mind if you admit that you're less than superhuman. The one person who'll see your mistakes, your failings, and want you anyway."

Meg couldn't help herself. She was getting into the spirit of this. "Finding the person who gets excited about your dreams. And you get excited about his."

"The person," said Jack, "who wants to share your adventures."

"The person," said Meg, "who doesn't mind when you look awful in the morning."

"The person who looks awful right along with you."

"The person you can't imagine your future without," Meg added. "The person who's always been missing in your life, and you didn't even know it until you met him...."

They'd stopped walking. They stood gazing at

each other, even as other pedestrians hurried by. In spite of the noise and bustle all around her, Meg felt a stillness deep inside. And Jack...she saw no amusement in his expression now. Only intentness, as if he were trying to see right through to the core of her.

Someone jostled them. They began walking again, no longer hand in hand. The moment passed, almost before it had begun.

"Well," Meg said, her voice brittle. "It sounded good, anyway."

"Yeah," agreed Jack. "It sounded damn good."

"Wishful thinking."

He didn't answer, but he paused in front of a jewelry store.

"We'll be late to meet Kathy and Gary," said Meg.

"This is the surprise," Jack said.

She stared at a window display of diamonds on burgundy velvet. "I don't get it," she said flatly, trying to ignore her unease.

"The engagement ring," Jack said with a slight smile. "We told your friends we were working on it. Can't be found out as liars, can we?"

"This is going too far," she said. "Way too far."

"Afraid we don't have any choice," he said. "It seems Kathy got a little carried away again. Apparently she was trying for some more authenticity, so she told Gary that you and I were ring shopping today, and that we'd meet the two of them at a jewelry shop. She called me in a panic, informed me what she'd done. Seems we have to help her out.''

Meg shook her head in disbelief. ''She's running amok. She's told a lie, and now she's compounding it by telling more and more lies, as if that will somehow turn everything into the truth. But who am I to complain? I'm a collaborator!''

''You have to admit,'' Jack said, ''there's something almost impressive about what she's doing. It's foolhardiness on a grand scale. She must really care about this guy.''

''Oh, great,'' Meg groaned. ''You fall in love, and you lose your head.''

''Something like that.''

''It wouldn't happen to me,'' she stated firmly.

''Don't be so sure. Aren't you already doing something ill-advised because you care about your friend? Maybe you'd do something even worse for a guy.''

''A comforting thought,'' she said. ''I'll just have to make sure it doesn't happen.'' She pushed open the door of the store. ''Let's get on with the show. I imagine Kathy and Gary will be here pretty soon.''

He looked at his watch as he followed her. ''Twenty minutes. Gives us some time to rehearse.''

Meg stifled another groan, just as the saleslady came forward.

''May I help you?''

Jack put his arm around Meg's waist. ''We're engaged,'' he announced. Meg tried to jab him dis-

creetly with her elbow, but that didn't make him tone
things down. He merely held Meg closer and gazed
into her eyes as if he really *was* in love with her.
Jack Elliott was turning out to be a very good actor.

"Congratulations," said the saleslady, and she
produced a tray of rings.

Diamonds confronted Meg, and she had to blink
at the sudden dazzle. Jack picked one up. "Impressive," he murmured.

"Too big," Meg protested, and then, under her
breath, added, "not that it matters."

Jack didn't seem perturbed. "How about this
one?"

"Too plain," said Meg. "If two people are crazy
enough to get engaged, they might as well make
something of a statement."

The saleslady gave her a peculiar look.

"This one," said Jack. Meg stared at the ring he'd
chosen. It was neither too showy nor too simple. It
was, in fact, just right. The setting of gold and amethyst was lovely.

"How…nice," Meg hedged, trying to sound noncommittal, but Jack seemed to hear something in her
voice. He took her left hand and slipped the ring on.
"Too loose," she said immediately, relieved to have
found something wrong with it.

"That can be remedied," the saleslady assured
them.

"I like it," said Jack almost reluctantly.

Meg slid it off her finger. "We'll keep looking,"

she said, her tone forced. And so other trays were brought out, and Meg and Jack went through the motions of picking out an engagement ring. When Kathy showed up with Gary, surely it was a convincing tableau: Meg trying one ring after another. But her gaze kept wandering back to the diamond nestled in amethyst, and she felt a longing that she could not possibly have put into words.

KATHY HAD GONE camera-happy. All the rest of the day, no matter where the two couples ended up, Kathy snapped pictures. The South Street Seaport, city hall...the customs house, Ellis Island. She captured every possible scene on film, as if *that* would turn fiction into reality. Meg wanted to shield her face, refuse any more photos that took her and Jack unawares. But she couldn't say anything, not when her friend continued to look so hopeful that everything would work out.

By evening they'd shared a meal at another of New York's superb restaurants, and they ended up at Central Park. Jack suggested that each couple appropriate a carriage for a ride in the park, which was a relief; for the first time in hours Meg and Jack would have a little privacy and not have to pretend they were in love.

Now she sat snugly with Jack. The old-fashioned carriage creaked enjoyably as they went along, complemented by the clip-clop of the horse's hooves. Up front was the driver in his top hat, and overhead the trees spread their canopy of branches. The sky had turned the color between dusk and night: darkest blue softened by violet. Meg's shoulder was pressed next to Jack's, his familiar warmth enfolding her.

"I thought the day went well," he said.

"Which part?" Meg asked sardonically. "The time when Kathy got carried away and asked us when we were setting the date? Neither one of us could think of a single thing to say."

"Only momentarily," Jack reminded her. "We recovered."

"Yeah, right. You said you pictured a winter wedding, and I said something about June."

"Engaged couples aren't supposed to agree on everything," he remarked.

"Well, if they can't even agree on a wedding date, they're in big trouble."

"The rest of the day went well," he said.

"Have you forgotten the time when Gary asked us where we were going to live?"

"At least we agreed that time," Jack said. "We both told him we didn't know."

"We're not doing a very good job of this," Meg said. "He probably already suspects something is up."

"We'll just have to try harder." Jack tilted her face toward his and kissed her. For a long, enchanted moment she couldn't think about anything but his nearness and the taste of his lips. When at last they broke apart, she felt herself trembling.

"Are you cold?" Jack murmured.

"No...that's not the problem."

He put his arm around her, shared his warmth. "What is the problem, Meg?"

"Everything...the fact that we're pretending to be enthralled with each other. And the way you keep kissing me when there isn't any need."

"There's need," he murmured, capturing her mouth once more with his. This time they both prolonged the kiss, the night deepening around them and cloaking them with its magic.

A very long moment later, Meg rested her cheek against Jack's shoulder and drew a ragged breath. "Oh Lord," she whispered.

"You know that nothing's changed, Meg," he said, his voice very low. "I still want you."

"I don't see a future for us. Do you?"

"I'm not thinking about the future. I'm thinking about tonight."

How tempting it was. Perhaps they could end up in another hotel room, and Meg could once again know the rapture of being in Jack's arms...

She straightened. "No. It wasn't right the first time. And it wouldn't be right now."

"I wasn't thinking about right," he said. "I was just thinking about you, Meg."

She heard the regret in his voice, and her own regret twisted inside her.

"Jack, this engagement nonsense has actually taught me something. It's made me think about all the ways two people *could* get it right, if they were ever lucky enough. And so, unless they can achieve the ideal, they shouldn't try at all.''

''You're setting pretty high standards,'' he said. ''Maybe impossible ones.''

''Am I? At least I'm starting to admit that two people could trust each other…and they could give everything to each other, if they were brave enough.''

''But giving everything—isn't that what you're afraid of?''

''Oh, yes, I'm afraid. That hasn't changed. You see, I don't think I'm the type who ever could give everything. It's a lovely thought, that's all…knowing that maybe somewhere there are people who really do love each other enough to let down all the barriers.''

He took her hand between both of his. ''The problem with all or nothing is that most likely you end up with nothing.''

''So what's your solution, Jack? Sex in a hotel room now and then? Relationships that never quite fulfill, that leave you with an emptiness worse than anything you had before? Give me 'nothing' any day.''

''I don't know the answers,'' he said honestly. ''Especially not right now. If I ever figure out my life, where it's headed next, maybe I'll see more clearly. Or maybe not. I only know one thing, Meg…''

He didn't have to say the rest of it. She knew what he was thinking. He wanted her, just as she wanted him. But it wasn't enough. No matter the ache inside her, it just wasn't enough.

The carriage ride came to an end. Jack climbed out, then reached out his arms for Meg. He brought her down beside him and kept his arms around her. Another kiss, stolen in the night...

"Hey, you two," came Kathy's voice, sounding pleased. No doubt she thought Meg and Jack were playing their parts exceedingly well. Meg drew away from Jack and tried to pretend that nothing was the matter, tried to make believe she'd been sharing a lighthearted moment with her fiancé. Make believe...that was all this day had been.

As they made their way back toward Meg's apartment building, Kathy and Jack fell into step and began chatting. That left Gary and Meg lagging behind. Gary didn't say anything at first. Meg couldn't seem to think of anything to say, either. But then Gary surprised her.

"So," he said awkwardly, "you're pretty happy, huh?"

She searched for an answer. "Well...yes...but you know me, Gary. I've always been a cheery person, haven't I?"

"You're happy with this Jack." He said it as a statement, not a question.

Now Meg had to search even harder. "We all had

a good time today, didn't we? So we were all pretty...happy.''

Gary, usually reticent, wouldn't let it go. ''What's the big deal? You're happy, right?''

She thought about the undeniable enjoyment of Jack's company. But today it had been something more...something deeper, richer. Whenever he had held her hand or looked into her eyes, she'd felt as if the sky had grown just a little bit sunnier, the afternoon a little more special.

Now she felt the oddest tightening in her throat. ''Gary,'' she said. ''I'll tell you this much. There were times today when...when maybe I was happier than I've ever been before.''

He didn't say anything else. Meg was left to ponder the confusion of it: how could she have known those happy moments, when it had all been such a pretense?

They arrived at the apartment building. Kathy began to make a long, convoluted explanation about her plans to spend a few moments at Gary's hotel. Before she could finish, Gary dragged her off down the street. Jack watched them go.

''Why is she so afraid to admit she's going to spend the night with him?'' Jack asked.

''I think it feels different to her, having Gary in New York. She's behaving almost the way she did when they first started dating...all of ten years ago.''

''A decade's a hell of a long time,'' Jack said.

''You wouldn't keep a woman dangling that long?''

He glanced at Meg. ''Sometimes it's the woman who does the dangling. But either way, guess I wouldn't want to be in limbo.''

''All or nothing,'' she murmured. ''Maybe that applies to you too, Jack.''

''Maybe,'' he said, looking thoughtful.

They went into the building and up to 7C. Meg knew she should just say good-night to Jack at her door. But somehow she didn't want him to leave…not just yet.

''How about a nightcap?'' she asked awkwardly. ''Or coffee.''

''Coffee's good,'' he said.

She ushered him into her apartment. She had to admit that the place felt empty without either of her friends there; Kathy was occupied with Gary, of course, and Lena was caught up in her whirlwind romance with Nathan.

Meg gave an ironic smile. ''Girlfriends,'' she said. ''We spend a lot of time together until a man comes along and takes our attention. Always put the man first, that seems to be the motto.''

''With guys it's the opposite,'' Jack told her. ''We get together every Thursday night for a couple of beers, and we don't want to change that for any woman.''

She led him into the kitchen. ''Is that what you

do back in Maine—get together with the guys every Thursday?''

''Not every week,'' he said gravely. ''But I have good friends on my construction crew. We like to congregate at Lou's Bar.''

''Lou's,'' she echoed as she started the coffee. ''Sounds very picturesque.''

They sat across from each other at the table while the coffee brewed. Jack glanced around, seeming to take in all the little details: the old-fashioned tins on the counter, the bright pot holders hanging on the walls, the colorful scarves Meg had improvised as curtain ties.

''Didn't expect your place to be like this,'' he said. ''So…homey.''

''Why on earth not?''

''I figured you thought of the hotel as your real home.''

Meg drew her eyebrows together. ''Just because I spend a lot of time there doesn't mean I'm a slave to the place.''

''It wasn't an insult, Meg. Just an observation. And I've never thought a woman had to be domestic.''

Meg gave a shrug. ''Well, domestic—have to admit that's not me. If you open my freezer right now, you'll see nothing but frozen dinners. Gourmet dinners, perhaps, but frozen, nonetheless.''

''I'll take your word for it.''

She gave him a hard look. ''When it comes right

down to it, though, most men think women should have a domestic side. I can't believe you're any different.''

"I'm open-minded," he said imperturbably. "Why shouldn't the guy be the one who does the cooking?"

"Do you cook, Jack?"

"Not much," he admitted. "But my point still stands."

"I don't believe it," she said. "If you ever do settle down, you'll be expecting pancakes in the morning and roast beef at night."

"Never did care for roast beef."

The coffee was ready, and Meg poured two cups. "Sugar?" she asked. "Cream?"

He helped himself to the sugar bowl. "You don't need to wait on me."

"Jack, I can serve you a cup of coffee without feeling threatened."

"It's just everything else that threatens your independence." He spoke mildly, as if to take the sting from his words.

"Okay," she admitted, "so I'm a little protective of myself... Make that a lot protective. With most men, it's the way you have to be."

He didn't argue with her. They sipped their coffee in a silence that was unexpectedly companionable. When they finished, it was Jack who took the cups to the sink and rinsed them.

"You've proven your case," she said. "You don't expect me to wait on you."

He turned off the faucet. "Guess it's time to say good-night."

"Yes, well... good night, Jack." She rose to stand beside him. Maybe that was a mistake. Because it seemed to lead, quite naturally, to a good-night kiss.

The kiss led to something else...a gathering of warmth deep inside Meg. She put her hands against Jack's shoulders, leaned near to him. His arms came around her and brought her close. And ever so quickly it happened—the warmth sparking into desire, fanning into need. It carried her along, sweeping away her misgivings. So quickly the wanting happened.

She clung to Jack, trembling. Her mouth opened to his, and she knew that silently she was beseeching him for more. His hands moved over her back, found the swell of her hips. She moaned softly as she pressed closer to him. She sensed his breath accelerate, his heartbeat match hers. They kissed and touched, and surely both of them knew where they were headed next.

But it was Jack who drew away, Jack who gazed at her with darkened eyes. He brushed a finger against her parted lips, his face seeming to tighten with regret, and then he stepped back.

"All or nothing," he murmured, his voice husky. "That's what you said it had to be, Meg. All or nothing."

She held her arms against her body and turned away from him. Maybe she should be grateful that he'd stopped, but all she felt was a hollowness inside. "Good night, Jack," she said, her voice low.

She didn't look at him again, and a few seconds later she heard the front door open and close. All or nothing. So this was how nothing felt.

CHAPTER TWELVE

"So," SAID MEG'S brother, "are you in love with the guy?"

Meg wondered grouchily why conversations about Jack Elliott seemed to lead inevitably to this question: Did she love him…?

"I shouldn't have told you about him," she grumbled. She and her brother sat in a subway car rattling its way beneath New York City. Shaun had said he wanted to ride the subway before leaving town. Meg suspected he was just trying to find any way he could to outdistance his personal problems. Somehow he seemed to think talking about *her* personal problems would help him forget his own.

"You didn't answer my question yet," he reminded her.

She couldn't answer. Her feelings about Jack were too muddled, too chaotic. Last night in her apartment, she'd wanted him so much. Needed him so much, and yet he had been the one to turn away.

She made an effort to quell the turmoil of her thoughts. "Shaun, you've delayed going home to Barbara, but you said you were going to call her. Have you done it?"

Darkness streamed by on either side as the train moved along. Shaun and Meg had this corner of the subway car to themselves, but still he seemed reluctant to speak. When at length he did, his voice was wooden.

"Yes, I called her. Now she's saying that maybe we should consider a separation. And maybe she's right."

"Oh, Shaun." Meg stared at him in dismay. "Surely something can be done."

"I don't know, Meggie. I just don't know anymore. Maybe we've both changed too much."

Meg sat there with a heaviness in her heart. The train carried them onward. Passengers got on, others got off, but she and her brother had chosen no particular destination. Perhaps both of them were trying to outdistance their problems.

"Shaun," Meg said, "has it ever occurred to you that maybe you and I and Ryan have spent our whole lives doing everything we can not to be like Mom and Dad?"

He gave her a skeptical glance.

"Think about it," she said. "Ryan swears he's never going to get married. I'm not much different. And you, well, you married, but you chose a woman independent and resourceful in the extreme. You figured no way could she end up like Mom used to be—frustrated and unhappy. But now Barbara *is* unhappy, and you're scared history will repeat itself, after all. Shaun, maybe being scared isn't helping the situation. Maybe you just keep remembering how things were when we were kids, and it doesn't help you to see how things are now. Because Barbara isn't Mom. And you're sure not Dad.''

He gave her another skeptical look. ''Can you do that in your own life, Meggie—forget the past?''

It was one more question she didn't know how to answer. All along, Kathy and Lena—and Jack—had pointed out how much Meg feared ending up like her mother. Maybe, all along, she'd been too afraid. Or maybe her fears were justified. Maybe love simply wasn't worth the risk.

THAT EVENING, Helen Elliott wanted to hear all the latest about the hotel. She listened attentively as Meg described her ongoing plans to host a charity ball at the Alexander, and her problems trying to find replacements for two more employees who had quit. Most of all, however, Helen wanted to hear about the London job offer.

''I finally talked to Mr. Riley on the phone today,'' Meg said. ''I realized I couldn't avoid him forever. And I told him that I'd have a decision for him by next week. He wasn't happy about the delay, but he agreed to it.''

''That still doesn't give you much time,'' said Helen. ''This is a very important decision, one that could change the whole direction of your career.''

Meg settled back in her chair in Helen's living

room. Chester had placed his head on her knee, and she gave him a pat.

"My big question is whether or not I can trust Mr. Riley," she said. "He doesn't seem worried about the way employee morale is plummeting at the Alexander. He just keeps telling me that in London everything will be different—I really will have full control. Should I believe him?"

"You should use this opportunity," Helen said promptly. "Maybe it won't be perfect—nothing ever is—but it will be a stepping stone. Just think, you'll have international credentials in the hotel business. Oh, Meg, how I wish I'd been facing those types of decisions when I was your age! I waited too long, and now I'm struggling just to hold on to the job I *do* have."

Meg gave the older woman a sympathetic glance. "Are they still trying to make you retire?"

"I'm pretty sure that's the idea. My boss refuses to let me work while I'm in this damn cast. Oh, he tries to make it seem like he's being solicitous, just looking out for my welfare. But he keeps telling me about the fine benefits package they'll offer me if I retire. Apparently when I was hired, seniors were in with management. But now seniors are out—definitely out."

"I'm sorry," Meg said.

"Enough about me," said Helen. "You're the one with exciting, life-altering prospects ahead of you."

Meg grimaced. "Put it like that and I'm really starting to feel the pressure."

Helen observed her shrewdly. "Why do I get the feeling that my son is complicating the decision for you?"

Meg was unaccountably flustered. "Jack hasn't gotten involved. He would never ask me to stay behind—I'm positive of that."

"I'm talking about your feelings for him. You do have them, don't you?"

Meg wished Jack's name hadn't popped up in the conversation. "I like your son. Who wouldn't like him? He's a wonderful man."

"Cut the bull, Meg," Helen instructed. "Are you in love with him, or what?"

Meg stared at the other woman in exasperation. Always that question! "I...I don't know. How can I possibly? When you think about it, I've barely just met him."

"I worry about you, Meg," said Helen. "I'm afraid you'll discover that you are in love with him, and you'll make your decision based on that. You'll stay behind when maybe you *should* be moving forward...to London."

"I thought you wanted Jack to settle down," Meg said wryly. "Grandkids and the whole bit."

"Don't get me wrong," Helen answered. "If Jack ever did get married, I'd want you to be his choice. Couldn't think of anything I'd like more. But, Meg, the truth is, I think you should be very careful about making decisions based on a man. Even if that man happens to be my son. Perhaps especially if he's my son.''

Meg had recently sensed a tension whenever Helen spoke about Jack. She wondered how the two of them had been getting along. Right now Jack was out taking his run; it was clear that he felt stifled in his mother's apartment. Maybe they were both getting on each other's nerves. Meg didn't want to be caught between them.

''When I make my decision, I won't let Jack be part of the equation,'' she said, wondering if she was trying to convince herself or Helen. But Helen was already speaking, obviously intent on her own train of thought.

''Before I met Jack's father, I had such plans,'' she recalled. ''Ambitious plans. I'd decided I was going to take the business world by storm. And then, well, I took one look at Andrew Elliott, and that was it for me. Somehow, before I quite knew how it had happened, his plans seemed much more important than mine. I did everything I could to help him succeed, and when he finally got his doctorate I was as proud as if I'd done it myself. To have him land such a prestigious teaching job—that made me proud, too. I was the perfect faculty wife, because that was what he needed from me. But when I started searching for something of my own…Andrew never understood that. It was always about what he needed in a wife—not about me.''

Meg remembered that Jack had used almost those exact words about his father: *It was always about what he needed....*

"When my son was born," Helen continued, "I wanted him to be different, more sensitive to the wishes of other people. Even back then I knew that my husband was too rigid, too lost in his own world. So I tried to make sure Jack *was* different. Unfortunately, I don't believe I succeeded."

Meg listened with unwilling fascination. These were private family matters, and she didn't feel she had any right to hear them. But Helen seemed to be letting out emotions long bottled up inside, and Meg didn't know how to stop her.

"My son," Helen said, "has turned out to be very much like his father. They're both stubborn, both convinced they know what's best—what's right. Oh, Jack rebelled against his dad, but you always rebel against the ones most like you. Over the years I've seen the similarities grow more pronounced. The same mannerisms...the same drive. Jack is exactly like his father when it comes to accomplishing a goal. When Jack decided he was going to go back to school and make something of his life, he didn't let anything get in the way."

"That's a good quality," Meg said gently.

"Meg, I care for my son a great deal, and I do see his good qualities. But I also see the inflexibility in him that's so much like Andrew's. I'm afraid Jack won't bend for anyone. And that means, if you *do* love him, you'll have to bend to him. I wouldn't want that for you. It's something I did for too many years."

Meg didn't know how to answer. Helen's words struck too close to her fears. But Helen seemed to be feeling guilty about her criticism of Jack.

"I do care about my son," she repeated. "In fact, I have an idea for him. You know that tomorrow is his birthday, don't you?"

Meg was disconcerted. "Actually, I didn't know. He failed to mention it." When she gave the matter more consideration, however, she realized it was only in keeping with Jack. A man whose ex-girlfriend had accused him of being old wouldn't be the type to mention birthdays.

"It's the big forty," said Helen. "An occasion worth noting—so I've decided to throw Jack a party. A surprise party, to be exact."

"Hmm." Meg tried to be as noncommittal as possible, but Helen was already rushing on.

"You'll help me, won't you, Meg?"

"Hmm." Another attempt at being noncommittal, but then—for Jack's sake—she had to speak her mind. "It's a nice idea, Helen, but I don't think Jack will appreciate it."

"Why on earth not?"

"Well—it is the big 4-0," Meg said. "Some people don't like to be reminded they've reached a watershed. Trust me, Jack is one of those people. And New York isn't really his town. It's not as if he's back in Maine, where he can go to Lou's Bar with the guys and toss down a few beers.''

''You know about Lou's?'' Helen asked skeptically. ''That old dive?''

''Jack did mention it in passing. But, anyway, who could you invite in New York? His friends aren't here.''

Helen had accused her ex-husband and son of being stubborn, but she had an obstinate expression on her own face.

''Jack has been questioning my judgment of late. I certainly hope you're not doing the same thing. My judgment is perfectly sound, no matter what anyone else thinks.''

''Helen, I'm just saying—''

''I'm going to do it,'' Helen stated flatly. ''I'm going to throw a party for my son, whether or not he likes it. That's what families do. They celebrate birthdays and other special occasions. Jack and I are family...whether or not he likes it.''

Meg had the distinct impression she wouldn't be able to talk Helen out of this. She also had the impression there was a whole lot more to this than a simple birthday party. A battle of some kind was going on between mother and son. And Meg, through no wish of her own, seemed to be stuck somewhere in the middle.

JACK WAS FORTY YEARS OLD and feeling every day of it. It was no help that he'd walked into his mother's apartment twenty minutes ago, and a gaggle of strangers had yelled "Surprise!"

Okay, maybe they hadn't all been strangers. Meg had been there, as well as her friends Kathy and Lena. Not to mention her brother Shaun, a guy who appeared nice enough but who seemed as uncomfortable as Jack at this party. Jack had also recognized the neighbor from across the hall and Claudia the super. But otherwise, he had just heard "happy birthday" from twenty people he'd probably never see again.

Now, as he wandered through the apartment, feeling out of sorts, several of the party guests introduced themselves to him. Friends of his mother's, some of her co-workers, other residents of the building. Helen herself held court on the sofa, crutches and wheelchair determinedly out of sight. The entire place was festooned with streamers and balloons, all very festive. Too bad Jack wasn't in a festive mood.

He was looking for Meg, and at last he found her. She was in the pantry, grabbing more soft drinks from the cooler. When he came through the door, she glanced over her shoulder at him.

"Before you say anything," she warned, "you have to know that I tried to talk her out of it. I told her you'd hate the idea, but she wouldn't listen. When I could see I wasn't making any headway, I gave in. I helped organize the party."

"I don't see the jump in logic," Jack commented.

Meg looked a little defensive. "Helen's my friend.

She may be your mother, and she may be driving you crazy, but she *is* my friend.''

Jack stepped farther into the pantry, allowing the door to swing shut behind him. He leaned against the counter and studied Meg. She looked very pretty today in a slim skirt and a knit pullover. Her hair was slightly mussed, as if party organizing was starting to get the better of her. He took the sodas from her and put them on the counter.

''Something tells me you need a break,'' he said. ''Hell, I need a break, too.''

''Jack...your mother had good intentions. Maybe you could pretend you like the party.''

''Pretending,'' he said. ''You and I are good at that. So, are we engaged today?''

She flushed. ''Of course not. The last thing I need is for your mother to think we're engaged. Anyway, I told Kathy she could come as long as Gary didn't. I need a reprieve.''

''Reprieve. That's what I need when it comes to parties.'' His gaze traveled over her.

''Jack,'' she said sternly. ''You can't be getting any ideas. Not here.''

He always had ideas when it came to Meg. ''We could just keep a low profile. Hole up by the cooler. No one would miss us.''

''I can't,'' she insisted. ''I'm in charge of the party.'' She scooped up the sodas and slipped past him with a determined look, the door swinging shut behind her.

Meg, it seemed, had helped to orchestrate everything. The drinks, the decorations, the music playing in the background...the birthday cake. How could Jack have thought he'd escape a birthday cake? It was chocolate, with four candles—one for each decade. By the time you hit forty, you had to start counting by decades. There'd be too many candles otherwise.

Meg carried the cake into the living room. Everyone crowded in so he could blow out the candles. Just what he needed.

"Make a wish...make a wish!" he heard. He had only one wish—for this damn party to go away. But his mother sat there, wearing a new dress that Meg had bought for her. Helen looked small and frail. She also looked defiant, as if daring Jack to gripe about the party. So he just smiled and blew out the four candles and said yes, he'd made a wish.

Later, after he'd wandered around the apartment some more and talked to Meg's brother a little, he found Meg again. She was peering into the living room, her expression hopeful.

"Something up?" Jack asked.

"The neighbor man's sitting there," Meg said sotto voce. "Talking to your mother."

"So this isn't just a party. It's a matchmaking endeavor."

Meg prodded him into the hall. "I figured why waste an opportunity. Having a group of people around, that's the best time to break the ice. The time

I arranged for Mr. Cooper and your mother to be alone in the apartment, it didn't work, believe me, so I had to try something new.''

"You mean you've done this before?"

Her expression grew wary. "Jack, I'm sure you have other things to worry about besides your mother's romantic life. I certainly didn't get involved by choice. She told me about Mr. Cooper, things snowballed and…''

"And now you're matchmaking,'' he said.

"Just facilitating,'' she muttered. "Time to open your birthday presents, Jack.''

Time to take evasive action, was the way he looked at it. Holding Meg's hand, he drew her out of the apartment and up to the rooftop garden. The sun was beginning to set, turning the roses to red and gold flame.

"Don't you want to know what I got you for your birthday?'' Meg asked.

"You bought me a present?''

"It *is* your birthday,'' she reminded him.

"So what did you get me?''

"You have to wait and open it,'' she teased. "Let's go back down, and you can open the other presents, too.''

Still holding her hand, he went to the brick planter and had her sit beside him. "I'm starting to think of this as our spot,'' he said. "This is where we got engaged.''

"Very funny, Jack.''

"You asked me for a favor, Meg. Now I have one to ask of you. It only seems fair."

She gave him a suspicious glance. "If I'd known there were strings attached..."

"I'm going back to Maine," he said. "I'm leaving tomorrow."

He felt her stiffen beside him. She didn't say anything for a long moment. When finally she did speak, her voice was carefully expressionless. "I suppose it's inevitable. Your life isn't really here in New York."

"No, it's not," he agreed. "I've already stayed away too long. But I'm asking you to come with me."

She turned her head to gaze at him in the waning light. "To Maine?" she asked incredulously.

"Only for a few days," he said. "I need your advice on something. And the only way to get it is to have you go with me."

"What advice?"

"I could explain it right now," he said, "but I'd rather you didn't have any preconceptions."

Meg looked exasperated. "Jack, you're leaving tomorrow? And just like that, you want me to drop everything and go with you? Without even knowing why I'm going?"

"This is something for which I need a fresh opinion," he said.

"So fresh you can't tell me anything about it?"

"Not beforehand. Trust me on this, Meg."

"I can't drop everything on the spur of the moment," she argued.

"Can't...or won't?"

"My friends are in town. And Shaun, too."

"Your friends are pretty much occupied. And your brother told me he's decided to fly back to Oklahoma tomorrow."

"Oh." This seemed to give her something to think about. He saw disappointment and worry cross her face. Obviously she cared a lot about her brother.

Meg sighed, pushing her hair away from her face. "Going to Maine with you—it's just not a good idea."

"I'm asking you to come with me as something of a business consultant," he said.

"So now it's business," she murmured.

"Yeah...something like that."

"Jack, you're being more mysterious than ever," she objected. "I don't like mysteries."

"You like surprises," he said. "You won't tell me what you got me for my birthday—that's a surprise."

She appeared to think this over, and then she gave a shrug. "I'll tell you what your gift is. I got you a baseball cap to wear with your in-line skates."

"It sounds great," he said.

"No, it doesn't. It sounds silly now. But at the time, well, at the time it seemed like the perfect gift for somebody *young*. And I do happen to think you're young, Jack."

"Thanks."

"Okay, I've spilled the beans. Now it's your turn."

"Meg," he said, "I still can't tell you why I want you to come to Maine. Just…come."

She stood and moved away from him across the rooftop. "I'll admit that I'm curious. But I can't do it, Jack."

He watched her go all the way to the door leading downward. He saw her open it, begin to step through. But then she stopped. She bowed her head a little.

"Dammit, Jack," she said, almost under her breath.

He went to her. "It's only a few days, Meg."

She raised her head and looked at him. "What time are we leaving?" she asked grouchily.

"Probably around ten. Unless you need a more convenient time."

"Oh, hell," she said. "Ten o'clock is fine." And then, without waiting for him, she disappeared through the door.

LENA SPRAWLED across Meg's bed, propping her head on her arms. "My, my," she said. "Going away for the weekend with Mr. Gorgeous. Things are moving fast, don't you think?"

Meg folded a shirt and put it in her suitcase. "I should have asked Jack how cold it is in Maine this time of year. Perhaps I'll need a sweater."

Lena held up her left hand and turned it this way and that, frowning as she studied the sparkle of her diamond. "Sometimes I wonder," she murmured.

"Sometimes Nathan almost seems *too* perfect. Is he putting on a front? I mean, *no one's* perfect...."

"Gee, maybe you'd need to know a man more than a week before you make any rash judgments."

Lena sat up. "Let's get back to you and Mr. Gorgeous. Are you sure you're ready for a sleep-over trip? It's a big step in a relationship, and I keep telling you to meet other men."

"And I keep trying to explain that this is not what you think. Jack wants to consult me about...about something. And it's only for a few days. We leave tomorrow. I come back on Sunday. I'll hardly be gone at all."

"The weekend away," intoned Lena. "The sleep-over. Call it what you want, we're talking major stuff."

Meg crammed some wool socks into a corner of her suitcase. "There are several good reasons for me to be taking this trip," she said. "First, it's advisable for me to take some time off work, especially when I have such an important decision coming up about my career. Leaving the city for a few days will give me some perspective, I'm sure. And if Jack has a favor to ask of me, it *is* only fair. He did that ridiculous favor for me."

"He did it very well," agreed Lena. "But I'll tell you why you're really going on this trip with Jack. You're going because you're scared to death that you're falling in love with him, and you're hoping that Maine will bring you to your senses. You're hoping that you'll see him in his natural setting, and you won't like either the man or Maine. But deep down you know there's a possibility you'll love Maine…and the man. You have to find out, one way or the other. And boy, does it scare you.''

Meg stood still in the middle of the room, clutching her best pair of jeans. ''Lena, that's the most absurd thing I ever heard—''

''Is it?'' Lena asked, sprawling on the bed again. ''Or is it the simple truth?''

Meg tossed the jeans into her suitcase, slapped the lid shut and zipped it up. ''I already know how I feel about Jack. He's a very nice man. An extremely nice man. But we don't have anything in common.''

''Honey, *nice* is too tame a word for Jack Elliott. You're going to be alone for an entire weekend with a man who's a whole lot more than nice, and I wonder how you're going to handle it.''

Meg didn't have a chance to argue because Kathy came into the room just then. Her face was glowing, and she almost seemed to be floating as she gave a little whirl.

''I have wonderful news,'' she said dreamily. ''The most wonderful news you can ever imagine. Meg, our plan worked. It really did. Because, you see…it's finally happened.''

''Spit it out, Kathy,'' Lena said inelegantly.

Kathy gave a radiant smile. ''I love both of you. I love the entire world. Because…Gary proposed!''

CHAPTER THIRTEEN

EARLY NEXT MORNING, Meg took a cab with her brother to the airport. She stood beside him as he checked his luggage, and then she walked down the concourse with him.

"I'm going to miss you, Shaun."

"I'm going to miss you, too, Meggie."

"Have you decided what you're going to do?"

"Hell, no," Shaun said.

It didn't sound promising. Meg wished she could say something—anything—to help. But she didn't seem to be too good at that.

"I hope…I just hope everything works out," she said.

"I don't know if it will."

It was time to say goodbye. Meg gave Shaun a fierce hug. He hugged her back. And then he went on alone.

SHORTLY AFTER TEN, Meg sat beside Jack in his rugged four-wheel drive. He'd been garaging the vehicle while in New York, and now it seemed out of place as they inched their way along the congested streets of the city. Meg had a suspicion Jack would be a lot happier driving along a forested mountainside or over a rutted track. He tapped his fingers on the steering wheel as traffic stalled yet again.

"I haven't owned a car since coming to New York," Meg told him. "It would be more of a nuisance than anything else."

"Can't imagine living someplace where I didn't get behind the wheel," Jack said.

"We really are different, you and I."

He glanced at her. "I have a feeling you're going to keep reminding me of that. Meg, I didn't ask you to come with me so I could convert you to the Maine life-style."

She gazed straight ahead. "No danger of that. I'm sure Maine is a wonderful place...to visit."

"I won't try to convince you otherwise."

The trip was only for a few days, Meg reminded herself. Jack wanted her advice on something, that was all. So why did she feel so nervous? Why did she feel as if she was leaving behind the world she knew for uncharted territory?

Her gaze strayed to Jack. "I liked the beard," she said. "I'm sorry you got rid of it."

He rubbed his jaw. "It was just an experiment."

"Did it make you feel older...or younger?"

He grimaced slightly. "Let's just say it didn't provide me with any answers."

Jack looked good clean-shaven or not, but Meg had truly liked that shadow of beard. "You don't have to wear the cap," she said.

He was, indeed, wearing her birthday present—the baseball cap that was supposed to go with his skates. Secretly, she knew that she'd also chosen the cap because its sea-blue color reminded her of his eyes.

"It suits me," he said.

She liked the way the cap sat on his head so comfortably, so attractively, as if he'd owned it for a long time instead of one day. At last Meg forced herself to stop admiring Jack, and she stared out the windshield again.

"Gary proposed to Kathy," she told him. "It happened last night."

"No kidding."

"It's awful," Meg said.

"I thought it's exactly what you wanted for your friend."

Meg sighed. "It's exactly what Kathy wanted. It appears you and I really did have an effect on Gary. He seems to think that if we can be engaged and not lose our independence, he can try it, too."

Traffic began to creep forward, and Jack went from neutral to first. "So everything's worked out," he said. "Why aren't you glad?"

"Because it's all based on a lie, Jack! Of course we seemed like two people who hadn't given up our independence. That's because we were only pretending. Gary proposed on the basis of a misconception."

"Give the guy more credit," Jack said. "He must have been thinking about it, anyway."

"Maybe. Kathy says that all he needed was a little

nudge in the right direction, and that's what we provided. But I still don't feel good about it. If I'm going to provide a nudge, I'd like it to be a legitimate nudge. I let Kathy talk me into it because *she* wanted it so much. Frankly, I didn't expect Gary to propose. I thought he was a die-hard case.''

"Too late now," Jack said.

"None of this bothers you?"

At last the traffic moved freely, and he accelerated. "I'll tell you something, Meg. At first our 'engagement' seemed like nothing more than a joke. But then I realized you and I were doing a surprisingly good job of convincing other people. It occurred to me that maybe there are some things you shouldn't joke about.''

Meg nodded. "I agree completely. Now we'll have to wait a decent interval, and then get... disengaged.''

"So we're going to break up," Jack said. "Too bad. I was just getting used to the idea of us.''

She gave him a sharp glance. "I thought you weren't going to joke about this anymore.''

"I'm serious. We're talking all sorts of complications here. What'll Gary do when he finds out we couldn't make it last? Maybe he'll have second thoughts.''

"For crying out loud," Meg said. "This whole thing is way out of control. I never expected Gary to propose, but now that he has, it'll just have to be because he loves Kathy. He can't go around making decisions based on what other people do.''

"It's looking more and more like that's exactly what he does.''

"Jack,'' Meg said. "You're not helping.''

"I'm just saying we shouldn't be so quick to break up. We don't know what kind of effect it will have.''

"The pretending's over,'' she said. "Gary and Kathy are going back to Oklahoma next week. She can give him the news of our split when *she* thinks the time is right.''

"Splitting up,'' Jack murmured. "A real shame.''

"You're hopeless,'' Meg grumbled.

It took some time, but at last they were out of the city and headed northeast. The miles rolled by…an hour passed, then another. They stopped to buy snacks and a few sandwiches, but Meg refused Jack's offer for a more substantial lunch.

"Let's just keep going,'' she said.

"You figure if we hurry up and get there, the visit will be over faster. Relax, Meg. A little time in Maine isn't going to hurt you.''

She honestly tried to relax, but Jack was right—she wanted to hurry up and get it over with. But when they reached Boston, Jack refused to do any more hurrying.

"We're stopping for a very late lunch,'' he said. "A real lunch. Whether or not you say you're hungry.''

In downtown Boston, they found themselves in another traffic jam. This time, however, Jack didn't seem to mind. Now that they were officially in New England, a subtle tension seemed to have left him. He leaned back more comfortably in his seat, his hands easy on the wheel. Meg didn't think it was just him. There was a different energy in Boston than in New York. The drivers here didn't seem as tense or worked up. When the traffic moved again, cars drifted haphazardly, cheerfully in and out of lanes.

Jack took Meg to a restaurant in one of the old brick buildings of Quincy Market. Jack recommended the classic clam chowder, and Meg found she was hungry, after all. She and Jack sat across from each other, sharing a loaf of crusty bread with the chowder.

Meg studied Jack. "You really are a New Englander, aren't you? You belong here."

"Is that a diplomatic way of saying I'm a stick-in-the-mud?"

"No one would ever accuse you of that," she said. "There's nothing wrong with caring about a place so much that it's your one real home."

"The point being," he said, "that your real home is in New York—and mine is in Maine."

She wished it were that simple. "If I take the job in London, I'll have a new home to get used to."

"You haven't decided yet?" he asked.

"No, but I have to make up my mind this weekend. Monday's the deadline. I need to tell Mr. Riley by then, one way or the other."

Jack nodded, his expression carefully noncommittal. If he was disappointed at the thought she might be relocating all the way across the ocean, he didn't let on. What had Meg expected? That he'd ask her to stay? She didn't want that, surely. So why did she feel disappointment?

They lingered over dessert, cheesecake topped with fresh strawberries. But finally it was time to get on the road again.

"Ready for the main attraction?" Jack murmured.

She smiled a little at his play on words. "Ready as I'll ever be," she said. She just didn't know if she'd convinced herself.

IT WAS EARLY EVENING when Jack and Meg arrived in Cape Anne, Maine. As they drove through the town, diverse images drifted over Meg: shingled houses, a row of old shops on a cobbled street, a church spire gleaming in the late sun, boat masts rising from the harbor. And, beyond, the ocean spreading out dark and mysterious, seeming to go on forever.

"It's beautiful," Meg said. "Everything about this place is beautiful."

"Some people say we're too quaint," Jack told her.

"If that's the worst they can say..."

Jack took her to a hotel, a small, tidy building surrounded by fir trees. "I made a reservation for you here," he told her.

"Thank you," Meg said, suddenly feeling too formal.

"I didn't think you'd want to stay with me."

"We could have handled it. We're both adults."

"That's the problem," he murmured. They came to a stop in the parking lot.

She swung open her door and scrambled out. Inside the hotel, she found that Jack had already paid for the next few nights. He'd taken care of everything. In short order she was ensconced in her room, and Jack was preparing to leave.

"I'll let you get settled," he said. "I'll give you a couple of hours, and then I'll come back so we can go to dinner."

"And so you can show me whatever it is you want advice about," she reminded him.

He looked thoughtful, but then he shook his head. "Not tonight. Tomorrow will be soon enough."

"Jack—"

"See you in a few hours, Meg." And he was gone.

Left to herself, she glanced around. Jack had chosen well. The room had a deceptively simple appearance, pine floors, pine furniture, combined with touches of luxury: a plump comforter on the bed, original seascapes on the walls, deep-pile rugs scattered about. And, in the bathroom, a glorious old-fashioned tub with claw feet. Several moments later, Meg was immersed in hot water and a froth of bubbles. In her expert opinion, any hotel that provided bubble bath for its customers was first-rate.

Meg luxuriated in the tub, paying no attention to the passage of time. It was a novel feeling. Away from the Alexander, she had no business to attend to. Away from her apartment in New York, she was removed from her friends' rather turbulent romances. For tonight, at least, all she had to think about was herself...and Jack.

At last she emerged from the bath. She dressed in a cherry wool skirt and an embroidered tunic sweater; for all that it was spring, the night had a crisp edge. When Jack arrived to take her to dinner, he wore a herringbone sports jacket that she hadn't seen before. It struck her how much of his life she hadn't seen. Only now, in Maine, was she beginning to catch glimpses. His hair was slightly damp, as if from the shower. He looked more handsome than ever, and Meg couldn't resist when he took her hand and drew her toward him.

"Nice perfume," he murmured.

"It's the bath bubbles..."

"Wish I'd been here."

Meg felt a warmth gathering deep inside her. The look Jack gave her was outrageously sexy, but then he escorted her from the hotel room. He took her to a restaurant that fronted the ocean. Lights shimmered on the dark water as they savored grilled salmon, romaine salad with sherry vinaigrette and cranberry torte.

Meg took a sip of white wine and gazed out the window at the ocean. "It doesn't seem real," she said. "It's too beautiful for that. If I didn't know better, I'd say that you conjured up the scenery to bewitch me."

"All scenery courtesy of Maine," he said. "I didn't have a thing to do with it."

"When you did all that traveling, weren't you homesick for this town?"

"Actually, no," he said. "I was too busy back then just trying to get away. I wanted to see other places. I thought they'd be different, more exciting. Less narrow." He paused. "I liked traveling, and I liked a lot of what I saw. But it gave me perspective. I realized no place was any more exciting than my hometown. Excitement being a subjective term, that is."

"I always thought excitement meant New York," Meg said.

"And now?"

She sipped more wine. "I'm still a city girl, Jack. Just because I can appreciate a little natural beauty doesn't change that."

"I don't know," he remarked. "I think New England is already working its magic on you. You're changing—giving up control. Do you realize that already today you've let me order twice for you?"

She set down her glass. "I don't think so..." But it was true. She'd been drifting today. In Boston she'd simply asked Jack what was good on the menu and let it go at that. She'd done the same thing here.

Very distinctly, she saw the amusement in Jack's eyes.

"You'd better watch out," he said. "Who knows what you'll give up next."

"I'm not that paranoid about losing my independence."

"Yes," he said, "you are. But that's what I like about you. You're the most independent woman I've ever met—and you're damn good at being independent, too."

She lifted her eyebrows. "I suppose that's a compliment."

"It is."

She thought it over. "You know what you really like about me? The fact that I don't want a commitment from you, not an engagement ring, not anything else."

The amusement was gone, replaced by a faintly disgruntled look. "Are you saying that I see commitment…marriage, and all the rest of it…as one more sign of getting older?"

She leaned back in her chair, studying him. "No, you're the one who said that. Is that how you really feel?"

"Hell, maybe it's true." He didn't sound too happy about it. "Why else did I get involved with someone like Kendra? Someone almost a decade younger than me. Someone who ran at even the mention of commitment."

"Maybe you're glad she ran."

"Maybe." Jack still didn't sound happy.

A short time later he took her back to the hotel. He escorted her to her door.

"Well," she said. "Thank you, Jack...for a lovely night." She knew she sounded way too formal, and that only made her feel silly. Jack smiled a little. He framed her face in his hands and gave her a long, breathtaking kiss. Then he stepped back.

"I'm not going to ask if I can come in. I want to come in...but I'm not asking."

Once again he left her. Meg closed the door and leaned against it, battling an ache of longing. All or nothing, they'd agreed. And so, between them, it was still nothing.

"THIS IS WHAT I wanted to show you," Jack said the next morning.

He'd brought her to the outskirts of town, to a house that sat on its own bluff above the ocean. It wasn't just any house, though. It was an utterly charming New Englander on a grand scale, rambling along the cliffside, shingles weathered by years of salt spray. It had a steep sloped roof with fanciful carved trim all along the gables, and dormer windows poking out. There were bay windows, too, on the bottom floor, and a long, meandering porch that looked out to sea.

"Jack," Meg said, "this place is practically a mansion." She gave him an inquiring glance.

"I'll tell you all about it," he said, "as soon as you've had a look inside."

The house was so large that a tour took quite some time. Each room had its own charm, but overall the house gave Meg a sense of spaciousness and light. It had something to do with the wealth of windows, the high ceilings...even the emptiness. There wasn't a stick of furniture anywhere, and it appeared that no one had lived here in a while. But Meg suspected that even if the house were filled with objects and clutter, it would still afford that sense of airiness—a sense of opening itself to sky and ocean.

Meg went upstairs and downstairs with Jack, poking into every corner, opening cupboards, discovering nooks. At last, in one of the spacious rooms, she propped herself on a window seat. "Okay, Jack," she said. "You really have my curiosity going. Why did you bring me here?"

He paced. "This is the house where I grew up," he told her.

"No kidding...it's a dream of a place."

"Didn't seem so at the time. This is where I learned to resent my dad. This is where I watched my parents grow further and further apart. Moving out at eighteen was one of the best days of my life."

"It's a shame for a house like this to have bad memories," Meg said. "It deserves better. But, Jack, you still haven't explained why you brought me here."

He kept on pacing, as if he still didn't know how

to be comfortable in his childhood home. "I'm getting to it," he said. "When my parents divorced five years ago, neither one of them wanted to go on living here. Dad moved into the center of town, closer to campus, and my mother set out for New York. But they've never gotten around to selling this house. I guess they've delayed because of the possibility I might want it someday. I haven't wanted it…so it's just been sitting here, in limbo."

"A shame," Meg murmured again.

"This is where I need your advice," Jack said. "Without going into all the details, my mother's finances have taken a nosedive. She had a generous divorce settlement, but she's not the most experienced investor in the world…you get the picture. She's also near retirement age—and she also has a lot of pride. I've been looking around for a way I could help her get into a better position but let her keep that pride. So I've been wondering if this place could be turned into a moneymaking operation for her…a bed-and-breakfast, perhaps."

Meg considered the idea. "And you want my professional opinion."

"Exactly. Look, Meg, I wasn't trying to be obscure. I wanted you to see the house before you had any preconceptions about it."

"That was probably smart," she conceded. "I get the feeling you want more from me than 'Oh, wouldn't that be nice.'"

"Like you said, I need a professional opinion. And

not just from anyone. Yours is the one I want. You
know the hotel business, probably better than anyone. And there's something else. My mother trusts
you—she'll listen to what you have to say. She'll
listen a lot better than to me.''

Meg stood and gave the room a circuit. ''Jack, *I'm*
not trying to be obscure. But if you want a real opinion—a real idea whether or not this idea is econom-
ically feasible—it's going to take me a little time.''

''Take all you want,'' he said.

She got her purse and pulled out the pad she always kept with her for ''to do'' lists and such. She
jotted down a few things, then glanced at Jack. ''I'm
glad you asked me to consider this. It sounds like
fun. And if it'll help your mother, that's a bonus.''

''I'm glad you came here with me,'' he said.

They gazed at each other. There was a stillness in
the air, a sense of waiting. Meg knew, all too deeply,
all too well, what she waited for. It was always like
this when she was with him....

She turned quickly, breaking the moment. ''I
should get busy,'' she said. ''When you're coming
up with a business prospectus, there's a lot to do.''

''Still rushing,'' he told her. ''We have time.'' He
clasped her hand in his and led her out of the house.
They went down a rough pathway and came out
upon a rocky cove. There was a slender curve of
beach…just enough to make Meg want to slip off
her shoes and go wading.

She gave in to the impulse. She sat down in the

sand to untie her sneakers and roll up her jeans. Jack did the same with his hiking boots and jeans. And then, hand in hand, they dipped their toes in the water. It was bracing cold.

"Invigorating," Meg said through chattering teeth.

"There's another way to enjoy the water," he told her. He led her scrambling over rocks and to another stretch of beach. Here there was a rustic pier, with a trim white sailboat tethered at the end of it.

"Oh, my," said Meg. "Yours…?"

"Mine."

They climbed aboard. Jack raised the sails and loosened the mooring lines, and soon the ocean waves rocked against the boat as it headed out. The boat had a cabin fashioned of dark, satiny wood, but Meg liked being out in the open with the salt breeze riffling through her hair. She stretched out her legs, flexed her bare toes.

"Jack," she said, sighing, "if I had a sailboat, I don't think I'd do anything else with my life. I'd just…sail."

"I do a lot of that," he said, his hands resting on the helm. He looked contented. The sails billowed, welcoming the breeze.

"I'm learning more and more about you," Meg said. "You're a sailor…what else?"

"I don't have too many more surprises up my sleeve."

But it seemed he did. Before long, he took the boat

skimming toward another pier, over which presided an old lighthouse built of granite.

"Beautiful," Meg said under her breath. "Just like everything else."

The lighthouse rose above them, an austere beacon. In contrast, the sky shone a brilliant blue, drenched with sunlight. The ocean was a deeper blue.

"Beautiful," was all Meg could say again. She looked at Jack, and from the expression in his eyes she knew he wanted her to be captivated. Despite all disclaimers, he wanted her to love this place. To care about it.

She was beginning to care. About some things, she was beginning to care all too much.

CHAPTER FOURTEEN

WEBSTER COLLEGE OF MAINE was a very exclusive institution that proudly dated from the early 1800s. As Jack walked across the campus quad with Meg, he reflected on how much of his youth had been spent resenting not only his father, but this college, as well. As a high-school kid, he'd sworn that he would never attend Webster, much less join one of its elitist fraternities. And just to make sure the college would never have him, he'd tried as hard as he could to get lousy grades. Sometimes failing in school had been more work than actually succeeding.

"You're deep in thought," Meg said.

He gestured at the venerable buildings of ancient brick, and the equally venerable oaks and birch trees. "From the time I was a kindergartner, I heard about my dad's plan that I'd attend Webster. It was all laid out. I was supposed to get my bachelor's here, and then move on to Harvard for graduate school. My father told me history would be the best major for me—only slightly less worthy than philosophy. If I decided on law, well, that would be tolerated, as long as I went to Harvard."

"Somehow," said Meg, "I get the feeling you never did go to Harvard."

"It became a point of honor not even to try. I drove my dad nuts, telling him how I was going to end up owning a lobster boat or working construction."

"Jack," Meg said, "do you ever wonder what you would have ended up doing if you *hadn't* been so hell-bent on rebelling?"

He gave a wry grimace. "Yeah, I wonder that all the time lately. I'm not sorry I built my own company—I'll never be sorry about that—but I can't help asking myself if it would've been my first choice under other circumstances."

Meg didn't answer, and they walked along in silence for a few moments. For the first time he could remember, he enjoyed being on this campus, and he figured it had to do with Meg's presence. He glanced at her. He'd enjoyed showing her the family house this morning, and taking her for a boat ride. He liked, quite simply, having her on his turf now. She didn't seem to mind, either. She looked relaxed and comfortable walking beside him. She also looked exceptionally pretty, her hair tousled by the breeze and her cheeks pink from the coolness of the afternoon. He took her hand, and he was pleased when she didn't pull away from him.

They reached the building where the philosophy department was housed, and where Jack's father had had an office for more than thirty years. Inside, Jack

led Meg along a corridor where every sight was
overly familiar. The same posters as always lined the
walls, announcing conferences that had come and
gone years ago. The tile floor was immaculately
clean, as usual, and smelled faintly of lemon polish—
as usual.

The door of his father's office was open. It always
was. Dr. Andrew Elliott prided himself on being ac-
cessible to his students at all times. He looked down
on those faculty members who tried to barricade
themselves behind closed doors or piles of books.
His desk was always clear so that he would have a
good view of whatever nervous or respectful student
sat on the other side.

Now Jack stepped into the office. "Hello, Dad,"
he said.

Andrew glanced up from the computer where he'd
been tapping away. "Jack," he said, a note of what
seemed genuine welcome in his voice. Jack had
learned long ago that was simply his father's manner...polite, urbane, welcoming...even when speaking to the son he considered a disappointment.

Jack introduced Meg, and Andrew put on all the
charm that made him so well liked. He shook hands
with Meg, asked her about New York, effortlessly
seeming to focus all his attention on her. Jack
watched the two of them, and he could see Meg being charmed. She smiled at Andrew Elliott, and no
doubt found the old guy delightful. It probably didn't
hurt that Andrew looked the part of the quintessential

college professor. He had untidy salt-and-pepper hair and wore horn-rimmed glasses so unfashionable they set a style all their own. The nubby jacket hanging over his chair back was frayed from years of use; it was often the only protection he wore against the brisk New England weather, as if braving the elements were the credo of a philosophy teacher.

Meg chatted with Andrew for another moment or two, then gave Jack a perceptive glance. "I imagine the two of you have things to discuss," she said. "I'll be outside enjoying the campus." With this graceful excuse, she made her exit. Jack was sorry to see her go. It was true he needed to talk to his father, but he wasn't looking forward to it.

"Have a seat, Jack," Andrew said. The two of them settled down, the desk between them. "Nice young woman, this Meg Danley. A vast improvement over your last friend. Kimberley, was that her name?"

"Kendra," said Jack.

"Yes, well, I hope we see more of Meg."

Jack supposed this was Andrew's attempt at father-and-son talk.

"I'm not seeing Meg," he said. "Not the way you think."

"Hmm. Sorry to hear that. How was New York?"

"Fine," said Jack.

"And your mother. How is she doing?"

"Mending, but not as fast as she'd like."

"She'll be better soon, I'm sure," said Andrew. "She's a trouper."

It was a facile comment, and Jack had to resist the urge to grit his teeth. His father was determined to keep this a superficial conversation, but Jack had other things on his mind.

"The reason I'm here," he said, "is because I have a business proposition for you. I want to buy out your share of the house."

Andrew looked mildly interested. "The family homestead...you actually want to live there?"

"No. I'm thinking about turning the place into a moneymaking operation. A bed-and-breakfast. The income would help support Mom."

Andrew didn't say anything at first, merely settled back with a contemplative expression. From long experience, Jack knew exactly what was going through his father's mind. Andrew Elliott was wondering how this affected *him*. Not anyone else...just himself. Jack had long ago realized the source of his father's self-absorption: all his life Andrew Elliott had been told what a brilliant mind he had. He'd been told how special that made him. He'd gained entrance to the best schools, won praise from his most prestigious peers. Perhaps it was no surprise that he'd come to believe so firmly in his own importance.

"Well," he said at last. "Interesting proposition. Something your mother came up with?"

"My idea. I brought Meg up here to look into it

and give me some advice. If she thinks it's a good idea, then I'll go ahead.''

Andrew laced his hands over his stomach, a deceptively relaxed pose. ''You'd only be doing this if you thought your mother needed the money. But she shouldn't need any. She has a decent job, from what I gather. And the divorce settlement…let's just say I wasn't petty.''

Andrew Elliott might be a self-involved person, but he'd behaved commendably throughout the divorce proceedings. He'd been more than generous. It was also a fact that he tended to mention on a regular basis to Jack, but no matter. It was the truth.

''I'm thinking over the long term,'' Jack explained. ''Mom hasn't worked long enough to have the greatest retirement package. She will have to retire at some point, and when that happens, she could use the extra income.''

''The extra income should come from the money I gave her. Unless she no longer has that money. What did she do with it, Jack?'' Only now did Andrew betray even a hint of annoyance.

Jack didn't want to discuss his mother's financial problems—not with his father, that was for sure.

''You'd have to ask her,'' he said.

''Your mother and I don't call each other up to chat. Especially not about finances.''

''Maybe it's time the two of you did talk,'' Jack said. ''Maybe you could resolve whatever's left between you.''

"There's nothing left," said Andrew.

Nothing but resentment and bitterness. Jack, however, didn't say the words out loud. Instead, he went back to the subject at hand.

"All you have to do," he said, "is sell me your share of the house. I'll take it from there."

An odd expression crossed his father's face, one Jack couldn't define.

"I'll have to think about it," Andrew said. "I'm not sure I like the idea."

"You have other plans for the house?" Jack asked.

"I have to think about it, that's all." By now Andrew sounded genuinely irritated.

Jack stood. "We can talk about it in a couple of days."

Andrew turned toward his computer. "I'm under deadline," he said. "I'll need more than a couple of days to finish this article."

Jack knew how deadlines went in the academic world. They weren't exactly urgent. His father was trying to put him off, for whatever reason. He hadn't expected this. He'd thought he could count on Andrew's generosity, at least.

Andrew was already tapping away again at the keyboard, clearly dismissing Jack. Not that Jack was offended. This was something he'd grown accustomed to over the years. He knew that the brilliant Andrew Elliott had hoped for a different type of family: a wife content to live in his shadow, a son who would follow in his footsteps. Instead, he'd ended up with an ex-wife who'd squandered his money and a son who'd gone into construction. Andrew's solution, more often than not, was to dismiss Jack. He'd already dismissed Helen.

"See you later, Dad," Jack said now, his voice expressionless.

"See you, Jack," Andrew said without glancing up. And Jack left his father to his brilliant thoughts.

MEG WANDERED across the campus lawns, enjoying the architecture that surrounded her. The buildings had obviously been constructed before the days of Victorian excess. One had a bell tower, but otherwise their simplicity was striking and truly ageless.

The students were something else again. They strolled or hurried along with book bags slung over their shoulders, looking very young to Meg. She thought back to her own college days. They seemed so long ago now. She couldn't imagine being that young—or that naive—again.

Meg saw Jack coming toward her across the quadrangle, and she compared him with the students all around her. Jack was virile, mature...a man. The college boys were just that—boys. Meg could have sworn she saw a few coeds give Jack an appreciative glance. She didn't blame them. She was giving him an admiring glance of her own. But then, as he drew nearer, she noted the tension in his features. She surmised that the meeting with his father hadn't gone all that well.

He didn't say anything when he reached her. They walked back in silence to the parking lot where Jack had left the four-wheel drive. A few moments later Meg climbed into the passenger seat. Jack took the driver's side, revving the engine a little higher than necessary, punching the gas as he wheeled out of the lot.

"I figure you can either talk about it," said Meg, "or you can go on driving like demons are after you."

Jack grimaced. "There's not much to say. Except that my father and I just aren't on the same wavelength."

"I'm sorry," Meg said.

"You liked him, didn't you?" Jack asked. It seemed to her that his tone was deceptively casual. She still sensed the tension underneath.

"He's likable," she couldn't help saying.

"Yeah, that he is. Regularly voted most popular teacher on campus."

"Too bad he's not so popular with his son," Meg said lightly.

Jack eased up on the gas. "I thought I was done being angry with him. I thought there couldn't be any new wrinkles to our relationship. But now..."

Meg waited, not pressing him. She figured he'd say what he needed to. And at last Jack did go on.

"My father doesn't want to give up his share of

the house. I never realized it before, but that place represents everything that went wrong between him and my mother. When they first moved here, she didn't want to live so close to the ocean, or in a house that big and grandiose. But Dad won out, so that ended up being the house where I grew up. I don't believe my mother ever really felt at home there. She said the sound of the waves made her feel lonely…though I suspect it was life with my father that made her feel that way.''

It sounded sad to Meg. But perhaps no sadder than the story of her own parents.

''You'd think both your mother and father would want to get rid of the place,'' she said.

''Funny—they've let it slide for five years. Everything else about the divorce, they found a way to agree on. But never the house. Holding on to that house is like holding on to their bitterness.''

''Jack,'' Meg said, ''you haven't told your mother about this bed-and-breakfast idea, have you?''

''No,'' he admitted. ''I don't want her to have a chance to shoot it down too fast. I want her to realize that the house should finally be put to use. It needs to be something more than an empty reminder of a marriage that went bad.''

Meg shivered a little. ''How bleak. I have to agree with you. I think it's time the house became something more.''

''Does this mean you're endorsing my idea?''

''Emotionally, yes. On a business level, the jury's

still out. I'll have to do some thinking, then I'll get back to you.''

He smiled a little. ''You far prefer having our relationship on a business level, don't you?''

''I wouldn't complain if I were you,'' she said. ''You *did* ask for my professional opinion.''

Jack went on driving, and it didn't seem he had a particular destination in mind. Meg stared out the window. By now she'd seen enough to decide that the town had two focal points: the college and the harbor. Neighborhoods seemed to eddy and flow around the two. It made Meg want to explore, get to know the place even better.

''Jack,'' she said suddenly, ''do you realize something? You've brought me to your hometown. I've been here almost twenty-four hours, and yet you haven't shown me where you live. You haven't shown me where you work. Except for letting me meet your father, you're keeping everything personal and private away from me. *You're* the one who wants things on a so-called business level.''

He didn't say anything for a moment, just went on driving. She glanced at his profile, saw his abstracted look.

''Okay,'' he said at last, ''maybe you've got me. Maybe I haven't given you the full tour. And maybe it's time to change that.''

Only a short time later, Jack turned down a street shaded by maples. He pulled into the driveway of a saltbox-style house: two-stories with a double row of latticed windows and a brick chimney, the roof steeply sloping in back. Gazing at it, Meg felt as if she'd stepped back in time to early New England.

"It almost looks like the real thing," she observed.

"Just a very good copy. About a hundred years ago, this town went through the colonial revival craze. I reaped the benefits. I have a house that's a century old, made to look two centuries old."

"I've lived in apartments for so many years," Meg told him. "Maybe there's something to be said for houses."

Jack took her inside, and she saw that he'd made some effort to keep the colonial spirit: a pine settle in the living room, chairs with rush seats in the dining room, a chestnut cupboard in the kitchen. All in all, a few well-chosen heirlooms scattered among the modern conveniences.

"Taking stock?" Jack said after she'd made a thorough inspection of the ground floor.

"In a manner of speaking, yes," Meg answered. "And here's what I've discovered. You've inherited your mother's love of antiques, but I suspect you try to dampen it because you'd hate to think you're anything like her."

The discomfited look on his face told her she'd hit close to the mark.

"Jack," she said, "sometimes I tell you that we don't have anything in common, you and I. But I'm wrong about that. We're both trying as hard as we can not to be like our parents."

"Maybe a person can try too hard at that," he said.

"Or maybe not. Maybe it's good to do all we can to avoid their mistakes." She settled down in an oversize easy chair that was very comfortable. "I'll bet this is your favorite place to sit," she said.

"Still taking stock, Meg?"

She couldn't explain why she was doing it, exactly. But it did seem necessary to learn more about Jack. After all, she'd already made love with the man. Supposedly she'd even been "engaged" to him. But until now, she hadn't even seen where he lived.

"Let's just say I've worked up an appetite," she told him. "Time to go out for dinner—and this time it's my treat."

"We can rustle up something here," he said.

"Am I going to find out one of us has culinary talents, after all?" she asked.

"Meg," he dryly, "they invented the microwave for people like you and me."

He proceeded to prove it: baked potatoes and halibut courtesy of the microwave. And a salad that they collaborated on—butter lettuce, tomatoes, radishes and baby carrots. It was a good meal. They ate at the dining-room table while the late-evening sunlight refracted through the myriad panes of the windows. As night fell, it was chilly enough that Jack laid a fire on the stone hearth. Soon flames were crackling. The two of them sat on a sofa before the hearth, sharing a dessert of chocolate-peppermint ice cream.

Meg slipped off her shoes and curled her feet beneath her. "You do very well for yourself as a bachelor," she told Jack.

"Is that your way of telling me that I'm meant to be a bachelor?"

"Only you can decide that."

He gazed thoughtfully into the fire. "Sometimes this house feels empty. And maybe a little bit lonely."

"Is that why people get married?" Meg wondered. "Just to avoid loneliness?"

"Maybe it's as good a reason as any."

"I don't think so," she said. "Once you start getting desperate for a warm body next to yours, you can make all kinds of bad decisions."

"Do you picture yourself going through the rest of your life alone, Meg?"

"Just listen to the way you phrase that question," she scoffed. "How can a person be alone when she has wonderful friends and work she loves? You know, Jack, you're just as bad as everybody else. Assuming that a woman is somehow pathetic, somehow completely solitary unless she has a man in tow."

"Take it easy," he said. "I wasn't accusing you. It's a question I ask myself from time to time. Will I spend the rest of my life without…a partner. A mate."

Something about that last word evoked feelings in Meg she didn't want to examine too closely. She folded her arms against her chest and stared silently into the fire.

"Jack," she said at last, "if you decide you want a...partner, will you just go out looking for one?"

"I suppose some people do it that way," he replied. "It sounds logical. You socialize. You go places where you might meet people. You pick out the likely candidates. You eliminate the unlikely ones. And if you find someone compatible, you credit your own resourcefulness, along with some luck."

"Oh, yes, it sounds logical," she said. "And also very calculated."

"If you want something, shouldn't you go after it?"

She heard the amusement in his voice and knew he was probably only playing devil's advocate. Nonetheless, she felt inclined to argue.

"Love is different," she objected. "It's not like driving up to the fast-food restaurant and ordering what you want. It's something that takes you by surprise, I'd imagine. Besides, if you're purposely looking for it, you probably don't have enough of a life."

"So your solution," said Jack, "is to keep yourself so busy you don't have time to look."

"Or the inclination."

"What about kids?" he asked. "You don't want those someday?"

She sighed. "Another assumption—a woman has to want children or something's wrong with her."

"I don't think everyone has to have kids." Now he sounded completely serious. "I was just asking about you."

He'd posed a tough question. "I don't know, I really don't know. I like children, don't get me wrong. But having one of my own…that's scary."

"You'd have to be crazy not to be scared," he said.

"What about you? Do you want kids?"

He leaned forward and propped his elbows on his knees, staring into the fire as if it would hold the answers for him.

"I never thought about it much until lately," he said. "But now, sometimes I wonder. I guess turning forty will do that to a person."

"Do you think children would make you feel younger?" she asked.

He gave her a sardonic glance. "I'd have to come up with a better reason than that before I'd start reproducing."

"Just curious," Meg said. "Some parents talk about their children giving them gray hairs."

He seemed deep in thought, but then he spoke again. "I don't know whether kids would make me feel younger or older or somewhere in between. But certain aspects appeal. Sharing what you've learned in life. Taking time to help another human being grow up. Maybe influencing the process a little."

If this sounded appealing to Meg, she fought it. "I'm sure you'd make a good father," she said lightly. "I hope someday you get the chance. As for me, who knows if I'm even cut out for the maternal thing."

He studied her. "Interesting," he said. "We're sitting here, having a casual conversation about parenthood, and you immediately use it as proof that we're not compatible."

"Well, we're not compatible."

"Why are you working so hard to prove it, Meg? We were just kicking an idea around."

She stirred. "Seems to me you're pretty certain you want kids. And I'm not sure about it at all. Might as well get it out in the open."

"Right now I think you'd say anything to reassure yourself that you're not going to end up with me."

She slid her legs out from under her and planted her feet firmly on the floor. "I'm being honest with you, Jack. I really don't know about children."

"Right," he said. "Because having kids would make you seem too much like your mother. And that's the biggest fear you've ever had…the possibility you'll end up like her. Trapped. Unhappy."

Despite the truth of his words, Meg felt annoyed—so much so that she had to stand up and move away. "Let's just get out of here, Jack, okay? We don't need to talk about this anymore."

He gave her a long, considering look. She was afraid he wouldn't let up, but then he gave a shrug.

"Fair enough," he said. "We'll get out of here. Where to, Meg?"

She could tell him to take her back to the hotel. She could say good-night to him and be safe from his presence. That would be the sensible thing to do. But there was a part of Meg that wasn't feeling at all sensible tonight. That part took over, making sure she would prolong her time with Jack.

"Oh, hell," she said. "Take me to Lou's Bar."

"Lou's," he echoed, sounding bemused.

"Isn't that where you go and hang out with the guys, or whatever? The place your mother calls a dive. I'd like to see it—find out if she's right."

He gave a faint smile. "Lou's it is," he said.

CHAPTER FIFTEEN

LOU'S BAR, in Meg's opinion, was not a dive. Unassuming, yes. Low-key, yes. There were no frills, just a pool table in back and a dartboard and a long oak bar that Lou herself kept rigorously polished. Lou was a stately woman of fifty or so who seemed to cast a skeptical eye on every patron who entered her domain.

"She's awfully dour, isn't she?" Meg murmured to Jack as they sat down with their beers.

"We keep trying to get a smile out of her," Jack said. "One of these days it might actually happen—it's something for us to shoot for."

"We" turned out to be Jack and three of his buddies: Carl, Del and Perry. Carl owned a local plumbing outfit. Del was Jack's construction foreman and Perry was one of the crew. All three men greeted Meg heartily and didn't seem to mind sharing Jack with her. They made concerted, if somewhat labored, efforts to include her in the conversation. Meg sat back and sipped her beer. She enjoyed watching Jack with his friends. This was a side of him she hadn't seen before: the Jack who was one of the guys. She liked the way he got along so well with the men who worked for him. She liked the way he told jokes, even though he didn't do it very well—always stepping on his own punch line and then laughing about it afterward. She suspected he knew how to tell a joke just fine, but had more fun this way, inviting some ribbing from his friends. And, most of all, she liked the way he included her so effortlessly, so generously in his circle.

Before the night was over, Meg played a game of pool with Del. Carl challenged her to darts. She lost the pool game and won twice at the dartboard. Altogether she had a grand time, and she was sorry to leave.

Jack drove her back to the hotel, and they sat together in the parking lot.

"You have good friends," she said.

"Hey, you told me that anyone with good friends can't go wrong."

"I was right."

"They liked you," Jack said.

"Did they like Kendra?" she asked.

"Come to think of it, not much."

"I guess I should feel flattered I made the cut."

"They asked when you'd be back. They never ask that unless they like a person."

When she'd be back... That she didn't know. She had this weekend with Jack, and perhaps not much else.

"It's late," Jack said. "I've kept you pretty busy. I should let you get some rest."

He didn't move, however. Neither did she. All she could do was stare out the windshield into the darkness. And all she could feel was the beating of her pulse.

"Jack," she said, her voice very low. "Take me back to your place."

"Meg…"

"Why question it? Dammit, if it's what we both want, and if we only have this weekend—" She couldn't go on, her throat tightening.

Jack reached out, took her hand. "Are you sure?" His own voice was husky.

She was unsure of so many things. But this one, she knew. She'd tried so hard to resist, tried so hard to tell herself that she didn't belong in Jack's arms. But now, she could resist no longer.

"Yes, Jack," she said. "I'm sure."

MEG BY LAMPLIGHT, standing next to Jack's bed. He didn't think there could be a sight any lovelier. He wanted to go to her, but something told him to wait. Right now she was determined to do this on her own. Chin held up almost as if in defiance, she began to unbutton her shirt. When she was finished she slipped it off, revealing a lacy camisole underneath. Jack saw the smooth skin of her shoulders, the alluring outline of her breasts. It took a great deal of willpower for him to remain standing where he was. She gazed at him as she unzipped her jeans, slid those off, too. Lovelier still.

"Meg..."

The expression in her eyes told him that she acquiesced. He stepped toward her and drew her down onto the bed. At first they sat on the very edge. Jack kissed her mouth, and then the hollow of her throat. He'd waited for this such a long while, it seemed. The first time they'd made love had given him only a taste of her. It had happened quickly, impatiently. But now, tonight, he would prolong what they had. He would make certain that together they learned so much more of what they could give, and take.

Meg's lips were soft and warm as they parted under his. They kissed, and kissed again. At last, gathering her close, he lay with her. Slowly he moved his hands over her. Slowly he helped her tug off her camisole. And, even more slowly, he pulled off the scrap of lace that passed for underwear.

Revealed to him, she was even more beautiful than he remembered. He cupped his hand over the soft mound of hair protecting her most private, intimate place. She gasped, arching against him.

"Oh...Jack...it can't be," she said, her voice raw. "How can I feel like this so soon...?"

He kissed her again. "Go with it," he murmured against her mouth. He pressed his hand against her, then stroked gently. She rose to meet him, over and over, straining toward him. He lifted his head so that he could watch her face as the ripples of pleasure came over her. He could feel her pleasure almost as intensely as if it were his own.

She collapsed backward onto the bed. "That was crazy," she said, her voice unsteady. "I'm sorry…"

He grazed his hand across her hip. "What are you sorry about?"

"I just…gave in. Jack, you haven't even taken off your clothes. And here I am…completely bare…and *indulging*."

"We're only beginning," he assured her.

She started to unbutton his shirt as if in a hurry. He put his hand over hers.

"We have time, Meg. We have tonight."

She gazed into his eyes. "Yes, I know. But, Jack, I don't want to be the only one…"

He smiled. "I like you completely naked."

She laughed shakily. "That's fine, as long as you're completely naked, too."

He obliged. In short order, he'd done away with his shirt, his jeans, his own underwear. Meg caressed him, gently at first and then more boldly. But still he prolonged this time, running his fingers over her arm, her waist, her thigh….

"Jack…" She gazed at him without shame, without prevarication. And now when she spoke, her voice was perfectly steady. "I want you. I know you want me, too."

He kissed her throat once more, then left the bed and went to the bureau. He took out a box of condoms, bringing it back with him.

"You don't think we'll need the whole box, do you?" she asked. "Then again…"

The look she gave him was enough to make him want to hurry, after all. He tore open one of the packets, but Meg took over after that. She appropriated the condom and proceeded to put it on him. The experimental things she did with her hands almost took the last of his control. She seemed to realize it and trailed her fingers up his chest. Now she was the one who delayed, enticing him with her touch, her kisses. At last a low groan escaped him.

"Meg..."

She poised herself over him in all her tempting womanhood. And then, smiling down at him, she opened herself to him, drew him inside her. She was ready, and so was he. They found a rhythm, as if both of them could hear the same sweet music. Even as Jack moved deep within her, he held back as well as he could, trying to gauge her pleasure. But then she brushed her lips across his cheek and whispered provocatively in his ear.

"Go with it..."

No holding back now. Faster and faster they rushed together through a world of sensation. Jack was the first to cry out, and then Meg. He felt her shudder, felt her rock against him as she moaned. He wanted her like this forever.

Long moments afterward they lay tangled together, bodies damp, breathing ragged.

"Oh, Jack..."

He kissed her temple. "Pretty fantastic, I'd say."

"More than fantastic."

"We could try to do even better than fantastic," he suggested.

She lifted her head, gazing at him in disbelief. "You can't possibly be thinking *right* now."

"Maybe not right this minute," he said. "But in a little while…"

They dozed in each other's arms, woke and dozed again. The passion they'd shared was more than a memory. It taunted them, holding them in its thrall, demanding that they give yet more.

And so, again, they made love. Again Jack caressed Meg, and again she opened herself to him. This time they looked at each other through every moment, as if greedy for each other's pleasure. And this time they cried out together as pleasure overtook them.

JACK WOKE sometime in the middle of the night. He'd turned off the lamp so that he and Meg could finally get some sleep. But now he reached for her in the darkness and realized that her side of the bed was empty. Getting up, he slid into his jeans and went through the house looking for her.

He found her in the kitchen. She sat at the table, a bowl of chocolate-peppermint ice cream in front of her. She was wearing his shirt with the sleeves rolled up and the buttons undone. From here he had a tantalizing view of bare skin and delectable curves.

"I was hungry," she said, sounding guilty.

He grinned and straddled a chair across from her.

"Does sex always make you hungry? I seem to remember you wanted room service the first time."

She attempted a frown. "The first time, we went sneaking off to a hotel."

"As opposed to this time, when we just came sneaking to my place."

"It's different," she said. "I have a confession to make. Because I work in a hotel, making love in a hotel isn't my idea of the perfect setting. Don't ask me to explain it."

"You probably just like having a change of venue," he suggested.

"Probably." She gestured at her bowl of ice cream. "Want some?"

"That's not what I really want," he murmured.

She flushed, and that only made her look more alluring. "Jack, don't you think we should regroup a bit?"

"Why not…we have the rest of the night."

She set her spoon down. "If you look at me that way, I won't be able to do anything but…anything but make love to you."

"I can live with that." He rested his arms on the back of the chair, and it occurred to him that he felt remarkably good. Maybe better than he'd ever felt. He smiled. "I love you, Meg."

She stared at him, her face suddenly tense. "What did you say?"

"I'm pretty sure you heard, but it's worth repeating. I love you, Meg."

She shook her head. "That's impossible."

"Why?"

"It just is, that's all." She pushed back her chair and stood. Then she clutched his shirt next to her, the tantalizing glimpse of skin vanishing. "You got carried away, that's all. Let's face it, the sex was incredible. Anybody could get carried away after that."

"It was more than sex, don't you think?"

"I don't think anything. We had a great time, but now…now it's over." She hurried out of the kitchen. Jack followed her and watched as she went up the stairs.

"Meggie—"

"I really wish you wouldn't call me that. It's just a silly nickname." At the top of the stairs she turned and disappeared into his bedroom. Jack didn't find that altogether unpromising. He went upstairs, too. However, when he reached his room, he saw that Meg was slipping on her underwear.

"Kind of late to be going anywhere," he said.

She put on her jeans, zipping them up. "You don't love me, Jack," she said. "Really, you don't. I thought we'd discussed everything. The fact that you live in Maine and I live in New York. I might even be living in London, for goodness' sake. And there's everything else. I don't want to get married. And the children issue—"

"Meg," he said. "I'm not asking you to marry

me. I'm not asking you to have children with me. I'm just telling you that I love you.''

She paused, giving him an uncertain glance. ''How can you say you love me and not have all the rest go along with it?''

He sat down on the bed. ''I'm just getting used to the idea that I love you. It only occurred to me five minutes ago. I haven't thought much further ahead.''

She started buttoning buttons. ''It'll happen,'' she said. ''You'll think ahead. And then we'll really be in trouble.''

''Why?'' he asked. ''Because you think I'll ask you to give up your life? And you think you won't be strong enough to say no?''

''It's not that simple,'' she muttered. ''What if I do go to London? What then?''

He rubbed the back of his neck. ''I rack up a phone bill. And frequent-flier miles.''

''It wouldn't work,'' she argued. ''It just wouldn't.''

''The sex alone would be worth it,'' he said.

''You're making a joke out of this,'' she told him. ''And not a very good one.''

''No joke, Meg. I do love you.'' It was intriguing to see how many times he could say that—and how little it had the desired effect on Meg. She kept on doing up buttons, until she realized that she was still wearing his shirt.

''Damn,'' she said. She began unbuttoning. Then she turned around and slipped off his shirt. He gazed at the slim line of her back and had the urge to touch her. Something told him that wouldn't be a good idea, though. She pulled on her camisole and her own shirt. More buttoning.

"I guess you want me to drive you back to your hotel," he said.

"That would be the best thing," she replied stiffly. "I'm sorry. We probably just need some time apart."

Not in his opinion. "Does it scare you that much, Meg? A guy says he cares about you, and you see the end of life as you know it? Don't you have more faith in yourself than that?"

"Jack," she said. "Just take me to the hotel…please."

He didn't appear to have any choice. He took his shirt and noticed that Meg's perfume lingered in its folds. He wished that she was still wearing it, and he could take her to bed in it. Instead, he shrugged it on. Next he put on his shoes, and Meg put hers on. All too soon they'd left his house and were driving to her hotel.

When he pulled into the parking lot, Meg opened the passenger door and climbed out before he'd even had a chance to come around to her side. He didn't catch up to her until she was inside the building. Whether she liked it or not, though, he escorted her to the door of her room.

She used the key, then turned to him. Her expression was determinedly neutral. "Thank you, Jack. I know this is awkward. But I think it's best."

"Best to run away from me," he murmured.

"Best to give ourselves some distance, so you can figure out how you really feel about me."

He already knew. He hadn't expected it; the knowledge of how he felt had simply come to him, with no fanfare. It hadn't seemed earthshaking to realize that he loved Meg. It hadn't seemed like a life-shattering epiphany. It had just seemed good. Why couldn't he get that across to her?

"Good night, Jack. Or good morning, or whatever it is." She disappeared inside the hotel room and closed the door. He heard her turn the lock on the other side.

He went back to his house. Everywhere he went, he found remnants of the night he had shared with Meg. A bowl of melting chocolate-peppermint ice cream in the kitchen. Rumpled sheets in the bedroom. And her perfume, lingering with him.

Remnants only. Never had his house felt this empty...or this lonely.

"NICE-LOOKIN' WOMAN," said Ron Ballard as he settled into the extra chair in Jack's office.

"That she is," Jack agreed. Ron was referring to Meg, who'd appropriated the receptionist's desk outside the office. It was the weekend and no one else was in, but Jack had agreed to meet with Ron.

"New employee?" Ron asked now.

"She's just visiting," Jack told him.

Ron waited for a minute. "Girlfriend?"

"Not technically speaking," Jack said.

"Too bad," said Ron. He added, "Think she'd mind if I asked her out?"

Jack gave him a warning look.

"Okay, okay," Ron said, taking the hint. "You know me. I never like to waste an opportunity."

Ron Ballard liked to fancy himself a ladies' man. The truth was something slightly different. He didn't go out all that much, mainly because he had such a hard time actually asking women for dates. He kept backing out at the last minute, worried that he'd be rejected.

Jack knew all this because he'd once worked for Ballard Development in Portland. He and Ron had gotten along pretty well. Even when Jack left and eventually formed his own company, he and Ron had maintained a casual friendship. Sure, Ron didn't appreciate the competition, but they'd gotten along. And now Ron was hoping to buy out the competition.

"You ever going to make up your mind, Jack?" he asked. "You know I'm making you a decent deal."

Jack flipped through the pages of Ron's latest offer. "I see you made all the changes I requested."

"No employee layoffs. No benefit trimming. It's all right there, and I'm somebody who keeps his word."

Jack knew that, too. You could trust Ron when it

came to business. You just couldn't trust him when he fantasized about life as a man-about-town.

"What's the holdup?" Ron persisted. "Wait a minute, does it have something to do with your girlfriend out front?"

"She's not my girlfriend," said Jack.

"So what's she doing out there?"

Good question. This morning he'd arrived at the hotel to see Meg. He'd expected her to boot him out the door so they could have more time apart—more time for him to come to his senses, supposedly. Instead, she'd greeted him in a distant but polite manner and said no, she didn't mind stopping by his office with him while he had a meeting—she'd be able to entertain herself. Jack had been sure she wouldn't want to go anywhere with him, not after he'd admitted that he loved her.

The cold light of day hadn't changed his mind any. It still seemed a simple, nonshattering fact: he loved her.

"So what's the holdup?" Ron's question intruded on his thoughts. "You know I'm going to treat your people just fine. You know I'm not going to ruin your work reputation. And you know you want to go on to something else."

"What makes you so sure of that?" Jack asked.

"You and I go back a ways," Ron said. "You've always been restless, Jack. I'm surprised you even kept on with construction, when you seemed itching for something else."

"What else?" Jack muttered.

"Hey," said Ron, "I'm not a mind reader. You tell me."

"You just want me to sell," said Jack.

"Yeah, I do. Just like you want to sell, if you ever make up your mind." Ron stood and went to the door. He glanced down the hall. "Sure is one fine-lookin' woman," he said with a bit of flair. And then he left.

Jack stayed where he was, feet up on his desk. He didn't want to go out to Meg just yet. He wanted to delay getting the day in motion. It was, after all, their last day together in Maine. Tomorrow he'd drive her back to New York, and after that they'd go their separate ways. That seemed to be how Meg wanted it, anyway. Jack himself had never been too good at looking into the future where Meg was concerned.

So he stayed where he was, delaying the future. He flipped through Ron's offer again, then tossed it back down on the desk. He owed Ron an answer. He ought to tell him yes or no.

If Jack said no, he could go on in the construction business. It wasn't a bad business, not by any standard. But if Jack said yes and gave up his firm, he had a dozen options in front of him, didn't he? Why didn't he take one and just get on with it?

Maybe it had something to do with his dad. Andrew Elliott would be pleased if he learned that Jack was leaving the construction field. Jack sure hated to give his father that kind of satisfaction.

"Hell," Jack muttered under his breath. He was forty years old. Wasn't it about time he stopped measuring his successes by his father's idea of failure?

He couldn't seem to sit still anymore, and he began pacing his office. Maybe he always *had* been restless, just as Ron said. And maybe now that restlessness was catching up with him. Maybe it required something more of him.

But meanwhile Meg was waiting for him. And the day was waiting to begin…his last day with Meg.

He went out to get it started.

CHAPTER SIXTEEN

MEG SAT at the reception desk down the hall from Jack's office, cradling the phone against her ear. "Thank you," she said into the receiver. "You've been very helpful...yes, that really is enough. Good-bye now." She hung up the receiver and saw Jack standing in the doorway, perusing her. She couldn't seem to look into his eyes. It had been that way ever since she'd made love with him last night...and then heard him say that he loved her.

"My," she said now. "That was the lady at the tourist bureau. I called her for a few statistics on your town, and I ended up learning everything from the state bird of Maine to the state animal. The chickadee and the moose, if you didn't already know."

Jack didn't say anything. He just went on studying her.

"Anyway," she said, "I'm ready to talk about your bed-and-breakfast idea."

"So it's back to business," Jack said.

"I think that's best." She still couldn't look him straight in the eye. Instead, she tore a sheet of paper from her notepad and pushed it across the desk. "I'll explain the figures as we go along," she said.

Jack remained standing where he was for a moment, but at last he pulled up a chair and sat down. Meg proceeded in her most professional tone.

"I've learned that your town does a healthy tourist trade. That was one of my big concerns—would there be a sufficient inflow to keep bookings high. No problem there."

Jack studied the sheet, his face impassive. Was he thinking about last night? Meg certainly couldn't get it out of her mind, but she forced herself to go on.

"I've estimated the approximate outlay to get the bed-and-breakfast going. Some redesigning of the house would be necessary. Additional bathrooms, extension of the veranda, turning that large downstairs den into two rooms, and so forth. Since you're in the construction business that shouldn't be a problem."

Jack continued to study her notes without saying a thing. He'd said that he loved her...he *thought* he loved her. Maybe great sex could do that. You started to confuse pleasure with love....

Her face heated, but once again she compelled herself to go on. "Everyplace needs some type of angle to draw guests. With the Alexander, it's sheer luxury—or it used to be, anyway. At the hotel where I'm staying right now, it's rustic simplicity. With your bed-and-breakfast, well, the house speaks for itself, doesn't it? Charming and grand all at once, rambling along the cliffs, overlooking the ocean. Who *wouldn't* want to stay there? Bottom line,

Jack—you'd have a solid moneymaking operation. Enough to provide an income for your mother.''

He nodded thoughtfully. ''I'll pursue it then, see what happens. Thanks, Meg.''

''Business concluded,'' she announced, still trying to sound professional. She stood and moved away from Jack.

''I guess that just leaves the personal stuff,'' he said gravely. ''You know, like me loving you.''

''Would you stop saying that?''

''It's the truth,'' he said, coming to stand beside her.

She wanted to turn and burrow herself in his arms. It took all her will to resist. ''Dammit, Jack, you make it sound as if being in love were something so…so impossibly lighthearted.''

''It is.'' She heard the smile in his voice. ''Look at me, Meg.''

She wouldn't turn. Gently he put his hands on her shoulders and swiveled her until she faced him. Then he tilted her chin so that she had to look straight into his eyes.

''Meg,'' he said. ''I love you, and yet my life hasn't turned upside down because of it. Don't you think the same could apply to you?''

''No,'' she disagreed. ''Real love *does* mean everything turning upside down. You're kidding yourself if you think otherwise.''

He searched her face. ''Why can't you trust what we're both feeling right now?''

She closed her eyes. "I don't know what I'm feeling," she whispered. "I just don't know...."

He kissed her once, gently. Then he stood away from her. "Meg," he said, "we have one day left here. Let's just spend it together and not think about anything else."

"It won't do any good."

"One last day," he repeated. "What can it hurt?"

She was afraid to answer. Most of all, she was afraid that she might already be falling in love with Jack, after all.

IT WAS A MAGICAL DAY. All morning, she and Jack wandered up and down the Maine coastline. They meandered on the beach and found their way to salt-water marshes where Jack named the birds you could spy: plover, eider, heron. After a leisurely lunch of lobster cakes and wild-berry pie, they went sailing, the afternoon spinning out its enchantment of sun and sky and ocean.

But the day wasn't over yet. Jack drove Meg to Portland for dinner. At an upscale bistro, they ate scallops and risotto and strawberries in wine. Afterward they walked on streets where other people strolled and where lights glimmered against the night. Meg felt a New England spell weaving around her.

Jack took her to a nightclub. They danced, holding each other close, and time seemed to lose its impetus. Meg couldn't say whether minutes passed, or an hour or more. One song blended into another, the sultry music wrapping itself around them. Meg wanted to stay like this, Jack close to her, neither one of them feeling the need for words. Music was the communication between them, sensual and languorous, the slow tempo a counterpoint to the beating of Meg's heart.

They drove back to Cape Anne somewhere between late night and early morning. When Jack reached the turn that would take him to Meg's hotel, he slowed down. But then, after a glance at her through the darkness, he didn't turn. He kept on going. Meg didn't question his destination. She knew where the two of them were headed. What would happen between them seemed inevitable. She would not deny that, not tonight.

When they reached Jack's house, they didn't speak. Together they went inside and up the stairs. Together they reached his bedroom and turned toward each other. They helped each other to undress and then sank upon the bed. Meg clung to Jack, still without words, showing him with her body what she needed from him. And when at last he filled her, everything else was blotted out. Nothing existed except the two of them, and the giving between them.

Afterward Meg lay with her backside cradled against Jack. He kissed the nape of her neck, smoothed her dampened hair away from her face.

"Tonight you made love to me as if you were saying goodbye," he said.

"Not goodbye. Not yet."

He molded her closer to him. "Stay with me, Meg."

"Jack—"

"Not a lifetime. Just the next few hours."

"For now," she whispered, "I'll stay." She didn't think sleep would come to her, and yet it did. She fell asleep in Jack's arms, as if this were the only safe haven she would ever find.

BY THE TIME Meg woke, morning sunlight was streaming into the room. Today they would be returning to New York. Meg stirred, but Jack slept on. As carefully as she could, she slid away from him to the edge of the bed. Then, however, she couldn't resist watching him. He shifted position without waking, sprawling on his back and taking up space in unabashed fashion. The sheet had pulled away from him, and she saw the strong muscles of his chest, the dark hair swirling down past his navel. It occurred to Meg that a woman could spend a lifetime with a man like Jack Elliott and never slake her desire for him. A whole lifetime...

She grabbed the first item of clothing she could find. It happened to be his shirt again. She put it on, then tiptoed from the room. The house was very quiet as she wandered through it. Everywhere she looked, she seemed to learn more about Jack. In his study, she found shelves stacked with books on all types of subjects: history, engineering, anthropology, language texts for Spanish and French. There were even a few philosophy books. A computer sat on a walnut desk, but Meg also saw a drafting board covered with felt and angled to hold the pieces of a jigsaw puzzle. Only a corner of the puzzle was put together. She wondered if Jack's doctor had suggested this activity as a way to relax and avoid that impending ulcer. If so, Jack hadn't complied too well.

She peered into two other upstairs rooms and found them unfurnished, as if he hadn't decided what to do with them yet. Downstairs, he had managed to fill up the house. One room held clutter—fishing poles, boxes of books, a sleeping bag hanging from a hook, a tennis racket propped against the wall, a backpack against another wall.

Meg ended up in the kitchen. She was scrambling a pan of eggs when Jack appeared. He wore only his jeans, his chest bare. It was a look she had come to like.

"Hungry again?" he asked with a grin.

"It's breakfast time. Sit down, and we'll both eat."

"Careful," he told her. "You're cooking for me. That's the first step on the road to ruin."

"Very amusing," she replied as she popped some whole-wheat bread in the toaster. Then she forked the eggs onto two plates and put them on the table. Jack brought orange juice from the fridge. As soon as the toast popped up, they had a meal.

"From here on," Jack said, "you can wear my shirt anytime."

Self-consciously she fastened one of the buttons. "So far," she said, "I've discovered that you like to sail, fish, play tennis and camp. So what's with the doctor telling you that you need to relax? You have all the pastimes required."

"I just haven't been able to indulge them," he explained. "I've been too busy until now. But if I decide to sell my company, it'll be different. I will have time."

Jack had told her about the offer he'd had from Ballard Development. "What about your crew?" she asked. "Del and Perry and all the rest of them. Will congregating down at Lou's Bar be the same if you sell your business?"

"It won't be the same," he said, looking thoughtful. "But maybe it'll be better...who knows? I haven't made the decision yet."

Meg didn't want to think about decisions; she had too many looming over her. "How're the eggs?" she asked.

"You should never have let on that you know your way around the kitchen. I'll be asking for more."

It was remarkably cozy, sitting here in his kitchen, wearing his shirt. It was the sort of thing she could get used to. Meg set down her fork. She couldn't seem to eat any more.

"I'm going to get ready," she told him. "We'll be on the road pretty soon."

"We don't have to be. We could forget about going back to New York right now. We could spend another day or two together."

It sounded so appealing. More time with Jack. More time making love with him.

"There's a lot you haven't seen yet," he said. "Lakes and mountains I'd like to show you. Camping out…"

Camping with Jack. Sharing a sleeping bag, sharing his warmth.

"I can't," she said, her throat aching with all the suppressed longings inside her. "I have to get back to my real life."

"This is real, Meg. You and me here together— that's as real as anything you'll find."

She took a deep breath. "Jack, you don't want me to go to London, do you? I know you've avoided saying it. You keep telling me we'd work it out, one way or another. But the truth is, you don't want me to go."

He didn't say anything to that, but Meg wouldn't let him get away with silence.

"You want to be the good guy," she told him. "You want to come across as the modern, enlightened male who won't stand in the way of a woman's dreams. You'd hate to think you're anything less. But Jack, you have to be honest with yourself. And with me. If you really *do* love me, then you have thought about the future. At least a little, you've thought about it. And you don't picture me in London. You don't picture yourself on an airplane half the time, getting jet lag.''

His expression was rueful. ''Okay, Meg, I'll be honest. I don't want you to take that job. I don't even want you to live in New York. I want you here in Maine. But I sure as hell wouldn't expect you to stay home and cook for me. Instead, I'd expect you to keep your career. There are plenty of hotels in this area that would line up to hire you. Maybe I'd even ask you to work with me on that bed-and-breakfast.''

She stared at him. ''You're offering me a job?''

''More than that. I'd expect us to be partners. What I'm offering right now is a business proposition, pure and simple.''

''Nothing,'' Meg said, ''is pure and simple. What are you really telling me—you want us to live together?''

''That's a beginning.''

''So I move into this house…your house.''

''It would be your house, too, Meg.''

She shook her head. ''No, Jack. It's yours. I'd be like a guest.''

''I don't see it that way,'' he said. ''You've already left your imprint here. When you're gone, the place doesn't feel right.''

She closed her eyes briefly, saw herself picking up everything and moving to Maine. Jack's hometown…Jack's house. Jack's ideas for her career. Maybe she'd be happy. She could go sailing with him—not to mention camping and fishing. She could even take up tennis. All Jack's pursuits.

She pushed back her chair. "I have to get dressed," she said. "In my own clothes. I can't…I can't think when I'm wearing your shirt."

Upstairs she put on the outfit she'd worn yesterday: jeans, a flannel shirt she'd purchased in a Cape Anne shop and a cable-knit sweater. Even her clothes were beginning to look like Maine—rugged, able to withstand brisk weather.

Jack leaned in the doorway. "Can you think now?" he asked, and his tone seemed purposely casual.

"I suppose you'd like an answer," she said. "You'd like to have me…resolved. I mean, it would be awfully convenient for you to have me within reach all the time. We can have some of that great sex on a regular basis, and then you can get on with the rest of your life."

"Meg—hell, I don't see it like that. You make it sound as if I'd put you in a compartment and take you out only when I needed you."

"That's the way it feels," she said. "You keep saying love isn't earthshaking, that it doesn't change anything."

He frowned. "I was trying to reassure you. Trying to let you know that you could give in to your emotions a little without risking the end of your world."

"You want me to give up everything."

"It wouldn't be like that, Meg. I've seen you the

last few days. I've seen how much you've enjoyed yourself here. If you need city life, Portland is close by, and we're only a few hours away from Boston. Instead of giving up anything, you'd have everything.''

"Right," she murmured. "All I'd have to do is turn down the biggest career opportunity I've ever had. All I'd have to do is move to your town, fit myself into your life."

His expression went hard. "I'm not asking you to give up who you are."

"Just as long as it doesn't conflict with your plans." She spoke very quietly. "Jack, you've already said it. You don't think love should turn your life upside down. For you, nothing would change. For me, yes, it would be everything. I'd start out whittling my life to suit yours, and I don't see where it would end. Does that scare me? Damn right it does." She stared at him. Suddenly she felt a calmness inside, a coldness deep in her heart, but she went on.

"I can't do it. I can't have a relationship knowing I'll be the only one to give—the only one to change. So I'm going back to New York...alone. Believe me, I can find my own way."

His expression was still hard. "Finding your own way... Your independence means everything to you, doesn't it, Meg?"

He refused to understand. It seemed there was little more to say between them. "Yes, Jack," she said in that quiet voice. "My independence does mean everything."

MEG TOOK a commuter flight back to New York—alone, just as she wanted. When the cab from the airport dropped her off at her apartment building, the sky was overcast. It seemed a reflection of her own somber mood. She was convinced that she'd made the right decision, leaving Jack behind, yet she felt no peace. All she felt was a heaviness inside.

It didn't help to open the door of her apartment and find a crisis in the making. Kathy and Lena were sitting on the sofa, and Kathy was sobbing as if her heart would break. Meg had never known anyone who could weep with such abandon, such fervor as Kathy. Now there was no choice but to go to her friend and join Lena in consolation efforts.

"Oh, honey, I thought everything was going so well for you. Tell me what happened." Meg handed Kathy a tissue. Kathy didn't seem able to speak, so Lena filled in the details.

"It's Gary, of course," she muttered. "The wretch, he's gone and broken her heart all over again. Basically, he's called off the engagement."

"But why—"

"I'll tell you why," Kathy said soggily. "I told him the truth, that's why. I had to do it. Everything was so perfect between us...but there was that one little lie. It kept weighing on me, so I confessed, Meg. This afternoon, I told Gary that you and Jack had never been engaged. I told him it was all make-believe, a fantasy just to convince him that engagement wasn't such a bad thing, after all. And he said he felt like a real ass because he'd walked right into our trap. And then we had a terrible argument, and then he said it was all over.''

"I'm sorry," Meg said inadequately. "So sorry." She blamed herself for ever letting Kathy talk her into the scheme in the first place.

"Gary was just looking for an excuse to get out of the engagement," Lena remarked indignantly. "He's not worth the trouble—not worth it at all."

Kathy pressed the tissue to her eyes. "He had every right to be angry. I lied to him—no getting around it. Maybe I did it because I love him, but it was still a lie. You know what he said to me? He said he'd really been convinced. He'd been sure as anything that Meg and Jack were happy…that they were meant for each other. And he said if he couldn't trust his feelings about that, how could he trust his feelings about anything else? Including me."

Meg felt a bleakness spreading through her. "Kathy, it's my fault more than anyone else's. Because deep down I wanted to pretend that Jack and I *could* be happy. I wanted to see what it could be like. I got carried away."

"If you were so convincing," Lena murmured, "maybe there's some truth to it."

Yes, there was truth to it. No man in the world had ever made her feel the way Jack Elliott did.

When she was with him, she seemed to forget about everything else. She got swept up in him. Her own goals and dreams didn't seem so important anymore. And that was what scared her most of all.

"Jack and I...it doesn't matter," she said, her voice low. "We're finished."

This was enough to make Kathy stop crying altogether. She stared at Meg with reddened eyes. "Are you sure this is what you want, Meggie? Are you sure you're not just running away from Jack? Are you sure you don't love him?"

"Maybe some things are more important than love," Meg said.

"I think love is more important than anything else," Kathy disagreed. "Am I so wrong?"

"Not if you move on to somebody new," Lena said. "Splash some water on your face, and I'll take you out to meet another friend of Nathan's. This one is a pediatrician, and very cute."

"No, Lena," Kathy announced. "I'm through with the man-hunt. I can't go frantically searching for someone to make me forget Gary. Because, you see, I've discovered that I can't forget him. And somehow I'm going to have to live with that. I'll have to learn." Kathy rose to her feet. She looked mournful but resolute. Giving each of her friends a sad smile, she turned and walked away, her long blond hair floating behind her. She went into the spare bedroom and shut the door.

Lena and Meg looked at each other. "Think we should try talking to her some more?" Lena asked.

"No," Meg said. "Let's give her some time. I think I've done enough damage. Why did I ever pretend to be Jack's fiancée?"

"Because Kathy wanted it so much, and you're a good friend."

Meg sighed and buried her head in her hands. "I didn't do it just for Kathy. I can't ignore the selfish reasons. Jack said it was a way to try out being with someone, yet avoiding the risks. That's what I was doing. I was experimenting, but not taking any risks."

"What happened in Maine?" Lena asked gently. "Did you do some more…experimenting?"

Meg gave a humorless laugh. "I found out what it's like to be with a man who could fill your entire life. And I realized how easily my own life could vanish."

"I suppose," said Lena, "that love never quite works out the way you think it will." She studied her engagement ring with a brooding expression. "It's funny, but a bit of the sparkle seems to have gone out of this diamond. A bit of the sparkle's gone out of Nathan, too. I can't figure out why."

"Want to talk about it?" Meg asked.

"Not really. But, Meg, at least one of us has to get it right. Kathy has to stop pining for Gary. And maybe you have to admit you're in love with Jack. Sure, I told you to sample other guys. But, Meggie, even I can tell when somebody's got it bad. And maybe Jack Elliott is actually worth it.''

He was worth it, all right—except for one problem. He didn't want to give up anything for love.

CHAPTER SEVENTEEN

HELEN ELLIOTT SEEMED in remarkably fine spirits. She sat on the sofa in her living room and for once scarcely seemed bothered by the cast on her leg. Meg sat beside her.

"You're doing great," she told Helen. "Before you know it, your ankle will be healed and you'll be on both feet again."

"Just watch me," Helen said, petting her dog. "Chester and I may take up speed walking. Better yet, marathons. I feel up to all sorts of challenges. Meg, I've already confronted one challenge. There was something I wanted to do—and I just did it. Today Russ Cooper popped in to see how I was doing and I asked him to go on a date with me next Saturday night. And you know what? He said yes!"

"Helen, that's fantastic."

"Of course," said Helen, "until I'm completely better, I'll have to be a little inventive about this dating thing. But it's a beginning, don't you think?"

"A wonderful beginning."

Helen looked vibrant and pretty in her ruffled robe, her silvery hair curled attractively around her face. A bright afghan covered her knees, and she gave the impression that at any moment she would toss it aside and bounce to her feet.

"When you *are* completely well again," Meg said, "I suspect Mr. Cooper is going to have a difficult time keeping up with you."

"Don't you know it... Meg, I have you to thank. If you hadn't given me the courage, well, I never would have gotten to know Russ. Because of your help, I've gone from wishful thinking to having my wishes come true."

"You just needed a little encouragement," Meg said.

"After all this time, I might just have a man in my life. I guess I'm not over the hill yet, although my son seems to think I am." Helen's tone grew a bit caustic. Meg was wary about discussing Jack. Two days had gone by since she'd left Maine, and she still couldn't shake the heaviness she felt. Helen, however, seemed to have a lot to say about Jack.

"He called me up yesterday and told me he'd found a way to solve my financial problems. Can you believe it? He wants to support me with some scheme about a bed-and-breakfast."

"Helen, Jack consulted me about the idea. And I think it's a very good one."

This seemed to give Helen pause, but only momentarily. "I'm sure you mean well, dear, but I can't possibly take income from my son. He says it's a way for me to be independent, but I don't see how it qualifies as self-help."

"Half the house belongs to you," Meg reminded her. "You'd finally be putting it to good use."

"And what about the other half?" Helen asked. "My dear ex-husband doesn't want to give it up."

"Surely he can be persuaded," Meg said. "He can't be that unreasonable."

"He is," said Helen.

Meg knew she was beginning to step on treacherous ground, and she told herself she should just let the subject go. It really wasn't any of her business, was it? And yet for Jack's sake, she couldn't seem to give up.

"Helen," she said, "the way I understand it, your ex-husband is a generous man, whatever his other faults. Why would he need to keep the house from you?"

"Jack asked me the same question." Helen gazed toward the window. Her expression was distant now, as if she was searching into the past. "When we bought that house, it was the first time we'd disagreed over anything. I'd found a place I thought was perfect. A smaller house, more manageable, on the west side of town. But Andrew thought that house by the ocean was a good representation of his status. Already back then he was the renowned intellectual and had to have a place that expressed that. He didn't want a home that expressed *us*. It was the first time I realized that Andrew saw himself as the important one in our relationship, but I gave in. And I ended up living in that house for over thirty years. Maybe

I was a fool for staying so long and trying so hard to make Andrew care about the marriage as much as I did. All I know is that I finally got out.''

Meg was silent for a moment. "But the house," she said at last. "Neither one of you has resolved that.''

"I don't have simple answers," Helen said. "I was ready for us to sell the place five years ago, when we got divorced. Andrew's the one who could never come to an agreement. Don't ask me why. He doesn't want to live there—he just lets the house stand empty.''

"It's a shame," Meg said. "Jack has come up with such a good idea.''

"He's just like his father." Helen's voice was stony. "He belittles me. He doesn't think I can handle my own life. This scheme of his is only a way to take control. We're supposed to pretend it's my business venture, but he's the one who wants to make all the decisions. For goodness' sake, Meg, he didn't even consult me before he consulted *you*. He didn't even ask me if it was something I'd like.''

Admittedly, Meg could see how it might seem dictatorial on Jack's part, but she had to defend his actions. "Helen, he was afraid you'd dismiss the idea if he didn't have more to back it up. He knows you're prejudiced against him.''

"Prejudiced against my own son? That's ridiculous.''

"It's not ridiculous," she said. "It's the way

things are. You've got so much bitterness, so much anger toward your ex-husband that you've let it spill over onto Jack. It means you suspect Jack's motives, no matter what he says or does. And it means Jack has tried as hard as he can not to be like either you or Andrew. That's his way of trying to distance himself from the bitterness, I think. But in so many ways he *is* your son—and Andrew's, too. He's inherited Andrew's love of learning. I can see it in all the books he keeps at his place. Sure, he tries to hide that he's an intellectual like his dad, but it's there. And Jack has also inherited your penchant for beautiful things. That's something else he tries to hide, but not very successfully. Wouldn't it be a relief if all three of you could finally let go of the bitterness?''

Helen stared at her. Meg didn't know what to expect next. Maybe Helen would yell at her for interfering where she didn't belong and tell her to get out. Meg wouldn't be surprised at that. And yet, when Helen spoke, she surprised Meg in another way.

''That,'' observed Helen, ''was a good kick in the butt.''

''I'm sorry—''

''Don't back down now,'' Helen said. ''You had to tell me something, and you did. You know what, Meg? I can't help wishing that if you're not my daughter, you could at least be my daughter-in-law.''

Meg felt a tightness in her throat that made it dif-

ficult to answer at first. After a few moments, she
squeezed the older woman's hand.

"Thank you," she said. "Thank you for wishing."

But wishful thinking didn't always turn into
wishes come true.

ONE WEEK LATER Meg carried her gardening basket
up to the rooftop. The sun was setting, casting a
golden hue over the city. She hoped that she would
have some solitude. Instead, she saw Jack kneeling
at one of the flower beds, spade in hand.

She stopped and considered making a retreat. But
Jack had already glanced up at her.

"No use running away," he said. "You'll have to
talk to me sooner or later."

She set down her basket. "I didn't know you'd
come back. And I thought we'd already said everything there was to say."

"Not quite." He gestured with the spade. "We
could discuss whether or not to plant some dragon-
head over there. Or maybe some jupiter's-beard."

She raised her eyebrows. "You've been brushing
up on your gardening. Trying to impress me?"

"Is it working?" he asked.

"I'm impressed," she said. "But I suppose there
is something I should tell you, Jack." She took a
deep breath. "I've accepted the job in London."

"Congratulations." His voice was expressionless.
"When do you leave?"

"Next week."

He frowned. "That soon?"

"Mr. Riley wants me to get started as soon as possible. It's what I want, too." She tried to ignore the hollowness inside her, a sensation that never seemed to go away.

Jack laid down his spade, straightened and came toward her. She took a step back.

"Jack, don't...please."

He stayed where he was, but now his expression was intent as he gazed at her. "Meg, I have some news of my own. I finally figured out that I didn't want to sell my company. I realized I wasn't in the construction business just to drive my dad crazy...I was in it for myself."

"That's great."

"There's more," he said. "I don't want to stand still. Instead of Ron Ballard buying me out, I'm in negotiations with him right now to take over *his* company. Seems he's been meaning to play golf more, and this might be his opportunity."

Meg couldn't help smiling a little. "So much for all that extra time to camp and fish and sail."

"Maybe I'll find a way to take it easy," Jack said. "Maybe I'll learn to delegate more."

Meg studied him in the waning light. Jack Elliott...virile, dynamic. She didn't see him ever standing still—he wasn't the type. "I'm happy for you. I get the feeling you're doing exactly what you want. What else matters?"

This time he did take a step toward her. "You and me, that matters."

She held her arms against her body. "Jack, don't ask me—"

"Meg, taking over Ballard's company means I have to stay in Maine. But if I could go to London with you, I would."

She turned away. "This isn't a simple matter of geography."

He put his hands on her shoulders and turned her to face him. "What is it about, then? Why can't we work something out?"

She closed her eyes and battled the longings inside her. "I can't shake the feeling that somehow, if we start, you'll always find a way to put your life, your goals ahead of mine. And I'll go along be-cause...because I'll be so caught up in you."

"Listen, Meg. Don't believe that just because it happened with my parents or with yours. Give us a chance to make our own mistakes. Don't weigh us down with everyone else's."

It would be so easy to give in. All she wanted right now was to go into Jack's arms and mold herself against him. She wanted to forget about everything she'd dreamed or hoped before meeting him. But that was exactly why she couldn't do it. She couldn't for-get herself...she couldn't lose herself. Not even for a man like Jack.

"I'm going," she whispered. "And you're staying. And somehow the two of us will make the lives we're meant to make...apart.''

JACK STOOD outside a classroom at Webster College, watching his father in action. There could be no question that Andrew Elliott was a superb teacher. Right now he was conducting a fourth-year philosophy lecture, going over material that he'd probably given countless times before. Yet he behaved as if he was still fascinated by it. He probably was. He lectured with energy and style, knowing where to place a comment that would get a chuckle from his students, knowing when to be more serious. In the rarefied, elite and somewhat narrow world of Webster College, Andrew Elliott was both respected and well liked. He deserved his success. Jack couldn't deny that.

The class ended, but Jack knew his father would stay behind in the lecture hall to speak with lingering students. That gave Jack time to think about the subject foremost on his mind lately: Meg.

She'd been in England a month now. According to her friends Kathy and Lena, she was doing well. The two women were subletting Meg's New York apartment until more permanent arrangements were made for the place. They kept Jack informed about Meg, but it wasn't enough. Only one thing would make him happy...having her by his side.

His father finished and came out of the classroom. ''Jack,'' he said with the same easy attentiveness he gave to his students. "Good to see you, son. I'm walking back to my office, if you'd like to come along."

They crossed the quad together. Andrew nodded to other professors, said hello to a few students and called them by name. That was another thing that made him such a good teacher: he took the effort to remember his students' names. It made them feel special, singled out.

"I suppose," said Andrew, "you're here because you want to talk me into selling my share of the house."

"No," said Jack. "I'm no longer trying to tell other people how to live their lives."

"In other words," Andrew concluded, "your mother didn't go for the bed-and-breakfast idea."

"That's about the size of it."

Andrew seemed to think this over. "All right, you're not here to twist my arm. So why the unexpected visit?"

"Maybe I just wanted to say hello."

"Come on, Jack. Can't fool your old man," said Andrew. He had a habit of using certain phrases like "Hello, son" and "I'm your old man, aren't I?" Perhaps he thought they sounded fatherly, but they never rang quite true. It was as if he were attempting a foreign language, one he'd never genuinely mastered.

"For now," Jack said, "I'm just here to say hello." He wouldn't tell Andrew the real reason he'd come—so he could prove to himself that he wasn't like his father. He wanted to take a long, thorough look at Andrew Elliott and reassure himself that he wasn't anything like his "old man."

So far it wasn't working. He had a suspicion that he and Andrew shared at least one similarity—they both put the women in their lives second to other concerns. Why else wasn't Jack in London with Meg? Why else wasn't he showing her exactly how he felt about her?

Because she's being unreasonable. Because she could fit her life to mine a whole lot easier than I could fit mine to hers.

That was one voice. Another voice told Jack that he was merely standing on principle. It was a damn lonely place to stand.

He and his father reached Andrew's office. Jack expected a few polite but dismissive remarks. Surely Andrew had another article to write, another monograph to research—lofty pursuits that did not require father-son interaction.

Instead, Andrew seemed uncharacteristically at loose ends. He sat down, tapped his fingers on his desk, twirled his chair a little. When he spoke, his voice was abrupt.

"Jack, I know you don't think I've been a very good father. I know you think I'm a self-centered son of a bitch."

"I wouldn't have put it that way," Jack said.

"The sentiment is the same, though, isn't it? And

you're probably right. It's something your mother tried to tell me for years. Not to mention every woman I've been involved with since. They've all told me I'm too wrapped up in myself. One particularly belligerent lady informed me that I'm so fascinated by my own intellect I can't make room for anything or anyone else.''

Jack hoped he wasn't going to hear about his father's romantic life. Having been introduced to his mother's was bad enough. But Andrew was already moving on.

''So maybe I am that way. Maybe I never consider anybody but myself. Maybe I'm selfish…self-important, self-indulgent.''

There was irony for you. Andrew, in discussing his self-involvement at such great length, managed to sound nothing but self-involved.

''Dad, don't sweat it,'' Jack said. ''I'm starting to think everybody's at the center of their own little universe.''

''You know something? I really did want my marriage to work out. I was a lot happier with your mother than she was with me. Of course, when you're self-centered, I suppose you're oblivious to other people's discontent.'' Andrew was taking the self-centered motif and running with it. But then he gave a shrug. ''My point being, Jack, that I realize my limitations as a husband and father. It's no doubt too late to do anything about them now, but I suppose I can make one concession. I'll sell my share of the house to you. Then you can do with it as you please. Bed-and-breakfast, whatever.''

As simple as that, Andrew Elliott was giving in. ''Are you sure about this?'' Jack asked.

''As sure as I'll ever be. At first I held on to that house because I thought your mother would come back. Humiliating to admit it, but it's true. And then, when I had no choice but to see that the divorce was permanent…let's just say I was sentimental. The first few years your mother and I lived in that place were some of the best of our marriage. Maybe I didn't want to let go of the memories.''

Andrew Elliott would be self-involved to the end, perhaps. He'd probably never understand how unhappy Helen had been in that house, listening to the lonely sound of the ocean waves and living in her husband's shadow. His memories would not be the same as hers. And yet, it seemed Andrew did know how to come through.

''Thanks, Dad,'' Jack said. ''Meg is right about one thing—it's time for that house to move on.''

''Speaking of you and Meg…''

''Not much to speak of right now,'' Jack told him.

Andrew studied him. ''I like your Meg. If you get a chance, please tell her that for me.''

''If I get a chance,'' Jack headed toward the door, then gave his father a faint smile. ''See you around.''

''Stop by anytime. I like unexpected visits.'' Andrew sounded as sincere as when he spoke to one of his students. But maybe there was something else, too, just a little extra warmth reserved for his son. Maybe Jack hadn't really listened for it until now.

As he retraced his steps across the quadrangle, Jack watched the students milling around him. Impossibly young students, for the most part. He couldn't imagine being that young ever again. In his forty years he'd made mistakes, learned from them, gone on. Most of all, he'd discovered that what he'd accomplished so far was okay. He built things. He was going to build more. Maybe, in some ways, forty wasn't so bad.

As long as you were with the woman you loved.

HELEN WAS DRIVING the nurses crazy again. At this moment, the usually unflappable Mrs. Jansen was the nurse in question.

"I am perfectly capable," Helen insisted, "of walking back and forth across the room by myself."

"You *know* what the doctor said," Mrs. Jansen told her in an exasperated tone.

"Yes, I know exactly what the doctor said. And he's an overcautious old coot." Helen gestured menacingly with one of her crutches.

Mrs. Jansen looked as if she were about to blow a gasket, and Jack knew it was time to intervene.

"I'll take over from here," he said.

Mrs. Jansen sped past him, giving him a grateful look as she went. A moment later the front door of the apartment opened and slammed shut. Mrs. Jansen was wisely taking a breather.

"Thank goodness you got rid of her." Helen sounded exasperated. "That woman is truly getting on my nerves. I don't see why I even have to have her around anymore."

"Because we're listening to the doctor, no matter if he is an old coot," Jack said. He helped his mother walk the rest of the way to the sofa. If she resented his assistance, she didn't say so. But she gave him a shrewd look as soon as she'd settled down.

"So, Jack," she said. "Why did you come all the way back to New York this time? Still trying to convince me I should let you take over my finances?"

"Just thought I should give you a piece of news in person," he told her. "I talked to Dad yesterday, and he agreed to sell his share of the house to me."

"Imagine that. What made him change his mind?"

"The realization that you're not going back to him."

"As if he ever wanted me back," she replied witheringly.

"Maybe at one time he did."

"Jack when will you learn that he likes to make grandiose statements? He tries to sound sincere, but he isn't."

"He has his faults," said Jack, "but maybe he's not so bad."

"You, defending your father?" Helen shook her head. "So he really did agree to it?"

"He did."

"And you expect now I'll fall into line."

"I've learned not to expect anything," Jack replied honestly.

"Well, then," said Helen. "Let me tell you how it is. My boss called me again this morning to ask how I was doing. And of course he hinted about me taking early retirement. Well, I've had quite enough of hints and innuendos. I told him that I quit. I told him I wasn't coming back to work for him, period."

Jack rubbed his neck. "Guess we'll need that bed-and-breakfast sooner than I thought."

Helen gave him a triumphant glance. "Not necessary. I have other prospects. Russ Cooper has offered me a job as advertising director of his stationery stores."

"Russ Cooper..." Jack tried to place the name.

"The gentleman across the hall, of course," Helen said. "We're seeing each other, if you must know. Can you believe that up until now he's handled his own advertising? He really needs someone to take him into the new millennium—and I'm going to be that person." She sounded very pleased with herself. "You see, Jack, you *have* been underestimating me. I know I've made some bad financial decisions in the past, but I'm perfectly capable of handling my own future."

Jack supposed he had underestimated her. "So much for the bed-and-breakfast then."

She gave an imperious wave of the hand. "No need to dismiss it just like that. Do what you like with the house. If you make money off it—fine. You can give me fifty percent, you keep the other fifty. Fair enough?''

"Fair enough," he said. He wouldn't point out that she'd just given in. He didn't think her pride would tolerate thinking of it that way.

"After all," Helen went on, "Meg thought the bed-and-breakfast was a good idea."

"Meg knows what she's talking about."

"Speaking of Meg," said Helen, "have you called her yet?"

More than a few times he'd picked up the phone to dial her in London, but he'd always stopped himself.

"Not yet," he said.

"Don't let her get away. Surely the two of you can work things out."

He wished it were that simple.

"I'm taking some very good advice from a dear friend of mine," Helen confided. "I'm leaving bitterness behind. Maybe you should do the same thing, Jack."

She had a point. He and Meg had parted in what amounted to bitterness. But maybe their chance was already gone. That was what the empty feeling in his gut told him...his chance with Meg was already gone.

CHAPTER EIGHTEEN

MEG DIDN'T HAVE a single complaint about London. There was so much to see, so much she'd wanted to experience since she'd been a kid: Trafalgar Square, Piccadilly Circus, Westminster Abbey, Buckingham Palace. And, amazingly, she didn't have a single complaint about her new job. So far, Thomas P. Riley had been true to his word. He'd given her complete authority to create the hotel of her dreams. No decision was countermanded, no request denied. She even had a whole suite in the hotel to herself, a place to live with every comfort.

So why, given all these wonderful circumstances, did she feel so miserable?

She knew she could answer that question in two words: *Jack Elliott.* Or, rather, the absence of Jack Elliott. But she'd been trying so hard not to think about him. She'd tried as hard as she could to immerse herself in work, and not remember those magical few days in Maine. Days spent wandering with Jack, nights spent lying in his arms....

She was lonely, but she told herself that was natural when you'd just moved to a new country. She tried to keep the loneliness at bay with frequent phone calls back and forth between herself, her friends and family. One night, as she sat alone in her hotel suite, Shaun called.

"Hey, sis. Taking England by storm?"

Meg smiled as she held the receiver. "Shaun, it's so good to hear your voice." And then, more cautiously, she asked, "How are things going there?"

"In other words," he said, "you want to know how it's going with me and Barbara." He paused. "We're talking, Meggie. Working it out. Barbara finally admitted how damn scared she was. She'd failed at her job and she thought she'd fail at everything else, so she quit trying. And that's what set off all my fears about unhappiness and failing at marriage. But just talking about it seems to bring out the strength in both of us. We're pulling together. We're going to beat this thing."

Meg heard the hope in his voice. "Shaun, I'm so relieved."

"What about you, Meg? Are you still running scared?"

"What a way to put it," she chided. But after she'd said goodbye to her brother, she sat and stared at the phone for a long moment.

It rang again, startling her. "Hello," she said.

"Meggie, have you done like I told you and met any devastating Brits yet?" Lena asked from across the Atlantic.

"Of course she hasn't," Kathy said on the extension at Meg's New York apartment. "She has other matters on her mind."

Meg pictured both of her friends at the apartment, and a wave of homesickness came over her. She thought about her cat, Daisy, no doubt being spoiled outrageously by Kathy and Lena, but perhaps missing Meg nonetheless. It hadn't seemed fair to uproot Daisy yet, but that was just one more thing that made her feel lonely—not having her cat around.

"Do the two of you ever start out a conversation with a simple hello?"

Lena ignored her. "What Meg has on her mind," she said, "is Jack Elliott."

"I couldn't agree with you more," added Kathy.

"Guys, please," Meg protested. "The world does not revolve around Jack Elliott."

"If it doesn't," said Lena, "why haven't you gone out with any of those devastating Brits?"

"Lena—"

"We won't torment you any longer," said Kathy. "We have news of our own. First of all, can you believe that Lena broke up with Nathan? The engagement is off!"

"Oh, Lena, I'm sorry," Meg said. "Really sorry."

"Don't be," Lena replied, sounding her usual irrepressible self. "Once Nathan and I got to know each other a little better, the glow was off for both of us. The truth is, Meg, we all know I rushed things with Nathan. I was so determined to keep that vow of ours. But maybe I'm just not cut out for marriage, or romance, or all the rest of it.''

"Oh?'' came Kathy's voice. "Then what about that cute architect you met at the deli?''

"We're going on a date,'' Lena said virtuously. "That's all. A simple, ordinary date.''

Cradling the receiver, Meg settled into an armchair, tucking her feet beneath her. This was almost as good as having her friends right beside her.

"Well, *I'm* going to keep our vow,'' said Kathy. "I told Gary our wedding had to be no later than December thirty-first so we can make the deadline.''

Meg sat up straighter, gripping the receiver. "Kathy, don't tell me—''

"Isn't it wonderful?'' Kathy sounded blissful. "Gary flew all the way back to New York to propose again. He said this time it's going to stick.''

"He'd better make it stick,'' said Lena, "or he'll have to answer to me.''

"Oh, Kathy,'' Meg said. "Congratulations!''

"You know what he told me, Meggie? He told me that just because you and Jack refused to admit you were meant for each other, he wasn't going to make the same mistake. He said he and I *were* meant for each other, and he was through being scared. Okay, maybe he looked scared when he said it, but it was a lovely proposal.''

Meant for each other. Those words resonated in Meg's mind and in her heart. The rest of the phone conversation passed in a blur. When she hung up, she sat for another long moment, just thinking. And then she scrambled to her feet. She hurried to the closet and pulled out her suitcase. Willy-nilly, she began throwing clothes into it.

"Lord," she whispered to herself. "How stubborn I've been. How incredibly stubborn! Please don't let it be too late. Please..."

Somehow she would explain to Thomas P. Riley why she had to resign after only five weeks at her new job. Somehow she would make him understand. But that would come later. Right now the only thing that mattered was getting out of here. She had to call the airport, book the first flight she could—

A knock came at the door. She yanked it open, impatient at any interruption. She had to get home to Jack...

Except for one thing. Jack Elliott was standing on her threshold, looking improbably gorgeous in the baseball cap she'd given him for his birthday. She wondered if she'd conjured him up out of sheer desire and need.

"It can't be you," she said. "Can it?"

He stepped into the room and gathered her into his arms. He felt wonderfully solid. He was real, all right. And he was *here*.

"Jack...oh, Jack...I love you."

"I figured as much. Because I love you, Meg."

The kiss he gave her left her trembling. She clung to him, reveling in his touch.

"I was on my way to you," she said in wonder. "I almost had my suitcase packed."

"Good thing I got here when I did," he said, "or we'd be on opposite coasts all over again."

She laughed shakily. "Jack, kiss me again. Just to make sure I'm not dreaming."

She wasn't dreaming. She felt as if a London fog had suddenly lifted from her soul. She was in the most beautiful, most wonderful city in the world. Of course, she'd feel that way about any place, so long as Jack was there with her.

"I was wrong," he said, his voice husky. "Love does turn your life upside down. I couldn't be without you, Meg. It's as simple as that. So I'm here to stay. I can run my business long distance. Why not?"

"But, Jack, I was just about to quit my job. Let's go to Maine..."

He kissed her yet again, deliciously. "Maybe we'd better slow down. Maybe we're getting ahead of ourselves." He fished into his pocket and brought out a small velvet box. When he opened it, she saw a ring. Not just any ring, but the one she and Jack had found at the jewelry store. A diamond, the perfect size and shape, nestled in amethyst. She took it out of the box and slipped it on her finger.

"Does that mean we're engaged for real this time?" he asked.

"Yes," she said. "A million times, yes." She put her arms around him and drew him close, convincing herself one more time that he was really here.

"Meg, about that rule you have…the fact that you don't like making love in hotels…"

"Rules are meant to be broken." She took the Do Not Disturb sign and hung it outside the door. Then, very firmly, she closed the door. She went into Jack's arms again, right where she belonged.

A FEW HOURS LATER, Meg stretched luxuriously in bed. Her fiancé took that as an invitation to lean over and kiss the pulse at her throat.

"Jack, you're not thinking…"

"Not just yet," he said. "Maybe we could order room service and get back some of our strength."

"I'll scandalize all my employees," she teased. "Make that my ex-employees, since I'm going to quit my job and move back to Maine with you. I've decided to trust myself—and you. I've decided I can give my love to you and not lose myself in the process. Because I figure you'll be doing some giving, too."

"A lot of it," he said, his lips trailing over her collarbone. But then he settled back on the pillows, drawing her with him. "Meg, we have to talk. I have the feeling you're going overboard. You're so ready to prove your ability to compromise that you're going too far. I don't want you to quit your job."

"But Jack, you just expanded your business. And I know how you feel about Maine."

"Maine's been around a long time. It'll still be there by the time we decide to go back. And I told you I was going to delegate more. I have good people working for me. Sure, I'll have to fly back and forth, but nothing I can't manage.''

She rested her cheek on his shoulder, wondering if it was possible to feel this happy. Apparently it was.

''Jack, we won't stay here forever. Just a few months, long enough for me to get this hotel up and running exactly as I'd like. After that, I think I'll be ready for new horizons. Maybe that bed-and-breakfast...''

''I'm going ahead with it,'' he told her. ''I'd appreciate your help. But I envision a whole string of hotels for you, Meggie. I'm in the construction business, after all. Let's build one in Boston. Another in Portland. And why stop there? You already know your way around New York.''

''Now you're the one going too fast,'' she said. ''Although I like the sound of it. The Danley and Elliott hotels. They'll be known for their rooftop gardens... We could cooperate on a lot of things, Jack. Parenthood, even. Kids with you might not be so daunting.''

''It'll be daunting,'' he warned, ''trust me. But we'll be in it together when the time comes. Right now we don't have to worry about it. I have other things on my mind.'' He gave her a long and leisurely kiss.

''Just as long as we're married by the year 2000,'' she murmured.

"I think it can be arranged."

"I love you, Jack," she said.

"I love you, Meg."

They held each other close, lost in each other's arms. And Meg discovered that wishful thinking really could mean wishes come true.

HARLEQUIN SUPERROMANCE®

**From April to June 1999,
read about three women whose
New Millennium resolution is**

By the Year 2000: *Revenge?*

The Wrong Bride by Judith Arnold.
Available in April 1999.
Cassie Webster loves Phillip Keene and expected to marry
him—but it turns out he's marrying someone else. So
Cassie shows up at his wedding…to prove he's got
The Wrong Bride.

Don't Mess with Texans by Peggy Nicholson.
Available in May 1999.
Susannah Mack Colton is out to get revenge on her
wealthy—and nasty—ex-husband. But in the process
she gets entangled with a handsome veterinarian,
complicating *his* life, too. Because that's what happens
when you ***"Mess with Texans"!***

If He Could See Me Now by Rebecca Winters.
Available in June 1999.
The Rachel Maynard of today isn't the Rachel of ten
years ago. Now a lovely and accomplished woman,
she's looking for sweet revenge—and a chance to win
the love of the man who'd once rejected her.
If He Could See Me Now…

Available at your favorite retail outlet.

Looking For More Romance?

Visit Romance.net

Check in daily for these and other exciting features:

Hot off the press

View all current titles, and purchase them on-line.

What do the stars have in store for you?

Horoscope

Hot deals

Exclusive offers available only at Romance.net

Plus, don't miss our interactive quizzes, contests and bonus gifts.

PWEB

IN UNIFORM

There's something special about a man in uniform. Maybe because he's a man who takes charge, a man you can count on, and yes, maybe even love....

Superromance presents *In Uniform*, an occasional series that features men who live up to your every fantasy—and then some!

Look for:

Mad About the Major
by Roz Denny Fox
Superromance #821
Coming in January 1999

An Officer and a Gentleman
by Elizabeth Ashtree
Superromance #828
Coming in March 1999

SEAL It with a Kiss
by Rogenna Brewer
Superromance #833
Coming in April 1999

Available wherever Harlequin books are sold.

HARLEQUIN®
Makes any time special ™

HSRIU

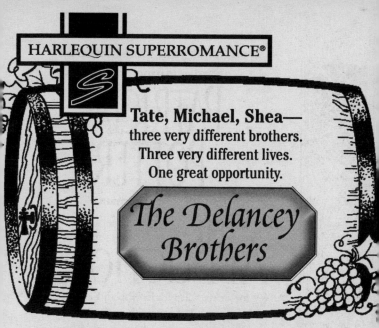

COMING NEXT MONTH

#826 A MAN FOR MOM • Sherry Lewis
By the Year 2000: Marriage
Sharon Lawrence's two daughters are determined to find a
man for their mother by the year 2000. Sharon seems
unaware of their scheme and the fact that she's "accidentally"
meeting one inappropriate man after another. She has,
however, noticed Gabe Malone—who may be the only single
man in the neighborhood who's *not* part of the Man Plan.

#827 MIXED MESSAGES • Dawn Stewardson
Carrie O'Reilly gets a frightened message from her younger
sister, Jenny. Turns out Jenny's on the run—from a killer. The
same man who intends to pin the murder he's just committed
on Sam Evans. Carrie and Sam team up. It's the only way she
can save her sister and the only way *he* can save himself. As
they search for Jenny, Carrie finds herself falling in love with
Sam—but can she *really* trust him?

#828 AN OFFICER AND A HERO • Elizabeth Ashtree
In Uniform
Army Captain Kaitlin McCord, an attorney in the Judge
Advocate General's Corps, falls for a handsome enlisted man.
That's bad enough. Worse, Master Sergeant Daniel Wilson is
a paralegal assigned to her office. As Kaitlin very well knows,
a relationship with a subordinate is a court-martial offense.
And as she quickly discovers, Army life—and love—in the
nineties can be complicated indeed.

#829 FATHERS AND SONS • Carolyn McSparren
Atlanta lawyer Kate Mulholland is facing her greatest
challenge. Her client—nineteen-year-old Jason Canfield,
charged with murdering his high-school sweetheart—is the
son of Kate's ex-husband. Kate divorced David Canfield
twenty years ago for an act of infidelity that resulted in the
birth of the boy she must now save from prison.